DEATH TIME

Chris pulled over and watched the car bank over a hill.... He should have driven up the road with a kind of single-minded dedication. But he hesitated.

All of a sudden, he realized he wasn't ready. He never had been. Meacham was a killer. Chris was nothing—a camera-carrying shithead. For Meacham, this was life; for Chris...what—an obsession? He had never before killed; he couldn't now, even in self-defense. Meanwhile, up and over the hill, that was the land of killers. That was the place where Meacham had gone, and now Chris would have to go...

THROUGH A LENS DARKLY

JAMES COHEN

WARNER BOOKS

A Time Warner Company

WARNER BOOKS EDITION

Cover design by Tony Greco
Cover illustration by Edwin Herder

This Warner Books Edition is published by arrangement with Donald I. Fine, Inc.

Warner Books, Inc.
1271 Avenue of the Americas
New York, NY 10020

 A Time Warner Company

Printed in the United States of America

First Warner Books Printing: February, 1993

10 9 8 7 6 5 4 3 2 1

*For Jonathan
and Monique Levey*

PART ONE

ONE

DORSEY had been explicit with his instructions. "Give me the perfect death." Not the perfect murder—there had been scores of those filmed, time and again, in every studio around Hollywood. "The perfect death," Dorsey had said. "A real capper. Exactly three minutes' worth of tape."

And Matt understood. By "perfect," Dorsey meant catching not only the details of death, but also the emotion, the consequences, the losses . . . the full trauma of being killed. Something that followed a car crash from the moment the steering wheel locked, to the car breaking through the railing, to the bodies being scraped off the cement. Except it couldn't be a car wreck, because they had too many of those. No; Dorsey would want something completely different. A capper. In fact, a three-minute capper. That was a hell of a lot of tape. On video, an eternity.

"I'm giving you just seven days for this one, Matt," Dorsey said. "Can I trust you? Because if I can't, I'll phone Chris."

"You can trust me," Matt said.

"Tell me the truth, because I can't have you screwing around in the editing room. If you got a problem, you better—"

"I'll take care of it, Al."

But a week had gone by, and Matt was still short the tape. He had busted his balls every day, and no matter how hard he looked, he couldn't find anything near the right footage. Car wrecks, police tapes, newsreels . . . He knew what Dorsey wanted—he had a nose for what was fresh, just like Chris; maybe *better* than Chris—but despite all the effort, Matt was left squatting on his apartment floor, sitting on a carpet of junk video cartridges, free-basing coke and trying to forget that, with only two hours left to deadline, he was going to fuck up. Completely. There was no way for him to win, not only because the footage had to be perfect . . . not just because it had to be new and fresh and graphic and emotional and stomach-turning . . .

It also had to be real.

That's what they were selling. That had been Dorsey's brilliant idea after five years of producing L.A.'s worst soft porn, after scrambling, under a pseudonym, for any manner of local, state or federal government film contract. People wanted action? People wanted violence? When it came to special effects, Dorsey couldn't compete with the big studios, but what about marketing a death tape—a sixty-minute cartridge to sell directly to video stores? A compilation of real murders, accidents and suicides clipped from whatever his company could dig up. And to make it come together, he could find two assholes who'd work for nothing and hustle their butts off, digging up leads, acting like detectives, ferreting out bad footage, begging off the good. A couple of film-school grads who were already used to busting their balls and would eat buttered shit if it meant a screen credit.

A couple of dumb asses like Matt and Chris.

Eleven months ago, almost to the day, they had been brought on board as associate producers of Dorsey's new division, R.I.P. Productions. Their mission: to produce the first video, *Raw Death*. And now, eleven months later, they were already finishing work on *Raw Death II*, with Dorsey going so far as to boost the publicity budget thirty percent, the money had been that good.

That was part of Matt's problem—beating his own success. *Raw Death* scored the minute it hit the stores, and now Dorsey wanted more than a sequel—he wanted to move it from a Grade B project to his version of a Grade A. He had the ridiculous idea that *Raw Death* could turn into a long-term, multisequel industry. But to make this dream happen, he needed bigger and better true-life deaths, and that was absolute hell, because when Chris and Matt clipped together the first tape they figured it would be a one-shot deal. They had already used the best footage—in fact, had gotten sick to their stomachs as they reeled through the murders and assaults and all other manner of abuse. Matt was left with nothing except, of course Dorsey's warnings.

"Keep off the historic shit," Dorsey said. "None of that Kennedy garbage or Oswald or any other big names . . . People want to see *people* get hit by trucks, not millionaires. Except I don't want accidents either. We used too many last time."

Dorsey talked now as if he were an expert on good death. As he gave Matt his final instructions, Dorsey paced the room with the air of some Ph.D. heavy.

"Nothing black and white, either," Dorsey said. "They're colorizing movies, not the other way. And no home footage. That stuff looks like shit. It's got to be professional. I want it to look like it came from the studios, but it shouldn't cost the same. I just want that professional look. Good lighting, close detail . . . The footage should tell a story. People like it more if there's a story."

Story? Utter crap. The first one never pretended to have a plot; they just divided it into segments by type: ten minutes of suicides, eight of car wrecks, three of airlines, ten of homicides, five of cult deaths, eight of multiple killings, another five of female victims—Dorsey's idea. And the film's capper: tape of a San Bernardino rape/mutilation/homicide—amazingly graphic footage that had once been used for evidence, and which Chris had managed to buy from a police hold. A remarkable tape because the killer, Ned Braddock, had been given a video camera from his wife just hours before he went crazy. It made Matt sick just thinking about it—Ned sitting on his wife, thumping his knife into her body, waiting for the police and telling jokes to the camera like Johnny Carson. When they saw the clip, Chris wondered if Dorsey would let it run. Dorsey did more than run it; he planned to use Ned's picture on the box for the next video—as if the murdering maniac had given the product his seal of approval.

"You've got to do it for me again, Matt, except bigger and better. I want us to see everything fall apart. We have to follow the action. Move about the room. Feel with the victim, see his eyes, know what's going through his head. Above all, Matt, we need to see the Moment. Understand? We need a good, close shot of the Moment."

The Moment. The precise second of death, the exact point in time when a person crosses the threshold from life to death. Of course, blood was always important, but what gave the footage meaning was staring into the victims' eyes and trying to see inside them as they made the jump from the living to the dead. People wanted to go inside death, see what was coming when you're lying on the floor with Ned Braddock sitting on top of you, chopping down . . . ravaged, raped, broken, ripped apart muscle and soul . . . when it was time to turn off, and you looked up, and instead of your husband you see nothing, except sometimes you smiled, so maybe you did see something . . .

The Moment. They tried recreating it in the studios. They spent a fortune so people could see fake gangsters riddled with fake bullets, or aliens bursting out of people's stomachs, or hatchets coming down on teenage heads. Thousands of people, all nestled in L.A., bleeding over their typewriters, trying to come up with new ways to have some Bel Air actor stare into the camera and die. The Moment. Probably the most powerful few seconds in any film, and not once had the studios come close to even the opening minute of Dorsey's *Raw Death*. There wasn't any question, Dorsey deserved his success. He was bringing an audience to the brink and then plopping them safely back on their couches.

"You can get that for me, right, Matt? Because if I can't trust you. If you think Chris should come in . . ."

Fuck Chris. Like Chris was the only one who could make Dorsey happy. If Dorsey really felt that way, he should have given Chris the job, not him.

And maybe that wouldn't have been such a bad idea. Matt had spent too much time cropping nightmares. He had stared into so many sets of dead and dull eyes that he really, truly didn't give a shit anymore. You could stare all you wanted into the faces of dead people; in the end, there was only one way to make sense of it, and anyone with a cross-beam and shoelace knew how to get the answer.

"We got a standard, Matt. We got to beat that standard."

Matt took another deep breath of smoke, then reached for the telephone. It was only nine in the morning, but there was a chance Dorsey was at work.

"Ruth?" Matt asked. "Is he in?"

"Not for an hour," said the secretary. "How're you doing?"

"Tell him to send a messenger around eleven."

"He wants you to bring it yourself."

"I'm not gonna be here," Matt said. "Tell the messenger to come upstairs to my door. I'll leave instructions there."

"But he—"

"Just do it, Ruth. Tell Dorsey the footage is great. It's really going to make his day," he said, hanging up.

Now, where was Chris? Where had Dorsey sent him? It was a Department of Agriculture contract; that much Matt remembered. Somewhere in the Midwest. Indiana maybe, or Wisconsin, or...

Matt walked to the kitchen and checked a list tapped to the refrigerator. There it was—*Sunrise Motel, Hayden, Iowa*, followed by a telephone number. He reached for the hall phone and dialed.

"Room eleven, please," he told the motel clerk. Matt waited, listened to the phone ring, tried keeping his patience as it rang a full minute. Finally the clerk rescued him. "If he's not in, I'd like to leave a message."

"Yes?" the clerk asked.

Matt thought a moment, "Tell him Matt called, and the film's finished, and that it's his now."

". . . it's his now," the clerk repeated. Matt could almost hear him writing.

"One other thing," he said. He tried hard to get all his thoughts together, to really let Chris know what he thought of him, of the film, of Dorsey and himself.

"One more thing," said Matt. "Tell him, 'Fuck you.' " The clerk hesitated.

"Don't worry," Matt said. "He'll think it's funny."

" 'Fuck you,' " the clerk repeated.

"Thanks," Matt said, hanging up. Now, was there anyone else to call? His sister? No, she'd be out of the house anyway. Maybe his mother? But if he called her, then he'd also have to talk to his father or else someone would be jealous.

He sat a full five minutes before looking up at the kitchen camera.

"Excuse me," Matt said, "Forgot you were there."

He smiled and headed back to the living room and Camera #2. He reached down for his coke, took a last hit, then blew smoke into the ceiling.

"Clouds," he said. "Thought I'd try a special effect," giving an even bigger smile.

The video cameras were almost quiet, emitting a long, low hum.

"Actually, Al, you probably won't want to use any of this. It's just a little lead, in case you need filler. I'm going to get everything ready now."

Matt excused himself and walked in front of Camera #3. First, he pulled up a small bowl with dog food. Then he rested the bowl on one end of a plank and tied a string to the opposite end. The string ran to the kitchen cabinet, where a small bottle sat at the edge of the shelf, waiting to be tripped into a long plastic gutter. The gutter made a run across the living room, then ended several feet over a brick, which in turn sat atop a five-pound plastic bag of sand. The bag rested on a crate pocketed with tiny holes, and inside the crate was a pot. The pot sat atop a bedspring, which also had a wire. In this case, the wire ran from the spring, across the room, through a pulley and to the living room sofa.

Here, it attached to the trigger of a shotgun.

Matt had the butt of the shotgun hammered into a wood shelf. The barrel pointed down, its tip no more than two feet from where he would rest his head. When he finished testing the wire, he did a last check of the cameras. They seemed right. Dorsey wanted moving shots? Matt had a remote so he could zoom in and out to follow his contraption. Then, when it was time to pull the trigger, the moves would be truly impressive. Matt had three angles for that—one from the POV of the shotgun, another from his POV and a third to take in the entire picture.

It was just what Dorsey wanted, and Matt would give it to him. He only hesitated once—walking past his coke, standing over the stash, wondering if he should take an extra hit. But he murmured, "Fuck it," and headed to a closet. He unlocked the door, tiptoed back to the sofa, lay in place and positioned his forehead just in front of the barrel.

I hope you appreciate how much work I put into this, Al. No one else would have done it." He looked down and pressed his remote, pulling back the frame. With that, Matt turned his head and shouted, "Food, Herc."

A Scottish terrier came out of the closet, skidded briefly on the living room floor, then nosed the bowl of food.

"Pretty funny, huh?" Matt said. "Man's best friend."

Herc wasn't eating a half minute before he jarred the bowl. This tugged the bottle, which in turn rolled down the gutter and dropped on the brick. The bottle broke and the acid poured down the brick and onto the plastic bag. Soon the sand was running through the crate and into the kettle.

As the kettle filled, the cord to the shotgun tightened.

"I worked long and hard on this," Matt said. "Got it timed perfect. Three minutes, on the nose. Couldn't ask for anything better."

He hit the remote, and the camera zoomed on his face.

"Fucking great, huh? Bet I'm taking up the whole goddamn TV."

Matt heard the spring creak, and he dared to glance toward the crate. Then he again rested. Tied to the shotgun was his wristwatch, so he could tell precisely how much time was left.

"Forty seconds," he said. "This is when it gets rough. This is when your brain really starts messing with you—one second, saying stick around, the next, jump out. You just gotta stop thinking, just blank it out. Relax. Relax . . ."

Matt saw the time on his watch. Less than fifteen seconds left. He was ready. The cameras were running, the shots were close, he could sense the cord tightening . . .

The spring under the pot slipped.

Matt lifted his head. Across the room, the pot had tilted off its support.

"Fuck," he said, still leaning forward, his head against the barrel. "Typical, right?" he said. "I mean, just plain, fucking *typical*."

Then the trigger pulled.

Matt was thrown off the sofa and across the floor. He didn't stop rolling until his body tipped the tripod for Camera #4. Then he stopped completely, his arms slouching, the only movement coming from the wet meat of his opened skull.

Above the shotgun, his watch clocked it. Start to finish, total death time: two minutes, fifty-seven seconds.

If only Dorsey were here to congratulate him. All things considered, it was a near-perfect death.

TWO

THE way Chris figured it, God was mind-fucking him. After a year of "deathploitation," he was making Chris pay dues by turning him into a Grim Reaper. A month earlier, Chris had said as much to Dorsey. He walked into the office, closed the door and declared, "I'm killing people, Al."

Dorsey looked up, grinning, as if he had anticipated the idiocy.

"I mean it, Al. I really feel like I'm killing people."

"So what does that make me? An accomplice to murder?" Dorsey answered.

Chris passed the couch and sat in the chair beside the desk, so Dorsey knew this was business. "I've been spending too much time with those clips. When I'm not filming them, I'm editing them. When I'm not editing them, I'm dreaming them. It'd be one thing if *I* was cutting *Bambi*, but when you're watching wacked-out psychos carve swastikas into their foreheads . . ."

"Jesus," Dorsey said. "You film-school grads. You bitch about making movies, then when you get the chance, your balls freeze."

"It's not just *my* balls. Matt has the same complaint."

"Matt hasn't earned the right to complain," said Dorsey. He leaned closer, squeezing Chris's arm, then walked to a small refrigerator for a lemon spritzer. "Will you listen to yourself? Everything you're complaining about—you think it gets easier? If it does, you're not doing your job. Hell, if you were cutting *Bambi*, you'd be having nightmares about killer deer. There's no such thing as a friendly film. Not if it's also a good one, and *Raw Death is* a good one. And the next one's going to be better."

Chris didn't budge. "I need a break."

Dorsey glared at him. "*You* need a break." His voice turned heavy. "And what do I need? Who's supposed to finish the goddamn video?"

Chris hoped he would find his own answer, but Dorsey waited. Finally, Chris said it. "Matt."

"Matt? Dorsey said. "You mean poor, tired, gumhead Matt? I thought he was tired like you? I thought he was—"

"Look, I don't care," said Chris. "Find someone else. It doesn't matter, just so long as it's not me. If you don't want Matt, you can—"

Dorsey cut him off, his expression snapping from frustration to consolation. Chris couldn't even pretend to understand what Dorsey was thinking. "All right," Dorsey said. "You want a break? I can work it out. I've got a government project. Should take about three weeks. You can get busy on that and we'll pass *Death II* to Matt. But if Matt screws it, you're coming back. This video's important for me and I hope it's important to you. That fair?"

Chris didn't answer. They both knew what was happening; Chris was getting a break and Matt was getting screwed. But Dorsey had played the guilt game before. Chris's silence was quiet assent, so Dorsey waved off his associate producer, letting him disappear into the Midwest while Matt stayed in L.A. to finish clipping.

So here was Chris, thousands of miles from the coast— thousands of miles from *Dorsey*—spending ten thousand dollars filming how frost can damage topsoil and feeling guilty as hell. And the irony was that after all his talk of escape, Chris hadn't escaped from anything.

Despite fifteen hundred miles, death was again staring him in the face.

They moved closer to the ice. Chris, his cameraman and his soundman—actually, sound*woman*—walked down the snow-covered slope and joined about a dozen people who had collected midway between a frozen pond and a fire truck. Everyone looked out at the pond, about six acres in size, with a hole almost dead center. Eight volunteers had worked their way half the distance to the hole, but from that point onward only the lead man dared approach, wearing a wet suit and anchored by a stretched rope.

In the heart of the hole floated a body.

Chris joined the tight semicircle of onlookers. They were whispering, frightened and fascinated. Chris had seen it all before, He took his place next to the outside man and asked, "Who is it?"

"Teenage girl from the neighboring farm," the man said. "Ice probably broke when she was crossing it. The stupidest goddamn thing."

"She's gonna be dead," someone else said. "Been missing all night."

"You can live a long time in icewater," the man said. "Body shuts down, heart stops . . ."

"Dead," a third person decided.

"Dead," another agreed.

Chris didn't give his prediction. He *knew* the answer. Dead. Dead the second Chris appeared. That was God's dirty trick. Chris's presence was the kiss of death.

"Maybe they'll take some coffee," said one of the group. Chris watched as the person carried a thermos to a smaller, tighter crowd standing near the fire truck, close to the emergency unit.

The family, Chris thought. *The mother and father.*

The rescue team was now close to the body. The man in the wet suit kneeled by the hole, then slipped into the water completely. There was shouting, but it was just the other volunteers moving a stretcher into place, ready to dash the girl to a medical center. Soon the diver and the body were back on solid ice.

She was the incarnation of a ghost, except a ghost has no weight, no being. The girl was heavy—her clothes waterlogged, a shoe missing, her winter parka hardening and freezing in the open air. For hours, an air pocket in the girls parka had kept the body afloat. Now, the only way the diver could lift the girl was to twist his hand under the parka's collar and carry her like a butcher carrying a hook of meat. He heaved the body away from the hole, then lowered it onto a foil heat sheet.

Moments later, the body was in the ambulance. Chris watched as the family was led to a sheriff's car, and the two vehicles drove off.

"Son of a bitch, huh?"

It was Billy, standing beside Chris and patting the camera.

"Man, I'd hate drowning." Billy rubbed his hands, seeming more concerned about the cold than the water.

Chris looked about the crowd. "You didn't see any other cameras, did you?"

"No," Billy said.

"Then you and Denny head back to the car," Chris said.

Billy left and Chris walked closer to the pond's edge. With the body out of the water, it was so goddamn peaceful. He put one foot on the ice, pressed down, placed another on it . . .

"Looks safe, doesn't it?" a volunteer said.

Chris turned. Some of the others had drifted onto the pond. The fascination never ended, did it?

"Ice always looks solid," the man said. "That's why the kids walk out." He nodded in the direction of the van. "What are you doing with the camera?"

"Filming."

"For the news?"

Chris shook his head.

"Bet you could sell it to the news. Is that what you're gonna do—show it on TV?"

Chris thought of R.I.P. Productions. "Something like that," he said. And he turned back toward the van, once again feeling guilty as hell.

Sometimes, all too often lately, Chris stared into a mirror and told himself repeatedly that, despite everything, he wasn't scum. He did this because you didn't work for Al

Dorsey without getting that wet, gummy feeling all over your soul. He also did it because he had grown used to living with indecency, and he realized this wasn't normal. Someone once said he had a compartmentalized personality: that the pieces of his life remained pieces, which meant he never had to add up the consequences. If true, it explained a lot about Chris, especially how easily he immersed himself in details without comprehending the final collective consequences of his actions. It wasn't a unique shortcoming, but his line of work gave it an almost evil twist. Billy was a reminder of this. The moment Chris was back in the van, the cameraman began pressing him to rush the tape back to California. Billy talked as if they had uncovered something vital, as if Dorsey needed a kidney transplant and the film were his matching organ.

Chris listened, but he had just enough sense to realize there was something wrong in storing the image of some poor, dead girl in the dark, dank vaults of R.I.P. Productions.

"How about it?" Billy pressed. "When do we show Dorsey the tape?"

Chris took a long breath. "Calm down," he said. "We still got footage to shoot on the farm, and I have a two o'clock interview."

Billy couldn't believe it. "We got film of a teenage girl getting pulled out of the water," he said. "A *teenage girl*, Chris."

"We got here too late," Chris said.

Billy turned to Denny for support, but Denny didn't give an inch. "Quit being a shit, Billy. It's too cold for that."

"*Denny*—"

"Just shut up," she said. "Dorsey won't care about this. All we got was her coming out of the pond. It's not like we got her going in."

Billy wanted to argue, but he knew what she meant. Dorsey couldn't care less about film of a dead body; he could get that by taking a camera down to the L.A. morgue. They returned to work and made it back to the motel by four-thirty. Denny went in first, taking off her coat, peeling off enough layers of winter clothing to give her body shape. Underneath it all, she was short, compact and muscular, not just sturdy but also strong. In contrast, the winter clothes gave Billy shape. Peeling off a sweater was like peeling off a layer of muscle. By the time he was stripped to his shirt and pants, all that was left was an electricity, an attitude, generated from a kind of tall, thin human conductor.

As for Chris, he was five eleven, with a medium build leaning toward thin and a deceivingly conservative haircut. He was also the middle ground between Denny's humorless pragmatism and Billy's possibly insane taste for catastrophe. He was the halfway house for humanity.

Billy and Denny carried in the equipment while Chris went to the front desk for messages. There were two: One from Matt, the other from Dorsey. "The first was your friend's idea," the clerk said. "He said it was a joke."

Chris read it: *The film is finished and it's all yours. P.S. Fuck you. Matt.*

Chris stared at the note. Was it meant to piss him off? Then he read the second message: a short note from Dorsey, telling him to call immediately. Chris did, using the lobby pay phone and calling collect.

"Chris?" Dorsey said. "Hey, you ever think of checking in?"

Chris considered whether to tell Dorsey about the pond, then decided it was an impossible secret. "A girl drowned and they just found her body."

"Tough luck," Dorsey said. "Anything good?"

"Nothing special," Chris said. "I got a call from Matt, anyway. He says the video's finished."

Dorsey started laughing. "Oh, yeah. He did a great job. Real impressive. I'm even thinking of giving him a promotion."

Chris knew he was being set up. "But?" he asked.

"But?" said Dorsey. "Just one small detail. Nothing big, really."

"What's the problem?" Chris said.

"A little technicality," Dorsey said. "Before I can promote him, first I gotta figure out how to scrape him together."

THREE

To the producers of Raw Death:
  Whoever the hell you are, each one of you must be fag-fucking, money-sucking scum. Did you ever think that children see this garbage? Is this what you let your children watch? If I ever get the chance to come out to that cunt city of yours, you better pray I don't see any of you on the street. If I do, I swear, you're going to star in your next movie.
  Sincerely, Lloyd D., Worcester, MA.

  Dear R.I.P. Productions—
  Just saw Raw Death. *I liked the stuff with the car crashes. You got anything else with car crashes?*
  John Tanner, San Antonio, TX

  To Al, Chris and John,
  I just finished watching Raw Death, *and I have to tell you, never before has a movie come so close to capturing the real death experience. Everyone involved should be congratulated.*
  In my covenant, we also work with death. Although we primarily sacrifice animals, once a year we try to perform a true sacrifice in the name of our lord. I was wondering; if I made a film, would you be interested in it? I have a home

video recorder, so it isn't a problem. As for the nature of the sacrifice, generally it requires the removal of the genitalia, as well as the clipping of all extending body parts (this includes the ears, nose, tongue and fingertips). Finally the sacrifice is rested on a fire, where he or she remains until death.

I'm not quite sure where this would fit in your next compilation. However, if you are interested, please leave a message for me in the classified section of my local newspaper. I'd be happy to contribute on your next project.

A Fan.

To the makers of Raw Death—
I have just one question: how do you sleep at night?
Sincerely, Disgusted.

"I appreciate your coming back, Chris," said Dorsey. "I'm going to need a little moral support. Not that there's anything to defend. And not like it's just my project. You and Matt have your names on the video, too. But it's not every day a guy films his death in Cinemascope."

"It's all right, Al," Chris said. Dorsey wrapped an arm about Chris and let him into the television news studio.

A set manager took care of them, checking their names off his list, giving them seats near a monitor so they could watch the show before their appearance. "I feel good about this," Dorsey whispered. "What about you? How do you feel?"

"I feel good," Chris said.

Dorsey nodded. "So do I. I think this is the right thing. Nip this in the bud. That's what we need to do, right?"

Chris agreed, which was all Dorsey really wanted. Chris glanced at the mail a last time, then handed it back to Dorsey. Dorsey waved the letters in the air.

"That's yesterday's crap," Dorsey said. "Did you read it? You'd think with all the crazies out there, these news stations would have something better to do. Maybe I should show them the letters. Maybe I should let them see just how sick this world is."

"I think you'd better put it away," Chris said, but the warning was unnecessary. Dorsey was already settling in his chair, the letters stuffed back in his pocket. He bit on a fingernail.

"Did you see Matt's footage?"

"I haven't had time," Chris said.

Dorsey frowned, thinking harder, starting on another nail. "Did you talk to his parents?"

"I called this afternoon."

"You told his father how sorry we are?" Dorsey said. "I got the morgue to ship off the body. You can tell him his son's nicely packed." Chris glared at Dorsey, but there was no point in saying anything. Dorsey was convinced of his sensitivity and a remark wouldn't shake his satisfaction. "Thanks for calling, Chris. I can't handle that kind of bullshit."

"Matt would have done the same for me," Chris said.

"Yeah, but he would have screwed up that, too," Dorsey answered.

Chris looked away. He was thinking of Matt's parents. When Chris had phoned, he wasn't sure what to say. How could he explain that the meaning of their son's death was a loud and clear "fuck you" at his boss and friend?

Matt's parents . . . They didn't even know what Matt did for a living. Matt had once told him this secret, and it surprised Chris. Sure, *Raw Death* was something you had to explain. At the same time, at least in L.A., it wasn't something to be ashamed of. On the Coast, the only thing that mattered were dollars, and the dollars had been good. Outsiders didn't appreciate this. The "buying public" judged you by your work, not your draw, but inside the business, what mattered was whether you made money. Since they had, Matt and he had jumped years ahead of anyone their age. They weren't no-credit filmmakers; they had become commodities. And any time Chris needed a reminder, he could wander down to a matinee show and walk the aisles, staring at the audience. Matinees on a workday in other cities struggled for business. Not in L.A. The theaters were packed with wannabes. Wannabe actors, wannabe writers, wannabe directors, wannabe producers . . . everyone watching, looking for the edge, seeing the same movie three, four times, trying to figure out what bit of magic picked the week's number-one film. Wannabes spent hours in the theaters, watching as if there were something more to it than the obvious; as if it were just a matter of sitting back and soaking in the projector light instead of getting your hands dirty, like Chris had.

Wannabes . . . Matt and Chris had climbed above all of them. They had produced one of the cult classics of the year, and even without the excuses, the bottom line was that after making money for Dorsey, Matt and Chris had value. Which meant that when Matt died—regardless of whether he had talent—the film business had lost something.

Chris might have told this to Matt's parents, but his call was passed to the family's lawyer, a man who cared less about condolences and more about whether Dorsey was ready to assume liability for the death.

Chris had so far spared Dorsey this news. He wanted Dorsey to learn of the lawsuit after Matt's body was too far for revenge. Instead, he encouraged Dorsey to send a wreath, and with it a trite little note: *We hope you are doing well in this sad time. Best wishes from R.I.P. Productions*—as if there was something normal in all of this, as if suicide was a job risk in L.A.

Chris also kept Dorsey happy by playing the servant, now searching for the makeup person, bringing him back to pat powder on Dorsey's forehead. Dorsey kept his eyes on a mirror and watched every touch of the pad. Then Chris took his turn under the powder. It was just seconds to their special appearance on a five o'clock news show. Like Dorsey had said, it's not everyday someone films his death in Cinemascope.

"I wish you'd seen the footage," Dorsey said again, a last whisper before standing and greeting the news anchor. The anchor was a woman, and she took a seat opposite them. Dorsey went for a smile, but there would be nothing friendly about this. The set lights flicked on, and Chris saw the director cue a cameraman. On the same cue, the anchor turned to a monitor and read aloud, "It was a tragedy only Hollywood could produce." Her tone was warm yet firm, her attention fixed on the camera. "I'm talking about a man who not only killed himself, but actually made a film of his suicide. What makes this story especially strange is what Matt Johnson did for a living—producing video collections of real murders and suicides.''

The red light flicked on the main camera.

''With me is Albert Dorsey, head of R.I.P. Productions, and Matt Johnson's colleague, Chris Thomas. We only have a few minutes, so perhaps one of you could quickly explain the idea behind your videos?''

Dorsey straightened. ''First of all,'' he said, ''what we're talking about is something we call nonfiction television. People have a genuine and understandable fascination with death, so what we've done is packaged one film—film which we've collected from very legitimate sources—that involves death, so that the purchaser can bridge in his own mind the difference between what he sees in fictional movies and what he sees in real life.''

''You're showing people getting killed,'' said the anchor. ''In one case a person getting shot, another time someone setting himself on fire.''

''That's part of what death is,'' Dorsey said. ''And as I said, the footage we get only comes from legitimate sources, including the news stations—including, I think, this one. But this isn't an exploitation film; it's not a bunch of naked kids running around a pool. It's just real-life footage.'' Dorsey leaned back, certain he was driving home the right point—that the film was legal, that it served a purpose and that it had something in common with everyday television, in particular something in common with this anchor. ''Now, as for Mr. Johnson, that's something different. People are speculating that his death had to do with his job.''

''What about Mr. Johnson?'' the anchor said. ''He filmed his suicide for your video.''

''We don't know that,'' Dorsey said. ''I can't begin to guess what was on Matt's mind. His death was a tragedy. Everyone who knew him feels that tragedy. But my understanding is that he wasn't exactly in a sober frame of mind when all of this happened. Provided, of course, that he did kill himself.''

''They have the death on film.''

"Yes, the death is filmed."

"And it was suicide," the anchor said.

"They have the death on film and it appears to be suicide," Dorsey said. It had been a bad attempt at a smoke screen. "The main point is whatever happened to Matt, it's incidental to the product we manufacture. Matt had his problems; I'm sure every company has employees with problems. My company is as legitimate a business as this station. And, like I said, we use a lot of the same tapes."

"And you feel the same way?"

Chris and the anchor fixed on each other. Dorsey had been doing so well, he hadn't expected a question. "Matt was a friend of mine," he said. "Anytime you spend months viewing and editing such graphic footage, you have to be careful with yourself."

"Which is a problem with your product, isn't it." the anchor said. "If this really could happen to anyone, then why make it in the first place? If it's only going to encourage people to hurt themselves or possibly kill people, should it be made?"

"Should the Beatles stop singing because of Charles Manson?" Dorsey replied. "Should Mike Cimino drop *The Deer Hunter* because a kid might put a gun to his head? If each creative industry had to worry about its audience, nothing would be made."

"Mr. Thomas?" the anchor said.

Chris answered carefully. "It's my job," he said, "to collect footage of people at the most private moment of their lives and that's the moment they stop existing." He paused, wanting to be sure of his thoughts. "If I'm to do my job well, I need to have the emotional freedom to get as close to a person as humanly and mechanically possible. That's not easy work. It requires a certain intensity."

"What about Mr. Johnson?" the anchor said.

"I think what happened to Matt was very unusual," Chris said. "There were definitely other things wrong with his life. If it was just the job, then I'd be dead too."

"God forbid," Dorsey said, patting Chris's arm and smiling. "The work we do—the work we *did*—demands concentration and caution," Chris said. "It's like handling poison-ous material; you have to keep on the rubber gloves. I wouldn't recommend it for everyone."

"Which leaves a last question, I suppose," the anchor said. "What about the footage? Mr. Johnson is dead, he filmed his death, you market a film on death. Are you going to use the footage?"

Chris shook his head. "Maybe it's not fair, but there's a big difference between running a clip of a stranger and running one of a friend."

"At the same time," Dorsey said, "we don't want to be hypocrites. If we use the footage about other people, it's only fair we consider ourselves victims to the same rules. I think Matt understood that, and that's why he provided the film. The main thing at this point, though, isn't the footage, but getting our lives in order. And all of us are doing our best to help Matt's family through the crisis."

Chris stared at him, not certain he understood Dorsey's answer. The anchor, however, again took command, speak-ing to the camera, and then, with the lights cut, directing them to the door. Dorsey didn't mind the quick treatment. He was on top of the world, certain he'd provided the perfect answers, giving Chris another one-armed hug as soon as they were in the elevator. A team, Dorsey kept saying. A one-two punch.

Chris just stared back. "Al, explain that last thing you said."

Dorsey looked confused.

"You aren't thinking of using Matt's tape, are you?"

Dorsey smacked his lips, trying to show Chris he had given the matter careful thought. "It's a tough call, Chris. I mean, I've got this deadline, and Matt—whatever his problems—did have the decency to think about his job."

"Al—"

"What's the problem?" Dorsey said. "Have you seen the footage? I asked you to look at it. He fucks up a little at the end, but—"

"You *can't*, Al," Chris said.

"Really?" Dorsey said. "Just because you know some-one you won't use the film? So in other words, it's okay showing a little girl hit by a car, but let a friend bang his head, and—''

''It may make no sense to you, but it does to me.''

''When I got a deadline, a lot of things don't make sense,'' Dorsey said. ''And maybe we wouldn't have this problem in the first place if one of us had stuck around long enough to finish off what he'd started.''

Chris had already thought the same thing; in fact, had thought about it several times that day. But he didn't want Dorsey distracting him.

''I've got some footage from Iowa,'' said Chris.

''A drowning, right?'' Dorsey said, sneering. ''A girl?''

''*Teenage* girl,'' said Chris, remembering Billy's pitch.

''But it only starts after she's dead.''

''Billy got good close-ups,'' Chris said. ''If you want to see it, I can—''

''You want to put up a drowner against someone blowing off his skull?''

Chris thought for a moment. ''Maybe I can dig up something.''

''Between now and tomorrow?'' Dorsey said.

''Why not?''

Dorsey grinned, enjoying the proposition. ''You really think you can do it?'' he said. ''After all Matt went through, you think it's that easy?''

Chris shrugged, and Dorsey, with great pleasure, patted Chris a last time.

''All right,'' he said. ''You've got until tomorrow,'' heading back for his car.

As for Chris, he bought a newspaper and turned to the metro section. People were killed almost every night in this city.

For Chris, the question was figuring out where the next murder would happen.

FOUR

"BECAUSE I love the movies."

That's what Chris said to anyone who wondered why he moved to L.A. The answer was pat because the question was wrong. There was nothing secret about why Chris had come here; like scores of other people, the movies had mesmerized him. Some came for the craft, others for the money, but everyone came for the immensity of it all. It was like the Kafka novel where a character spends forever trying to reach an unreachable castle. For Chris, the castle was the movie industry, except this time it wasn't just one character pounding on the door—*everyone* wanted in. And a few succeeded.

Why he loved the movies . . . The better question was how he could do such a good job on a movie like *Raw Death*.

"Everyone loves the movies," Chris said. "Isn't that why you came here?"

"Of course, but I thought my life would be a little more normal," said his date.

She was Chris's latest attempt at a relationship—a freelance film editor who would see him for another month and then drift off. Or so he presumed, since his move to L.A. had only brought a string of failed romances. In each case it was the woman who walked.

"We finish the rough cut three days ago," Gwen said.

"That's when I found out I'm dropped for the final cut. They had me working every day from six to ten and now they're taking me off the project."

"You've got a contract, don't you?" Chris said.

"They don't care about that," she said. "Look, never mind. Can we change topics please?"

They were in a restaurant and she took a moment to look about the room. Chris knew what she was doing: job hunting. While Gwen looked for connections, Chris stared at her. She had an anxious expression, a kind of tight-fisted energy that always kept some part of her body in motion—for the moment her hands, which drummed on the table. Nearby were a purse and clipboard. The clipboard was a mess of phone numbers and names, and the purse held everything from a wallet and a stopwatch to a diaphragm.

"Did you tell your family?" Chris asked.

"Of course not. Why would I?"

"Because you phone them every week," Chris said.

Gwen remembered. "Right," she finally said. "I forgot I told you that."

"Your father should have an interesting reaction."

"Interesting's one word for it," Gwen said. She looked about the room. "I should kill every damn person in that company. You're the death expert. How should I get my revenge? What's the latest rage in murder?"

"You aren't the killing type," he said. Chris reached across the table and picked up her clipboard. "Did you talk with Doug Beyer over at Running Dog? He's got something about POWs in Vietnam or Cambodia. Stars a football tackle."

Gwen glared at him.

"What's wrong?" Chris said.

"I said I didn't want to talk about it anymore," she said. "*You* answer some questions. Tell me how things went in America's heartland."

He shrugged.

"Did you ship off Matt's body?"

Chris nodded and Gwen looked amused. "Now you're a coroner," she said. "I swear, you're even doing crap jobs that haven't been invented. Is there anything else they have you doing?"

"I've got a job tonight," he said. "I have to find some footage for Dorsey."

"A job?" she said. Chris could tell she was thinking again, this time at the prospect of someone else working. Chris also saw a familiar look in her eyes—a look of exhaustion, and not simply with unemployment. She leaned back and shook her head. "I don't know, Chris. Our lives are on such different paths. I'm not sure this is going so well."

"We haven't had much of a chance yet," he said. "I wouldn't give up, if that's what you mean."

She let him hold her hand but offered nothing. "You're this kind of enigmatic presence," she said. "For someone who does as much as you, you're one of the least involved people. I know. I mean, you think about me, but it's like you're thinking too much. It's not even thinking—it's some kind of concentrated energy, and it's always concentrated on me. I feel like a guinea pig." She moved closer and whispered, "I feel like you're stripping me clean, Chris. It's the weirdest thing, but I swear, even when we're having sex, I feel like you're trying to steal my orgasms."

Chris stared at her. "You mean you're not having orgasms," he said.

"No, I'm having them, but I feel like you're not having your own. I feel like you're trying to ride off mine. It's like you're screwing and stealing from me at the same time."

Chris didn't know what to say. Gwen looked just as uncomfortable. "I just don't know what to make of you," she said.

She wiped her mouth and waited for Chris's reaction.

"I wish you'd say something," she said.

Chris raised his eyebrows and shook his head. "This is a new one," he said.

She glanced at her watch. "Maybe you should be going. You have a full night ahead."

They both looked relieved. They were leaving the restaurant when Gwen kissed him goodnight.

"You know something?" she said.

She was looking up at him, her expression almost tender. He waited.

"You stare too much," she said.

Chris didn't answer, choosing to remain silent, watching as Gwen went to her car and drove onto the highway.

If Chris stared too much, so had the rest of his family.

Chris grew up in a household that spent less time talking than watching each other's moods. It was a skill that became critical when his father died. His father had suffered a stroke, and for weeks he couldn't move or talk. All he could really do was die. The only way visitors communicated was by watching the soft changes in his mood. Chris did the same: staring at his father, paying attention to every movement of his lips, eyes and cheeks. When death came, Chris was beside him, watching him, pulling free every last lingering thought. His father was Chris's first Moment, and during that Moment, Chris felt more power in a split second than he'd ever felt in his life. But what was it? Was it love he felt? Was it fear?

When his mother died, Chris was already in California. He missed her death, and it was a shame because he loved his mother, but more than that, he'd wanted to be there and stare at her and feel the same closeness he'd had with his father. There was also something else he'd wanted to do. Something important.

He'd wanted to bring a camera.

Things were so different in L.A. It was as if his life had begun fresh upon reaching the city—a feeling shared by others who had moved west. The only things that survived were a few memories, part of a bank account, and some old, lasting habits. Like staring, he supposed. Gwen complained about it, but filming and staring was how he spent most of his days; it was how he'd spend this evening, with only ten hours left to find and film a murder.

It wasn't a new job for him. In fact, he'd already done it twice for the first *Raw Death*. The trick was being informed, and Chris began by checking the weather. He wanted a warm and clear night, provided of course warm didn't mean lazy. Lazy people either did nothing or stayed indoors. In either case, Chris would be screwed, because he needed good outdoor action; something with an unhindered point of view, and, preferably, reasonable proximity for sound.

So Chris started with the weather. Once satisfied, he turned to the city crimes. He underlined the robberies, assaults and homicides before turning to his map. After flattening his layout of L.A., he circled the locations of the crimes, and alongside the circles jotted the time of day for the various attacks. Finally, with an area sketched and picked, he headed to the production offices. No one was in, but Dorsey had left him a note plus the keys to the van. *Remember—no car wrecks,* the note read.

Chris went to the closet and pulled out two tape cartridges, one battery pack, one camera and a police band radio. The camera, tapes and pack he put in the back of the van; the radio he belted into the passenger seat. After setting the radio dial, he turned the ignition and headed downtown.

L.A. at night. Always interesting, particularly along the fringe of West Hollywood, not more than five blocks from Sunset Boulevard. This was Chris's destination. He pulled over by a curb, parked and turned up the volume on his police band. It was like a cop stakeout. He stretched, glanced out the side windows, looked behind him, relaxed, settled and waited, listening as the reports came in, knowing the biggest trick would be choosing the right call to track. He leaned forward when he heard a possibility, and leaned back when it turned flat. He did this until a quarter past one. Then came word of a gang fight six blocks northwest, behind a small shopping mall.

Chris knew the location. It was an outdoor yard with a fringe of incandescent, high-voltage lights. This was the kind of lighting worth gambling on, and he shifted into gear, reaching the scene in minutes.

There was nothing quiet about the fight. While Chris parked in the shadows and filmed, teenagers screamed and pummeled each other. He filmed, convinced the riot was beyond control, knowing this was all he could safely do, focusing tighter as a teenager fell and another placed a foot on top of the boy. The attacker swiped the air, his chain striking down, and with each flick of the metal, the boy beneath him tried to keep up a guard.

Chris tightened the shot. The boy had curled up, blocking any view of his eyes, and that was bad. Dorsey would want the eyes. Chris watched, filmed, tried to be patient, until finally the chain struck the boy across the temple. The arms dropped instantly, and suddenly Chris had everything. The look, the fear, the pain . . .

The police.

The teenagers scrambled for the dark. Some hoped fences, others scrambled down the ramp, a few dashed past Chris's van. Chris finally stopped filming, opened the side door, and walked over to one of the police officers. "Here," he said. "Maybe you can recognize some faces." He gave the tape to the cops. He did this to build favors and because Dorsey could care less about a tape of fighting kids. "It's crazy out tonight."

"Full moon on a weekend," one of the cops said.

"I was out doing night shots on the city," Chris said. "Any places I should watch out for?"

"Olin and Twenty-third," the cop said.

"Olin definitely," said a second cop. "But I wouldn't go anywhere on Twenty-third. It's turning into a fucking drag strip."

"Cars you mean?" Chris said.

"Yeah, cars. Turbo-charged nonsense."

"Drag racing," the first cop said.

"Right," Chris said. "Thanks," knowing drag racing meant accidents, and accidents meant a waste of time. He went back on the street, drove a few blocks, parked and continued the vigil.

One-thirty.

Ten hours to deadline.

It came together at five A.M.

He saw it right at sunrise, with the light coming over the mountains and the palm trees a fresh breezy green and the streets a sandy tan. Robbery-in-progress at a 7-Eleven on La Brea Avenue. The police were already there by the time

Chris arrived, but it didn't matter. Inside was a crackhead. The man was carrying a shotgun and pistol, and looked like he was having an argument with the Slurpee machine. There was a clerk inside, so the police treated it as a hostage situation, blocking the street and taking positions behind their cars. Chris didn't mind. It was so early and there were so few people, the cops weren't worrying about one guy with a camera. He moved freely, covering the robbery from every angle. Dorsey wanted that too. Lots of shots, lots of angles.

He also kept the camera steady, even when the gunman blew out the front glass door. The police jumped and so did an ambulance team, but not Chris. He kept firm, glancing at an officer and saying, "What's gonna happen?"

The cop ignored him, but that was all right too, because Chris knew the answer. Rifles were out and the safeties had to be flipped. Now the crackhead had to make up his mind; do or die. And if Chris hadn't spent so much time in the van, he might have been a bit more generous with the crackhead. Instead, he made a wish that would spare Matt any part of Dorsey's fame and fortune. He thought maybe the gunman would point his rifle at a cop, and that the cops would respond in kind.

Instead, the crackhead went berserk. Chris had him, full frame, when he stopped shouting at the slurpee machine long enough to grab the cashier and drag the man over the counter.

Then, while Chris was tight on the cashier's face, the gunman put the barrel against the man's chest and pulled the trigger.

Chris had it. The lunacy, the fear, in perfect close-up.

And it wasn't over.

There was still the crackhead to finish. After killing the cashier, the crackhead began screaming and running down the aisles, popping shots into the pretzels and chips, managing one last shotgun blast before the police opened fire.

Chris had it again. First one arm went out, then the other... The police fired until the crackhead's chest popped open. He fell backward, caught spread-eagled on a snack foods rack, his eyes staring out of the store and into the camera.

Into Chris's eyes.

Chris didn't move or take his finger off the camera's trigger. He only filmed, taping nothing more than this drug addict slowly gazing into death—someone not even aware he was dying. It was incredible. The eyes; they held steady. Not blinking, not turning . . . All the same, Chris could sense them sinking back. Retreating and drawing into the core. And Chris was following. His camera was with the addict every step into the abyss until, as always, there came that moment . . .

The Moment.

And Chris was again left with the living.

Later, he walked into Dorsey's office. He stood there with tape in hand, empty of all thought, waiting for Dorsey to take the cassette from him—to look at the tape and let him know he had succeeded.

Dorsey took the cassette and tossed it aside. There was no need to look at it; he had that much faith in Chris.

"Good," he said. "By the way, I've been thinking about who should replace Matt. You got any ideas?"

Chris shook his head, and Dorsey gave him a letter.

"I got this yesterday from a guy in New York. At first I thought it was another film grad, but it came with a tape. He put together some interesting footage. The guy has talent, I think. We might want to bring him in."

Chris couldn't read the letter now. He folded it and slid the letter into his pocket.

"Let me know what you think," Dorsey said. "It's your decision, yes or no. You're the man in charge." Dorsey also dropped an airline envelope in front of his associate producer. "When you get to Iowa, try finishing your soil shots by Wednesday, so you can fly back here Thursday. You'll want to be here for the budget meeting." Finally, Dorsey lifted his head. "I'm trying to figure how much to spend on *Raw Death III*."

FIVE

CHRIS sat in his hotel room, remembering what Dorsey's secretary had said as he left for his flight back to Iowa.

"I don't know how you did it, Chris," Ruth told him, talking about his all-night vigil.

"It was just luck," Chris said. "Luck and patience."

The secretary stared sympathetically at him. "That's not what I meant," she said. "I meant," her voice emphasizing the disbelief, the distrust in Chris's humanity, "I don't know *how* you did it."

She sat there, eyes curious, protected by pictures of her husband and children. All he could do was try being funny. "I guess God picked me to make his home movies," he answered, and they both smiled. At the same time, there was nothing funny about any of this. His one consolation was that spending a night on the street, waiting for disaster, wasn't any different from the work of a reporter. All Chris did was get to the scene a few minutes quicker. And with that perspective, who cared if the footage was for Dorsey or the evening news? Like Dorsey once said, after someone declared there was a difference between a star showing skin in a legitimate film and doing it in one of Dorsey's epics: "A tit is a tit and prick is a prick, no matter what the budget." The same was true here.

Except he knew it wasn't quite true. Context mattered. That was why Chris hadn't let Dorsey use the film of Matt. And now in Iowa—alone and recuperating, reorienting himself in some bread-basket town that would never make sense to him . . .

Presuming Hayden even qualified as a town. When they had arrived, Denny said that in the world of townships Hayden was not quite the lowest form, but also wasn't far from the bottom. Later Denny corrected herself and compared Hayden to split amoeba, since Hayden was in proximity to Marsh, another minor community.

Basic life, basic values, playing out among a network of farms, fields and small-town streets and—

Chris stopped himself. He was condensing; turning a living town into a single, neat thought, just as if he were back in L.A., pitching a movie for some wallets. And he knew why, too. It made him feel better than the town, and for the moment that was necessary. What would people of Hayden or Marsh think if they knew how he'd spent the previous night? Surprise? Disgust?

If, of course, they were shaken at all. After all, Dorsey's movies were a hit in the Midwest, some selling at two-for-one specials.

In a clothes drawer was one of their video cameras. Most of the equipment was film, but Dorsey liked Chris to frame a shot on video first, just to make sure it was worth the expense. You could do that with some video cameras—not only reuse the tape, but use the camera to play back what you recorded on television. Chris did that now: disconnecting the cable on the motel TV, then hooking his own wire to the set. When all the connections were made, he crossed the room and opened his suitcase, this time zipping back a sleeve he used for carrying his equipment. He dug about and pulled free the two boxes Dorsey had given him.

"Campo, Donald," the first box read. It was the video from Dorsey's job applicant. Chris slid out the cartridge, slipped it into the video camera and read Campo's letter.

* * *

Dear Mr. Dorsey:
I'm an assistant director for Two-Tone Productions in Manhattan, and now I'm looking to move west. For the last eight years I've been working on low-budget thrillers. I want to take my talents to L.A.

Please look at my clips. I pride myself on realism. Maybe you'll appreciate the quality.
Sincerely, Don Campo

Chris was still reading the letter when the footage began. He understood what Campo meant by low-budget thrillers. Chris sat and watched ten minutes of S&M film. In one clip, Russian female KGB officers tortured an American female spy. Chris watched as the Russians took turns at the American: first with a cigarette, then a whip, then knitting needles ... He watched, hoping to God it was all special effects. The burns smoked, the welts swelled, the needles drew blood. The second clip was more of the same, except this time a woman police sergeant and a male officer took turns interrogating a woman prostitute. Chris watched for a minute, then stopped the tape.

"I pride myself on realism," Campo had written. "Maybe you'll appreciate the quality."

Quality? It was some horribly conceived nightmare; as close as Chris had ever come to violence for the sake of violence. Of course, maybe that was the point—a kind of in-your-face hatred that Campo hoped you'd never forget. This was possible, but this probably gave Campo too much credit. The film, the film's victims ... you could stare forever at their agony and never close the distance. The torture was as soulless as pornographic sex. So what was the point? What was the point of anything without something real at stake?

Chris dropped the tape in the garbage, disgusted with the footage and Dorsey. He crumbled Campo's letter and reached for the second box. "Johnson, Matt," it read.

Chris removed the cartridge, set it in the camera and pressed the play button. The television snow flickered clear, and for a moment all he saw was a blank screen. Then, without any introduction whatsoever the tape began. Matt's tape, Camera #1, from the kitchen.

Chris sat down and watched.

"Over here is the dog bowl," Matt said, reaching into a cabinet. He grinned, finished straightening the kitchen, then walked back to the living room. For a full minute, Chris heard and saw nothing. Dorsey had made no attempt to edit the tapes; spliced together, each tape would recount the action from start to finish, from a different viewpoint. Chris was stuck in the kitchen, alone with the refrigerator, cabinets and the door frame. Through the open doorway, at an angle, Matt occasionally crossed into view. Chris saw him go through the motions of bending, then continue his walk, now breathing out smoke. But then he completely disappeared from view. For a moment, there was nothing. Finally, Matt, somewhere in the living room, shouted and Herc came racing into the kitchen. That fucking rat dog, Herc. The dog put the contraption into motion, and Chris watched as the string pulled and the acid began dripping.

There was little after that. Some muttered talk from the living room, a shout . . . really nothing until the sound. A sudden, jolting shock, followed by a heavy fall.

And then, without a break, Chris found himself at Camera #2.

This was a quick clip. Matt had set up a camera in the bathroom. Chris watched as Matt came stumbling over the toilet, threw open the lid and vomited. Thirty seconds later, he stumbled out of view. That was it for Camera #2.

Which left the three cameras in the living room.

Dorsey started with the establishment camera. Matt had it angled not only to include him, but the crate, the wire, the shotgun. As with the first tape, Dorsey ran it from the start of the action. He watched Matt go through his phone calls and finally position himself on the sofa. He listened as Matt shouted for his dog, then started talking, his eyes all too alive, his mind clearly conscious of everything that was happening. Chris had at least hoped Matt was in a sufficient stupor not to understand what was happening. Now it was all too clear how carefully plotted the day had been. And it was also clear that no matter how much coke Matt had smoked, the consequences were also on his mind. Chris watched, and the more Matt talked and stared at the shotgun, the more Chris wished Matt would stop fooling around. Hell, they had both been in worse slumps than this. It made no sense. Absolutely none, no matter what he babbled at the cameras.

"Fuck," Matt shouted, leaning forward, staring at the crate, "Typical, right? I mean just plain, fucking *typical*."

He almost didn't finish the sentence. The blast fired and Chris closed his eyes. When he opened them, the angle of the camera was wrong. Then he realized Matt had been thrown off the sofa and into the camera's tripod. It was over; at least for this clip.

There were still two to go.

It was a camera from Matt's POV. Matt had placed it inches above his head, to film the shotgun going off. It was almost overly dramatic, and Chris wondered if maybe all this was a way for Matt to feed his ego. No one, after all, got this kind of coverage, not even prisoners on death row. It was excessive. It was pure Dorsey.

Except Matt screwed this one. When he raised his head, he covered the camera's angle of the shotgun. It wasn't going to work, Chris thought. Then he realized exactly what was going to happen. He heard Matt curse, and Chris saw how his head lifted in front of the shotgun, and Chris wished like hell he was quicker than the tape player.

Instead, there was the shotgun fire, and the blast split Matt's skull, painting the lens with blood.

Last camera.

Chris dared to watch. He had to. He had to know exactly what Dorsey considered his property. He forced his attention to the television, already forewarned of the last camera angle and now finally seeing it. He stared down, along with the camera, upon the arm of the sofa. On the bottom of the screen, Chris could just see the tip of the shotgun barrel, and that was all he saw until Matt came into view. Then, instead of the sofa, he saw a full frame shot of Matt's face.

"Fucking great, huh?" Matt said. "Bet I'm taking up the whole goddamn TV."

Chris again watched and listened. He knew Matt's speech. Seeing him up close didn't change anything; not at this point. It only made things more pitiful. All that mattered was how Matt made his final delivery. If the joke was to be perfect, Matt would have to provide what they both knew Dorsey wanted. So Chris waited, his mind counting down to the Moment, his finger over the hold button, waiting . . . waiting . . . until he heard the cue words. "Fucking typical." That was it. Three, two, one . . . "Typical, right? I mean just plain—"

Chris freeze-framed. Matt was blurred. By lifting his head, he had moved too close for a clear focus. His focus was also off. Matt was looking across the room at the crate. Good, Chris thought. Saved. And he stop-framed forward, catching the moments in fractions of seconds, until—*shit*— Matt gave what Dorsey wanted. Matt stared into the camera. The rest of Matt's face was unreadable, but still, somehow, the eyes registered. And Chris saw the look of a raging lunatic. A freaked-out, killer stare. And the madness held, up to the moment that smoke puffed from the shotgun. Chris went that far, progressing carefully, frame by frame. Advancing until a single frame was distorted by another blur— perhaps the pellets frozen before Matt's face.

Then he turned off the television, turned off the camera and began disconnecting the wires. All the time, he thought of one thing. Not Matt, not himself . . .

He thought of Dorsey.

Why was Dorsey being so generous? Matt had handed Dorsey gold, and Dorsey had set it aside. Why? A moment of good taste? Was there some hope for Dorsey after all?

Or maybe this was just Dorsey's last joke on Matt. He'd always considered Matt a fuck-up. Maybe this was his way of keeping Matt from forever finding success on the screen.

Or there was another possibility. Could Dorsey just be

holding on to the tape for his next sequel, *Raw Death III?* Was there some advantage to *that?*

Chris went to the bathroom, washed his face and stared into the mirror.

Lines and boundaries, he thought. They were being crossed before he even saw them.

He stared a long time in the mirror, then finally managed a sickly grin. Under his breath, he whispered, ''You are not scum.''

He'd be whispering the same thing tomorrow evening.

SIX

"CHRIS," said Billy. "Remember the footage of that girl who drowned?"

Chris wasn't in the mood for this. If Denny was in the room, he would have passed him to her. But Denny was still at breakfast and didn't have to be on the job until lunch. In the meantime, all morning, it was up to them to go through the week's rushes.

"Chris?" Billy started again.

"Yeah, I remember," Chris said.

"Remember how you said it wasn't any good because we didn't see the girl before she drowned, so Dorsey wouldn't want it?"

"I remember," Chris said. "I talked to Dorsey, too. I was right."

There was a moment of quiet. Chris waited, knowing it wasn't finished, waiting for Billy to say how he'd sold the footage to a news station and for Chris to fuck himself.

"Chris," said Billy, "suppose we had film of her before she drowned?"

Chris looked up. Billy returned the stare—Billy not quite sure enough of his victory to gloat, Chris not certain Billy understood what he had said. At last, Chris left his seat and joined him, sitting by the editing machine. Billy was already rewinding the film. "Remember those establishment shots you wanted? Some time exposures of a sunset, that kind of crap?"

"Dorsey wanted it, not me," Chris said. "It was in the script."

"But you remember when we set up the cameras—one on a hill, the other by the road? We did that the day before the girl was pulled from the water. We set up the cameras and set them for time exposures and left the cameras running. Except the timing was off on both cameras, so I had to do the whole thing again the next day."

"I remember," Chris said.

"We got her."

"Got her how?"

"Got her driving the night she died," Billy said. "We got her with the road camera. She's riding in a pickup truck with her boyfriend."

Billy ran the film. It was exactly what Billy said: a time exposure that hadn't time-exposed, so the sun didn't set fast enough and the time crawled along at close to normal speed. Chris watched as one car sped by, then another, then . . .

"That was it," Billy said.

"I didn't see anything," Chris said.

"You weren't paying attention," Billy said. He backed up the film and ran it slower. Chris leaned in for a more careful look. The viewer had only a twelve-inch screen, and although it was more for guaranteeing exposure than seeing details, he could still make out the shapes. The pickup came around a turn and toward the camera. Chris could see a teenage boy behind the wheel and beside him a blonde-haired girl, her body turned toward the boy, raising a hand over her mouth. Then the pickup disappeared out of view.

"That's the whole thing?" Chris said.

"That's it," Billy said. "Ten hours later, they're pulling her out of the water."

"Why do you think it's her?"

"You haven't seen the other footage," Billy said. "I was looking at it yesterday and you can see her face clearly."

To prove his point, Billy switched reels. He also turned off the monitor and adjusted the viewer so the image projected on a wall. He fast-forwarded, then stopped when the rescue began. Billy really had done a remarkable job. He had a tight, close shot of the rescue team and, most important, a tight, close shot of the body. Chris watched, fascinated, as the man in the wet suit dropped in the water and the girl at first bobbed under the water, then again surfaced . . .

Billy stopped on a frame. "Just look at her a second," he said, and Chris did. Soft features, streaks of makeup smudging her eyes, her hair wet and shrouding much of her face.

"Seventeen I'd guess," Billy said.

Chris shook his head. "Fifteen, tops."

Billy kept the footage running a moment longer, then stopped it, rewound the film and returned to his first reel.

"You can see better with the projection," Billy said. "That's her, all right."

Billy ran the stop-frame, flashing forward a moment, then freezing, then forward again. When he finished, Chris knew Billy was right. It was her. She was talking to a boy—animated, making some point—then reaching to her mouth, carrying a lit cigarette. And the boy, he just listened. His head didn't turn, his mouth didn't bend with either a word or smile. He was a driver, his attention absolutely fixed.

"It's her," Chris said, "but it's still not her drowning. That's what makes Dorsey's prick stand up."

"Shit, this is probably the last time anyone ever filmed her alive," Billy said. "You don't think it means something, having a picture of her and her date, then the body coming up? I think Dorsey could dig that. Love and death. What more could you want?"

"It's not her boyfriend," Chris said. "Look at how they're sitting."

"What are you talking about?" Billy said, pissed off. "How would you know? When was the last time you had a date?"

Billy ran the footage again, and this time Chris concentrated on the boy. The teenager had a thin, drawn face, with a flushed look that came with the weather. Aside from the red, there was no color at all, although that could also have been the film's exposure. His hair was a dark color, but his eyebrows were thin, almost as thin as his lips. It wasn't a handsome face; just a worried one. At the moment, it struck Chris as unusually tight.

And familiar. Chris thought it was the clothes he recognized. And he did, but not because of a past memory. The boy and the girl wore almost identical parkas. Chris wondered if it had to do with the school.

Then the pickup truck ran out of view, and for the fourth time Billy rewound the film.

Finally, he began to see it. It was in the face, but mostly the way he focused: the way his attention fixed on the rearview mirror, so intently concentrating he completely missed the camera. Chris studied the eyes and knew exactly what he saw. He saw Matt. He saw the crackhead. He saw the line, or someone about to walk over it, or walk someone else over it. He saw the stars of *Raw Death*. Dorsey had a term for them: Moment Makers.

He saw a Moment Maker.

Billy flicked off the viewer. "So what do you think?" he insisted. "Tell me the truth for a change. Is this something Dorsey could use or what?"

Chris stared at Billy.

Chris walked into the sheriff's office, looked to a deputy, waved and waited. He had visited the officer on his arrival in Hayden, just so the police would know why three strangers had intruded upon the town. For now, the deputy waved back and lifted a finger. "Just a minute," he said, then returned to his phone call. Chris understood. No one was being rude; matters simply took their own pace in Hayden. Chris waited, and while he waited, he looked about the station house. It was a small county office that served the deputy, the sheriff and a single receptionist. For now, the deputy was alone, but on a busy day they would work together in the same room, their desks no more than an arm's length apart. If Chris and Dorsey worked under similar circumstances, they would be in a death grip by noon; here, however, everything had the certain ease of a small town.

The deputy hung up the phone, crossed the room and extended his hand. "Sorry about the wait, Chris."

Chris smiled back. During their first introduction, both had been friendly. Nothing had changed. "I don't mean to bother you," Chris said. "It's just I've got something that might interest you and your boss. It has to do with the drowning."

"Yeah," the deputy said. "I heard you were at the pond."

"I'm talking about before that," Chris said. "It's when the girl was alive. I got some footage of her with a boy."

"You got film of her before she died?"

"That's right."

"And you think it's worth us taking a look?"

"I thought you could use it," he said.

The deputy understood. "I'll talk with Tom," he said, meaning the sheriff. "I think we're both free around four. How about we stop by the motel then?"

"The sooner, the better," Chris said.

"Fine," the deputy said. "About two hours."

"Fine," Chris said, leaving, knowing he'd spend the time sitting in the motel wondering whether he should have been more direct.

Two hours. They passed with Chris watching the clock.

Dorsey called, and Chris said he'd call back later, hanging up. Billy stuck his head in the door every twenty or so minutes, asking when they'd be filming. Chris told him not until tomorrow, but Billy kept checking anyway. Billy knew something was up and wanted to be a part of it.

Denny was different. She checked in, Chris told her about the police, and she just shook her head and left.

Chris, however, knew this was right. And as the time passed, he thought less about the police and the girl, and more about the one person he didn't know.

He thought about the boy.

Who was he? Where was he? Why did he do it? Could he do it again?

At last they arrived, fifteen minutes late. Chris sat the officers down, ran the footage of the pond, and then ran the car footage. "You can probably see what got me worried," Chris said. "That teenager," pointing at the boy, "he's the one that got my attention. I keep wondering who he is. If we can find him—"

"Call him Todd," the sheriff said.

"Todd Meacham," said the deputy. "And the girl's Kathleen Donnelly."

They stared at Chris, appearing concerned but certainly not anxious. The sheriff began to make sense of what Chris was suggesting. "You were thinking, maybe, that Todd had something to do with her accident?"

The deputy shook his head. "There's nothing strange about Todd driving Kathleen home. They're neighbors."

"Nothing strange about it at all," the sheriff said. "We already talked to Todd. He told us exactly what time he dropped her off."

"Todd's a good kid," the deputy said. "They're all good kids around here, Chris."

Chris looked in pain. "See, that's just it," he said. "You know him, so you trust him. But I just know what's in the film, and from what I see, that's not two teenagers out for a drive. It is for her—maybe for Kathleen—but the look on the boy's face. I know that look."

Chris played the footage again, this time freezing on a frame. He walked into the picture and pointed at Todd.

"That's a dangerous person," Chris said.

The deputy chuckled. "To me, that's the look of a very careful driver."

The sheriff squinted. "Mr. Thomas, what makes you know so much about dangerous people?"

Chris thought about the question. He also thought of his change of status, from first to last name. "I once did some research on a few murder cases," he said. "There's nothing wrong with that, I hope."

"No," the sheriff said, "but it also doesn't mean you can stare at a picture and tell me he's a killer."

"Chris," said the deputy, "it's not that we just don't reach the same conclusion as you—we also know better."

"What we could do is make a copy of the film for Kathleen's parents," said the sheriff. "They could make a photo out of one of the pictures. They'd probably appreciate that."

The deputy stood to leave. "You did the right thing by phoning us."

"Of course," the sheriff said. "Coming out here was no bother at all," also standing and heading for the door.

A few minutes later, they were gone.

As for Chris, he stood in the room, alone, with Todd Meacham's face projected on his motel wall.

Chris was in a coffee shop. He wasn't angry with the police. They weren't real police anyway; they were people hired to protect a set of laws that were rarely broken. Good people, but not police.

On the other hand, how many people, cops or otherwise, knew as much about killing as Chris? How many had been given the opportunity?

Chris went from the coffee shop to a phone booth, where he checked on an address. Then it was back to the van, driving seven miles south, passing the pond where Kathleen Donnelly had drowned—the hole already starting to ice over, warning signs now facing each bank—finally slowing before a mailbox. He slowed enough to see the name, then turned onto the adjoining dirt road. He drove maybe twenty yards before thinking better of using his headlights. He cut them and went just over the crest of a hill, parking.

And from this distant vantage, he sat in the car, staring at the Meacham house.

He saw the shadows of people moving about the living room, people probably preparing for supper, unaware of death, unaware of life . . . unaware of Chris.

Todd Meacham. He wasn't running anywhere; he was in his room. He was probably upstairs reading, thinking about the girl or someone else.

It was all here. There was nothing to do but sit back and

wait for Todd to snap again. And Chris was sure he would, because there were few people who could muster that kind of restraint, especially once the cork had been popped. Especially someone who, intentionally or not, had committed Hayden's version of the perfect murder.

Chris stared at the shadows, possibly at Todd, thinking of what was to happen, wondering if this was another of those lines daring to be crossed. It was something new, he was sure of that. Maybe even a walk into the land of guns and maniacs.

He wondered, and rubbed his eyes, and ran the idea so many times through his head that the whole thing lost sense. Finally, he backed carefully, quietly off the dirt road and turned onto the highway. He drove to the motel, all the time crafting his pitch to Dorsey. He decided to be direct; Dorsey would be easier to handle with the cards on the table. He went to his motel room, dialed out, said something to Dorsey's secretary and waited.

"Chris," Dorsey greeted. "How're you feeling?"

"I'm doing fine, Al," Chris said. "I'm doing very fine."

"Yeah?" Dorsey said. "I didn't know how you'd be after seeing that stuff Matt filmed."

"I liked mine better," Chris said.

Dorsey chuckled.

"But I got something better than either of them."

"Oh yeah?"

"It's about that girl who drowned," Chris said. "She didn't just trip into the water, she was killed by this local kid. Except the police here can't see the noses in front of their faces, so the kid's roaming free. I've seen film on this kid, Al. I'm sure he's going to do something again."

"Yeah?" Dorsey said. "So what's that got to do with us?"

Chris knew Dorsey was onto him; still, he let Dorsey enjoy his game. "I don't think anyone's ever filmed a murderer before," Chris said. "I don't just mean when he kills someone; I mean every day of his life, up until it happens again. A real profile. Something that shows you what it's all about, instead of some pieced together, after-the-fact bullshit.''

"I've never heard of it," Dorsey said. "But what's that got to do with us?"

"I was thinking," Chris said. "As long as I'm here already, and I've got the film, and what I don't have you can send out, and as long as I also take care of the other film . . ."

"Yeah?" Dorsey said.

"I was thinking," Chris said, "as long as we've got all that in place, maybe it'd be okay if I missed next week's meeting.

"Maybe," Chris said. "I've got another video."

PART TWO

PART TWO

SEVEN

ODD felt sorry for Kathleen Donnelly.

He was there when they discovered the body, and was still there when the rescue team dragged it from the hole. He sat beside an evergreen, tucked against the wind, waiting until the pond was free of people. Then, at last, he walked down to the bank.

Todd was tall for his age; tall enough to make a habit of taking careful, loping steps. This time, he showed more than his usual caution. When he reached the ice, he stood on the shore and rubbed his toe over the frozen surface, as if the pond were something new to him. And perhaps it was, since death had altered everything. Todd thought of the summer, when heavy rains beat the water into a muddy cloud. There had been a similar change, at least in feel. Before, the pond had an overlooked gentleness; now, after being so forgettably quiet, it had a bottomless, frightening depth.

He stood on the bank much longer than needed. Then, with one last look about, he crossed the ice to the hole. He kneeled, bit the fingertips of his right glove and pulled the glove free of his hand.

Finally, Todd looked down at the water.

It was bad out today. A numbing cold was already hurting his fingers, but that was nothing compared to what came next. He lay belly-flat on the ice closing his eyes, forcing away the fear and pretending he was being pushed in. One minute, standing safely on the ice, the next, without any warning—

His hand plunged into the pond.

The *cold*. He had never before experienced such pain, and he almost pulled back; Todd, however, overcame his instinct. He kept his hand submerged, and the moment his body understood and gave in, something strange happened. Suddenly, the cold wasn't so painful. Yes, it hurt, but pain wasn't his primary thought. Instead, Todd found it almost calming. As soon as his body gave in, the water chilled him completely, making him as cold and clean as the rest of winter. The feeling crept up his arm and to his chest. If he just held still, the cold would draw him into the water. He would never again feel pain. He would never again feel anything.

A full minute passed before he lifted his hand. Instantly, his hand was struck by a terrible burning, as if it had been slipped into fire.

Was this what had happened to Kathleen? Had she felt this? He wondered, because that was why he had come: to know what she had experienced, to learn how death felt. To touch the water and the cold, to reach into the hole and feel like he was slipping his fingers into her grave and her pain.

No. The pain was the punishment for leaving the water. This was the price for trying to experience death without dying. Todd rolled on his back, his hand in agony, slowly realizing that by turning from the hole, he had slid onto a long, frozen slick that ran from the hole to the shore.

This was where Kathleen had been carried. Water had streamed from her wet clothes, leaving a broad path across the ice.

A week after his visit to the pond, he would think back to that slick, wondering if it was still there, certain that if he could find it, it would once again lead him to the edge of death. For now, however, Todd was forbidden to cross onto the Donnelly property, and the best he could do was walk the family farm, rubbing the snow in his palms and holding his hands to the open wind. And when it was cold enough, the numbness again took hold of his body, and he again had a taste of peace, of the cold.

He walked a half mile straight from his house, then traversed the snow until he came to a thin, bent mesh wire fence—the eastern border of the farm. He stopped and made a quarter turn, heading along the next border.

It was a long walk, and the cold hurt, but that was the point. The longer he walked, the more he became like a shell, walking almost blindly to a gate.

He stopped. If he opened the latch, he could cross onto Donnelly land. If he went forward, he could again be at the pond.

He stared at the neighboring field, then looked back toward the house. Was his father watching him? Could his father even see him at this distance?

Todd turned back toward his father's land and walked until he reached the rear of the barn. He entered through a back stall door, wondering if his father had fed the calves, then deciding to do it himself. While he fed them, his body grew warmer and he began thinking again. Maybe all of this really was his fault. Maybe he *was* dangerous. The idea came as he poured the feed and stared about the barn and once again saw the pitchfork: the one he had broken, the one with the bent prong.

Todd?

Todd stood up. His father's voice had been distant, but direct. William Meacham knew exactly where to find him.

Todd headed outside. He found his father near the doorway to the house, talking to a stranger. Todd hesitated, but William Meacham waved him closer. His father had that smile he saved for visitors—a kind of second personality that kept the family as secure and hidden as the land beneath the snow.

"Todd, come here," William said. "I want you to meet someone."

Todd stood alongside his father.

"My name is Chris," the stranger said.

"Chris makes movies," William said. "He's gonna pay

five hundred dollars to film here, so I don't want you causing him trouble, all right?''

Todd nodded.

"I mean keep out of his way," William said.

"Yes, sir," Todd said. "Yes, sir, Mr.—"

"Chris is fine," the stranger said, offering his hand.

"Mr. Thomas," William Meacham told his son.

Todd stared at Chris.

"Nice meeting you," Chris said.

William Meacham patted Chris on the shoulder. "Nice meeting you," he said for his son. Then to Todd, "He's gonna be filming around the farm, so don't be surprised if you see him." William Meacham still had on his smile, but Todd felt the undercurrent. He nodded to his father—the sort of nod that made it clear Todd understood. His father saw this and offered him a real smile. "Maybe if you're lucky he'll put you in his movie. Chris could make you a star, I bet. He could make this whole farm famous."

"Maybe a small star," Chris said.

William patted his son. Todd finally extended a hand, and the stranger reached out and shook it.

"Nice meeting you," Todd said. And then, with his father's encouragement, he also smiled.

It was a distant camera shot. Billy took it from the van, about eighty yards from the spot where Chris finally met the boy. But Billy had caught the moment, and now, back in the motel room, they projected the scene on the wall, the frame steady as Todd appeared from the barn.

"Todd come here," William called. *"I want you to meet someone."*

The voice was faint and static, almost impossible to hear. Denny shook her head. The sound had been her responsibility and she failed miserably.

". . . Chris," Chris said to the boy. That was all they heard: fractured sentences that barely reached the microphone.

"Chris makes movies," William told his son. *"He's gonna pay . . . film here, so . . . ouble."*

"You can't stick a boom mike under a van and expect to hear anything," Denny whispered.

Chris dismissed the problem. The sound hadn't mattered anyway; not this time. It was just a record of his first contact with the Meacham family; something to inaugurate the project.

"... *eep out* ...," William said.

"... *sir,*" Todd said. "*Yes si* ..."

"... *is fine,*" Chris said."

"... *omas,*" William said.

Denny, too disgusted, turned off the sound. The film, however, continued. Billy forced an extra turn out of his zoom, and the frame tightened on the boy. Todd adjusted, as if feeling the squeeze of the frame. When the clip ended, the boy could have been looking in the camera.

Denny turned on the light. "I know at least one thing," she said. "The sound is awful."

"We can work on that," Chris said. "What about the kid?"

Chris looked to Billy, and Billy said, "If I were a killer, I wouldn't hang around after I did a girl. I'd disappear."

Denny also looked unconvinced. "Chris, I don't see how you can just look at someone and say he's a killer. I'm not saying you're wrong, I'm just saying I don't want to spend a month finding out if you're right."

"We'd be staying to film his next attempt at a kill," Chris said.

"You don't know if he's going to do that," Denny said. "Even if he is, it wouldn't matter. We don't have the equipment for the job."

"Dorsey will send anything once we prove it's worth his time."

"You're dreaming," Billy said. "Al can't even squeeze out a shit unless you feed him Ex-Lax."

"We can manage," Chris said. "We got crap equipment and we can barely cover a room, but it's not like we have to film every moment of his life. We just need enough of the right footage to snag Dorsey. Then he'll send us hardware."

Neither was ready to support that notion. Denny headed

for the bathroom, Billy for the television. As for Chris, he went outside. He wanted time alone to think and to consider his choices.

He climbed in the van and drove to a local gas station. Along with gas, the station ran a small market, selling sodas, sandwiches and other quick food. He had come for something to eat, but then he noticed something else: several wire shelves loaded with video cartridges. Chris walked back and studied the tapes. Apparently the station did more than fill stomachs and gas tanks; it also supplied movie rentals. He thumbed across the tapes until the store manager saw him. "Mr. Thomas, how's your movie going?" In the small town of Hayden, Chris and his crew had quickly become celebrities—or at least notables. The shop owner wasn't the first, and wouldn't—as Chris hoped—be the last to know him by name on their first meeting.

"Fine," Chris answered, but his concentration was on the shelves. He wanted to see the kind of tapes that sold in Hayden. He was particularly curious about one tape.

He ran his finger across the Rs.

"You still shooting in the fields?" the manager asked. "It must get pretty cold."

"It's no fun," Chris said. He finished one shelf and tried a second.

"I'll bet it isn't," the manager said. "You make any of those?" He nodded at the cartridges.

"A friend did," Chris said.

"What's the title?"

Chris considered his answer. Was Hayden ready for a title like *Raw Death?* So far, all he'd found on the shelves was the usual Hollywood fodder: action films, bikini comedies, vomit horror. It made him uneasy because video marts were like magazine stores—they revealed how a town thought and relaxed.

"Does your tape have a name?" the manager asked again.

But a car honked and the manager left to pump gas. Chris took a last look. It wasn't here, at least not in the main collection. He was ready to give up when he glanced below the Zs and again stopped.

They *were* here: on the bottom shelf, away from the family films. Not his tape, but others. Pornographic sex, pornographic violence . . . films that didn't know the meaning of fade-out or cutaway. And when Chris found them, he felt vindicated. Hayden really did have its darkside—it *was Raw Death* country. That made all the difference in the world, because it meant that when he looked into someone's eyes, he was peering into familiar depths. This was proof that human nature, in all its possibilities, was alive in this winter land as elsewhere.

An hour later, Chris was back at the motel. He went to Denny's room and knocked on the door. She opened the door, wearing a bathrobe, her hair wrapped in the towel, but Chris talked as if he had been expected.

"I know we don't have much to work with, and I know you don't like the idea," he said, "but what if we narrow things? Let's pick a place where we can track the kid without having to move around. Maybe get a chance to film him doing something good enough to get Dorsey's interest."

Denny didn't know what to say. The door was open, the wind was cold, and she was in her bathrobe, wet and chilled. But the possibility of a solution caught her off guard.

"It would have to be the farm," she said.

There was a moment of quiet. Finally Chris talked, his tone was pleading. "Denny, I know I'm asking a big favor, but what if we go by tomorrow and give it a try?"

She seemed to listen and Chris moved closer, ready to plead.

"I'm trying to be reasonable," he said. "Can't you see I'm trying? Just one shot. Don't you think it's worth at least one shot?"

They were on the farm an hour after sunset.

Billy had picked three camera locations: one near the entrance to the Meacham farm, the others facing opposite sides of the house. He also set up a camera to run an overnight time exposure; this, however, was only backup. For now, Chris wanted them filming as long as possible, so he gave Denny responsibility for the first camera, Billy the second and himself the third—which was fine with Denny, since the first camera was with the van. Her job was to wait by the highway and film anyone going on or off the farm—a kind of security camera, so if Todd left the premises, he'd be taped. As for Billy, he knelt behind a wood pile, a blanket over his body and camera. All things considered, he was surprisingly warm, and that gave him the patience to only film when there was action. And there was action now: the Meachams were eating dinner.

William, Todd, the mother . . . what was her name? He did the establishment shot, then the pan, then kept shooting, because the father was talking. He sat and filmed, wishing that Denny could have placed a microphone in the room or that he could read lips.

The dining-room window wasn't especially large, but the angle was perfect. It reminded him of that Kubrick film where a computer eye peers through a window and reads the lips of two astronauts. Billy was playing the computer— watching them eat, filming the family meeting-ground. Mrs. Meacham, serving dinner, then sitting in a far corner of the table, no longer existing . . . Todd listening to his father, or perhaps not listening—the kid seemed to always look down— and William talking only to Todd, when he talked at all.

It made Billy think that perhaps what he saw wasn't so much a family in balance as a family entirely off balance, the collective weight precariously on the edges. He thought of this because he knew something about tension. These people hated each other. The wife hated the husband, the husband hated the kid, and the kid—the kid was left to swallow it in. Nothing showed on his face, but it was there. And when Todd got up to leave, something else was clear; the tension at the table wasn't unusual. It was the normal family hour. Billy—sitting in the snow, guarded by a cord of chopped wood—was witnessing life in the Meacham household, and life was miserable. Nor were things any better at the third camera.

"Chris?"

Chris looked down from the barn loft. It was Denny—her arms folded, hugging a thermos. She climbed a ladder, crawled over a scattering of hay and joined him near a hollow window.

"I was getting bored," she said.

Chris patted the camera. "I've got it on Todd's room."

Denny looked out and saw an upstairs light. It was an hour after dinner. Even without a zoom, she could see Todd Meacham sitting at a desk, bent over a book.

"How long has he been up there?"

"Twenty minutes," Chris said.

"What can you see through the camera?"

"I'm trying to see what he's reading, but I can't make it out."

"Probably schoolwork."

"I don't know. He looks like he's reading, but I can't see what's on the desk."

Denny took a turn at the camera, pressing against the eye cup, trying to make out what the boy was doing. Finally, she pulled back and rested against the wall. Chris had already opened the thermos.

"When we go tonight, I think I'll leave this on time exposure," he said. "Then I can come around in the morning and change cartridges."

Denny moved through the hay, reached the edge of the loft and looked down. Cows and cow shit. She sighed and made her way back to the window, settling beside Chris. "So how was L.A.?"

"A mess," Chris said.

"You see what's-her-name?"

"We had dinner."

Denny grinned—a kind of all-knowing, sarcastic look. "So, did she split? What's your warranty these days— ninety days?"

"That's about thirty days more than yours."

"I'm not the one dying for love," she said. "If I was, I wouldn't be spending the night sniffing cow crap."

"That's funny, Denny." Chris squinted through the eye

cup, again watching Todd. "What's the sound distance on the boom mike? Could we get anything if we pointed it from up here?"

"Maybe to the fence, but not all the way," she said.

"His mouth is moving, but I can't see his lips," he said. "What he's doing?"

"He's still by the desk and he's talking to himself."

Chris stepped back and Denny looked through the camera. She could tell that Todd was repeating himself, but she couldn't make out the words. "Maybe he's singing," she told Chris.

"Maybe he's psychotic."

Then another figure appeared in the bedroom: William Meacham, standing to the side of his son, virtually filling the boy's doorway.

Denny watched as William entered the room and closed the door. Todd stared as his father talked. William didn't seem angry—didn't shout, didn't frown or tighten—but he did keep talking and he did keep in motion: pacing about the room, sitting on the bed, standing just as quickly.

Finally, he leaned down, kissed the back of his son's neck and went to the window. With one hand, he pulled at a belt—a thick piece of leather, anchored by a heavy brass buckle. With his free hand, he pulled down the shade.

"Shit," Denny murmured.

She sat there, watching, as William's shadow blurred. the father was positioning himself over the boy.

"What's happening?" Chris asked. "What's he doing?"

She couldn't answer; her attention was locked on the shadows. It was awful—the shadow coming down on the boy, her ears imagining the sound of each strike. "He's beating him," she finally managed.

"Who's beating who?"

"The father's beating the boy," Denny said. "For Christ's sake, look for yourself."

Chris did, watching the shadows. "Someone's going crazy in there," he said.

"It's the father," she said. "Trust me—I saw him with the belt."

Now they were both watching—Chris at the camera,

Denny simply staring. They were waiting and watching while the camera filmed and the shadows became blurs against the blinds.

They were still watching when the shadows slipped out of sight.

"What's happening now?" she said.

"I don't know," Chris answered.

Someone turned off the bedroom light.

"What is it?" she said. "What's going on? What's he doing in there?"

Chris shook his head.

"Why did he turn off the light?" Denny said. "What's he doing in the dark?"

Chris refused to turn and answer her. His eye was to the camera, and the camera was running.

EIGHT

DORSEY stared into the box and wondered why the post office couldn't smell the stink of a dead, two-foot rat. It wasn't his first thought. His first was what kind of lunatic signs "God" at the bottom of his hate mail. It was something he should have wondered weeks ago, when the first letter arrived.

Demons will pull at your pants and tear your genitals, the letter read. *Long, thin needles will be squeezed up your rectum, then turned slowly until all you release is blood. Then you'll be forced to swallow that blood, Al Dorsey. It will be dripped down your throat, and then your penis will be cut off. It will be cut at the base and cupped, so the urine can be squeezed into your mouth . . .*

He'd received similar letters, of course, but never from someone claiming to be the Almighty. Now, at last, it was bothering him. Bad enough when someone in the name of the Lord threatened you with a plague of locusts; but to have "God" dream up tortures as personal as castration . . . It had to be sacrilegious. Presuming, of course, the letters weren't from God.

Dorsey took a last look inside the box. It was definitely a rat. The head had been twisted, and there was another note under the body. *This is what's going to happen to you, Al Dorsey. I'm going to stick a funnel up your buttocks. I'm*

*going to stick it deep, and then I'm going to take a bottle of
bleach and pour it down. Then when you're screaming in
pain and your mouth is wide open, I'm going to reach down
your throat and twist my fingernails into the cavity of your
chest. And I'm going to keep digging until I find your heart,
then pull it out for some fresh air. Think about that, Al
Dorsey. Your day is coming.*

Sincerely, God.

He put the lid back on, rubbed his head and sat back.
Finally, he paged his secretary. "Ruth, I got another dead
animal here."

"Skunk?"

"Rat."

"Who's it from?"

"God," he said.

Ruth came in carrying a dust bin and wastepaper basket.
She swept the package into a plastic sack, then looked at
Dorsey. "About time He wrote you," she said, thinking his
remark had been a joke.

When Ruth left, he considered taking a tranquilizer. But
then he kept wondering what kind of asshole thought that by
signing a letter "God," he'd make you believe a letter had
been postmarked from Heaven; especially when the real
postmark was Universal City.

A lunatic in L.A. . . . Was such a thought conceivable?

That *was* a joke, but a private one. He just couldn't get
used to the idea of being threatened. The truth was, he felt
secure in L.A. The city was made for him. The heat, the
pollution, the endless miles of pavement, the chemical
sunsets, the pissed-off Mexicans, the shit-rich wasp, the
palm trees and quarter-mile driveways and stucco bunga-
lows. Dorsey couldn't have been more at home if the real
God had dropped from the sky and asked him to manufacture heaven. Heaven? It was here, on the West Coast.

"Ruth," he called, "has Azeez called?"

"You had a message on the machine from Chris, and
there was a message from Don Campo in New York."

"No Azeez?"

"No Azeez."

"Christ," he said, then reached for the phone and punched in the number. "I'd like to speak with Mr. Azeez please. This is Al Dorsey. I thought we had a court date."

The secretary put him on hold, and almost five minutes passed before his lawyer was on the line.

"Mr. Dorsey, excuse me," Azeez answered.

"You didn't call," Dorsey said. "What's happening? Are we going to court today?"

"Let me check, Mr. Dorsey," Azeez said, again putting him on hold. Dorsey sat, waiting, fuming, cursing discount law services. It was worse than joining a group health plan.

The phone clicked back on. "Mr. Dorsey, I'm glad you called. You reminded me, the court date's been suspended. The other party wishes to negotiate."

"Negotiate how much?"

"They won't say," Azeez said. "They want to meet at noon."

"Meet with scum?" Dorsey said—an odd objection. Dorsey met regularly with scum.

"It could be beneficial, Mr. Dorsey," Azeez said. "Both sides could save money."

"If you're saving money, then you're still spending money."

"You can save court costs," Azeez answered. "My legal fee does not cover court costs."

Dorsey was too exhausted for this, especially after a threat from God. He listened, then gave his reluctant okay and hung up. "Fucking olive," he said, meaning his lawyer.

Dorsey settled back, then saw the phone was blinking. "Bob's on the line," Ruth told him. "He wants to know if they should start shooting."

"Jesus," Dorsey said. "He's got five naked people over there, right? They're gonna catch cold if they don't keep moving."

"But you told them to stop."

"Not if everyone's already there," he said. "For Chrissakes, tell him to start and when I show up, he can stop."

Dorsey glanced at his watch. It was already ten o'clock. Without another thought, he grabbed his coat, left the building and headed for the studio, which was a generous word for the place. The studio was really a large loft that had been quartered into working rooms, available for weekly rental. It was almost a communal arrangement, with the basement full of discarded costumes and props that, more times than not, dictated the plot of Dorsey's films.

Dorsey was met at the door by an assistant producer. "How's it going?" Dorsey asked.

The man shrugged, and Dorsey knew what it meant. The bad news was the footage wasn't sexy. The good news was that only a day had gone by, so they could easily get back on track, and that was important to Dorsey, because he had high hopes for this picture. Usually, his soft-porns were routine: boy meets girl, boy screws girl, girl screws girl, boy screws girl and girl. This time, he had made a special arrangement with a bigger film company, which had just finished shooting a futuristic, science fiction adventure/ horror movie. For pennies, Dorsey had gained the right to use their sets. He stood a chance at making a low-budget soft-porn movie with the look of a large budget film. But that also meant they had to get the right people doing the right job. Dorsey waited for a break in the filming, then walked quickly to his director and dropped a hand on the man's shoulder. "Bob, can we talk?"

Bob was on his knees, trying to reposition one of his actresses. He was kneeling in front of a wall of sheet metal, some technical-looking consoles and an elaborate, futuristic sexual gymnasium made out of a half-dozen water beds. While the actress reached for a bathrobe, Dorsey led his director to a quiet corner.

"Bob, I don't want to waste time here, so I'm gonna talk straight. The rushes stink."

Bob stiffened.

"I'm talking like this because we've worked together for—what is it, eight pictures? I mean, ninety-nine percent of the time, you do great, but this picture . . . it's miscast. The shots I saw yesterday, the girl was missing something, don't you think?"

"Her name is Jill," Bob said. "Use her name, all right? She's not a piece of meat."

"Fine. Jill. This isn't about names, it's about natural, God-given talent. I saw the rushes, and her talent isn't good enough. It's too flat."

Bob looked to the ground and shook his head—uncomfortable, insecure. Dorsey knew the motions. Directors were such shitheads.

"You know what I mean, Bob. You know what sells, what we need to make the picture work."

"Breasts aren't everything," the director said. "When Jill's on camera, she's expressive. I thought, just once, it wouldn't hurt to get some acting on film. Especially *this* film."

Dorsey wrapped an arm about his director. "You're brilliant, Bob. You're a pioneer. I don't think anyone else in the business would have had the guts to do what you did. Putting acting in front of talent . . . I admire what you tried. But there's a time and place for everything, and we've already got too much on the line. Sometimes you got to go with what you know works, and this is one of those moments." He looked across the room and pointed. "What's her name?"

"Donna," he said.

"Can she read her lines?"

Bob shrugged. "She's playing a psychokinetic deaf-mute mating queen. She doesn't have any lines."

Dorsey patted his shoulder. "Do me a favor and give her a try," he said. "Make Jill the queen, and send me the new rushes."

Bob nodded, and Dorsey left the studio. He got to his car just in time to answer his cellular phone. It was his secretary.

"Mr. Dorsey, you got another call from Chris and another call from Mr. Campo in New York."

Dorsey glanced at his watch. Christ, where was the day going? "What did Chris want?"

"I couldn't figure it out," she said. "I think he wants money."

Dorsey rolled his eyes. "Did you get Campo's number?"

"The same as before," she said. "He'll be there all day."

"If he'll be there all day, why bother me now?" Dorsey asked, hanging up.

That, of course, was stupid. Ruth was his lifeblood. Pissing her off was like poking a hole in your artery. But it was too late now, and Dorsey was going to be late for more things if he didn't stop worrying so much about hurting people's feelings. Bob, Ruth, Chris . . . sometimes half his life was spent finessing. What he needed was more people who didn't need coddling; people who had the confidence to run their own show. People, maybe, like Don Campo. Living and working in New York had to give him some amount of balls. *Campo,* he thought again."

Then the name slipped away as he thought ahead to another hour of finessing.

Dorsey reached the law office fifteen minutes late, which was just as well, because if he'd reached it in time, he would have hung out in the garage just to make them wait. Inside was Azeez, sharing drinks with the people that wanted to squeeze a hundred grand out of Dorsey's bank account: Geraldine Kimberly and her lawyer, someone something.

Dorsey nodded to Azeez, glared at Kimberly and took his place at the conference table.

"This is Mr. Franklin," Azeez said, introducing the man. "He's representing Miss Kimberly."

"Miss?" said Dorsey. "I thought it was missus? Isn't that why she's suing?"

Kimberly stared at Dorsey, her eyes hinting at a temper as deadly as that of her husband, Floyd Kimberly, the real cause of her lawsuit.

Floyd Kimberly was a street vendor who, after too hot a day, snapped a mental wire, climbed into his Buick and proceeded to play bumper cars with the early-evening traffic. The incident resulted in twelve deaths, as well as eight years in prison and thirty seconds in *Raw Death.*

Geraldine Kimberly brought suit against Dorsey not for the tape of Floyd's crime, but for using home-video footage of Floyd and herself eating with friends. Dorsey and Chris thought the footage added a "human" element to the story.

Now, Kimberly wanted payment for her unsolicited video debut.

"Would you like something to drink, Mr. Dorsey?" said Franklin.

"Scotch," Dorsey answered. "As long as I'm getting knifed, I better be numb."

Kimberly leaned closer. "You son of a bitch," she said. "None of this would be happening if you had some respect for people."

"Miss Kimberly would like to resolve matters quickly and avoid time in court," Franklin said, "provided an amicable agreement can be reached. She's suffered a great deal because of Mr. Dorsey, and I'd like to remind both of you that the footage Mr. Dorsey used in his movie was used without Miss Kimberly's approval or consent, and constituted in our judgment an invasion of her privacy."

"Please," Dorsey said, his tone annoyed.

"You haven't mentioned your settlement price," Azeez said.

"The original suit was for one hundred thousand," Franklin said. "Miss Kimberly is willing to cut that in half, provided Mr. Dorsey agrees to withdraw his countersuit, as well as cover the legal fees for both parties."

Dorsey took in the scene. Azeez was nodding, as if seriously considering the proposal, while Franklin glanced at his own watch, which only got Azeez curious about the time, so he did the same. Dorsey suddenly realized they were both discount lawyers.

"Fifty thousand is still too high," Azeez finally said. "Even one dollar would be too high, considering the nature of this case. Our position is that Mr. Kimberly killed those people, so his life became public. Everything and everyone associated with him became public. We are here only because Mr. Dorsey is a busy man and would like to avoid the trouble of a court case."

"We understand," Franklin said.

"I think that if you again cut your offer, we might be closer to an agreement. Provided Mrs. Kimberly also covers her own legal expenses."

Now it was Franklin's turn to soak in some thoughts, and Dorsey used the moment to collar Azeez. "Excuse me," he said, "but did you just offer to pay them twenty-five thousand dollars?"

Azeez felt obliged to speak with Dorsey privately and led him out of the conference room. "It wouldn't be a bad deal," Azeez said. "You'd spend twice that much in court."

"I shouldn't be spending anything. She should be paying me."

"Yes, but she doesn't have any money and you do, and the way these things work, the person with money pays the person who had nothing."

"I thought there was a justice system." Dorsey said.

"If you want to get out of this, you're going to have to give her something. Twenty-five doesn't sound like much to me, but if it's too much for you, then pick another figure. Just make it one they'll accept, because I have another appointment in half an hour."

Azeez headed back for the table and Dorsey followed. When they sat down, Kimberly and her lawyer had finished their own discussion.

"I'm sorry," Franklin said. "Twenty-five isn't enough."

Azeez looked to Dorsey, his eyes begging for negotiation. Dorsey never even glanced at him. Azeez was a mistake. Once again, Dorsey would have to do his own work.

"No," he said. "Truth is, twenty-five is too much. But my lawyer tells me I have to give you something, so I'm gonna give you what you'd get in court—a chance at making money."

Franklin was dubious; Azeez leaned back, also uncertain. Only Kimberly looked serious, since it was her money on the line.

"Tell me this," Dorsey said. "Why does everyone think I'm made of money?"

"This isn't about personal wealth, Mr. Dorsey," Franklin said. "It's about the grief and injustice that has been done to—"

Kimberly shut him up. "I'll tell you why," she told Dorsey. "Because your fucking movie made a ton."

"You think so?" Dorsey said. "All right—then screw this twenty-five thousand. You want a deal? Invest in the future. How about instead of money, I give you a point on the profits from *Raw Death?*"

Neither Franklin or Azeez said a word.

"A point," Dorsey explained. "that means if I make ten million, you get a hundred thousand. If I make twenty, you get two hundred thousand."

Franklin hedged. "But if you don't make a profit—"

"He'll make a profit," Kimberly said, again cutting him off. "He already has. We just don't know how much."

"Which is your gamble, because either you take my offer now or it's off the table."

Franklin thought a moment, then faced his client, talking in what was meant to be private counsel. "I don't think he'd make this offer if it amounted to more than twenty-five thousand," he said.

Kimberly listened, then said, "Make the deal."

"But—"

"Make the deal," she said, "but for two points."

Dorsey shook his head. "One point, that's it. A point and a quarter, tops, but that's a one-minute offer."

Franklin still looked perturbed, but now both lawyers were out of the picture. "Point and a half," Kimberly said.

Dorsey looked wounded.

"Point and a half, and we got an agreement. Point and a quarter, and we're going to court."

Dorsey tried looking angry, but he couldn't. For one thing, he was enjoying himself. For another, it didn't much matter how many points he gave away; like other production companies, Dorsey knew how to work the books so *Raw Death* wouldn't technically see a profit until well into the twenty third century.

"All right, bleed me," he said, reaching across the table to shake hands.

Kimberly accepted.

"You're a tough cookie," Dorsey said. "So now that you divorced that psycho, you seeing anyone?"

Twenty minutes later, everyone left happy—Geraldine

Kimberly with dreams of money; Franklin and Azeez with dreams of their fees; Dorsey with dreams of a sauna. Dorsey ate lunch, headed to his health club, took in a massage, met his broker, visited the distributor, phoned a dozen backers, rejected two dozen scripts. By four-thirty, he had made it back to his office, where Ruth gave him a handful of messages and a pissed-off look. "These are your calls," she said. "I would have phoned, but you didn't want me to."

Dorsey took the messages, grunting, nothing else. He might have apologized, but he had completely forgotten insulting his secretary.

"There's also some rushes from the studio and a package on the shelf."

Dorsey headed straight to his office, spreading the messages on his desk and deciding which to call. He did the important ones first—the calls from backers and investors, the people with the money. Then he returned a call from his Asian distributor and made another call to a movie chain.

At about six o'clock, he finally settled down to his messages from Chris. He stared at all five of them, thought better of it, pushed them aside in favor of another call. He picked up the phone, dialed, waited...

"Campo Productions," the voice said.

"Don Campo? It's Al Dorsey."

"Mr. Dorsey," Campo said. "How are you? Thanks for returning my call."

"It's been a fucking crazy day."

"I'm in New York," Campo said. "You don't have to tell me about crazy."

"I got lawsuits coming out my ears, I got one director who can't judge a good pair of tits, I got another out in Oshgosh spending money on some teenage bedwetter."

"I was calling because I'm coming out to L.A. tomorrow," Campo said. "Maybe we can get together."

"Definitely we can get together," Dorsey said. "Give me a call when you're in town and I'll arrange things."

"Anything you say," Campo said. "Thanks, Mr. Dorsey."

"Don't thank me yet," Dorsey said. "You haven't even met me."

Dorsey hung up, visited the refrigerator, sipped a drink, then went back to Chris's messages. "Jesus," he muttered, then did what he had do—dialing, waiting for yet another voice in the dark begging him for a few bucks.

"Hello?"

"Hello, Chris," Dorsey said. "Sorry it took me so long, but it's been a helluva—"

"This is Billy. How's it going, Al? You sending us the money?"

Dorsey rolled his eyes. "Put Chris on the phone."

"I'm gonna need equipment, too," Billy said. "The crap out here's good for nothing, and the battery packs are close to dead."

"Billy..."

Dorsey heard the phone being pulled free. "Al, it's me."

"Do me a favor and don't ever let him on the phone again," Dorsey said.

Billy was still talking, so Chris covered the mouthpiece, said something Dorsey could only imagine, then said to Dorsey, "You got my messages?"

"I heard you need money," Dorsey said. "In other words, you need what I don't got."

"We're really onto something here," Chris said. "We got some fantastic shots last night of this kid—late at night, upstairs."

"You were in his bedroom?"

"We shot through the window," Chris said. "It's okay. I got permission to shoot here."

"You got permission to shoot through his window?"

"Al, this is going great," Chris said. "We just need a little more money to get it right."

"*More*," Dorsey said, loud enough for Chris to hear his disgust.

"Come on, Al," Chris said. "Tell me what to do? How can I convince you?"

"A little proof might be a start," Dorsey said. "Chris, when you mentioned this idea to me before, I thought—hey, Chris Thomas? He's the best. I mean, you're a pioneer. I don't think anyone else in the business would have had the guts to do what you're doing.''

''But?''

''But this can get expensive. There's a time and place for everything, and we've already got too much on the line. Sometimes you got to go with what you know works, and this is one of those moments.'' He looked across the room, saw his package and reached for it. ''You can't even prove the first girl got murdered. The police don't even think she was murdered.''

''These aren't police, Al,'' Chris said. ''I explained that.''

''Well, the police may not be real, but the money is. Excuse me, but I'm sick to death of people jabbering at me like I'm a fucking bank.''

Chris wanted to shout back at him; Dorsey could feel the anger.

''What do you need?'' Chris said.

''What I need is proof,'' Dorsey said. He tore at the package wrapping, then cut the tape with a letter opener.

''What kind of proof?''

''Proof your idea is worth the bucks,'' Dorsey said. ''You said he's a killer? So where's the weapon? Did they find a knife in the girl's back?''

''She drowned. You know she drowned.''

''So find another victim,'' Dorsey said. ''I'd call that proof. Another dead body. A knife with his fingerprints. A piece of wet, rotting meat.''

Chris was quiet. ''Excuse me?'' he finally said.

Dorsey didn't answer; he was still staring into the open box. He used a pen to lift the thing out of the box.

That's what it was: a slab of wet, rotting meat, with a swell of maggots crawling over it. *Ashes to ashes; dust to dust,* the latest note read. *Sincerely, God.*

''Al?'' Chris said.

Dorsey sighed. ''This has been a shit day, Chris. Okay?''

''Sure Al.''

''I'll call you tomorrow.''

''Tomorrow's fine,'' Chris said, hanging up.

Dorsey did the same, then dropped the slab back in the box. He put the lid on top and did his best to reseal the paper. Then he went once around the outside with tape and reached for a magic marker. He had no idea if it would do any good, but it was worth a try.

Return to Sender, he scrawled across the top.

He turned off the office light and headed for the post office.

NINE

URING all his years in L.A., probably the oddest day in Chris's career was the time Dorsey sent him to Nevada for a sit-down with Dwight Hamisch, mass murderer and bit performer in *Raw Death*.

Hamisch was a fifty-nine-year-old retired sanitation worker who, in the course of a year, established a religion, amassed two hundred followers, bought a "church retreat" in a Nevadan desert, then proceeded to slaughter a quarter of his flock in private sacrificial ceremonies.

Chris met the murderer almost a full year after his arrest. The moment was occasioned after Dorsey called Chris into his office, pointed at the television set and said, "This man is money."

Chris faced the TV. Every day, Dorsey made a point of watching the talk shows. Geraldo Rivera, Phil Donahue, Oprah Winfrey—Dorsey watched as if he were in a board room and the TV was pitching him ideas. This time, he was watching a special on blood cults, and Hamisch was the guest star. "Look at him," Dorsey said. "How many people did he kill? Fifty? Sixty?"

"Forty-five," Chris said.

"Everything Manson did, Hamisch did better," Dorsey said. "I'm thinking feature film this time, Chris. I want you to go out there and see if I'm right. I mean, hell, I know I'm right, but I want you to make extra sure."

"Al . . ."

"I'll arrange everything," Dorsey said. "All you gotta do is go, all right?"

A week later, Chris was driving out to the Nevada state prison facility, a tape recorder beside him and a bottle of aspirin in a pocket. It was a rare rainy day, with thunder, lightning and a windswept storm. All things considered, it was the sort of overly dramatic weather one expects when en route to a meeting with a homicidal maniac. He turned off the highway and soon found parking near a two-story brick bunker marked Visitor's Entrance. Chris left the car, covered his head and ran inside. "I'm here to see a prisoner," he told a clerk, nervous about being there, embarrassed at requesting a visit with the state's most notorious criminal.

The clerk took his driver's license and began writing down the information. Soon a guard approached and walked Chris through a metal detector.

"I'm taking you to a private room," the guard said. He unlocked a door and led Chris into a virtually bare chamber—a table, two chairs, two paper cups and two pitchers of water. Fifteen minutes passed before a second door opened and Hamisch entered—a stocky man with thinned, graying hair and cheeks that sagged from age. In a prison uniform, he looked more like a public employee than a cult killer.

"Mr. Thomas?" Hamisch asked.

Chris nodded.

"You're in the movie business."

"Movies and videos."

"And you want to do a film on me?"

"Yes."

Hamisch looked bothered. "I'm not proud of myself, Mr. Thomas. I hate myself for what I did. I wish I could take it all back."

Chris relaxed and listened.

"When I did those things, I was hearing voices. I was out of work, I'd ruptured a disk, and the hospital had me on painkillers. I took to listening to preachers and between the pills and preaching, I started to get some bad ideas. I wrote them down, but they didn't make sense, they didn't have any shape. Then I watched too much TV and I saw a movie and things happened."

"What did you see?" Chris asked.

Hamisch tightened, as if it was impossible to explain.

"Pazuzu," he finally said.

Chris didn't understand.

"It was on TV," said Hamisch. "They were showing *The Exorcist*, and I was lying in bed, and suddenly I'm watching this kid smashing windows, breaking walls, twisting heads, without even lifting a finger. I lay there wondering who could do such a thing? Then the movie ended, and they showed the sequel, and I had the answer. Pazuzu, the demon god."

"Pazuzu," said Chris.

"I found myself watching what was going on and the world started making sense. And I have news for you, Mr. Thomas. Once you make sense of things, even if you're wrong, you're way ahead of most people. Suddenly everyone comes to you for the answer. People do anything you want."

"So you started killing your followers," Chris said.

Hamisch considered the remark, taking a long sip of water and letting Chris wait. "Mr. Thomas," he finally said, "I'm not proud of myself. That's what makes all of this awful, because I'm better now, but the people who aren't better—the ones who came to me for help—they're still out."

"They were the victims, Mr. Hamisch," said Chris.

"Those people *gave* themselves to me."

"Maybe they didn't think you were going to kill them," said Chris.

Hamisch leaned forward. "The last man I tried hurting was a doctor," he said. "That's why he escaped. This man was smart, educated . . . he knew how to hold his throat and stop the bleeding. But the police didn't find me because of what he said—they found me by following his blood. Even when he got better, he wouldn't talk against me. He never even testified. You know where that man is now?''

Chris obliged by shaking his head.

''He killed himself after I got my death sentence. He blamed himself for what happened to me.'' Hamisch opened his hands, as if overwhelmed. ''Maybe I did do wrong, but if I'd asked them to, they'd have done it themselves. I could have watched these people die. Instead, I became involved. I tried to help and now I'm going to die. Does that make sense?''

Chris listened. One moment Hamisch was begging forgiveness, the next he was absolving himself. None of it mattered, however, so long as he was coherent.

On the way out of the building, Chris asked the guard whether Hamisch was truly reformed. The guard said Hamisch was the model prisoner, spending nearly all his free time in Bible study. This had Chris thinking until he passed another visitor to the prison. ''I'm here for Hamisch,'' the man told the clerk. ''Triangle Associates. We had a two o'clock.''

And who was this person. A lawyer? Another film rep? What about Hamisch? Would he return to the table and open his heart to another stranger? Could he bare his soul on request?

Three days later, a New York author signed Hamisch to a series of exclusive interviews, all for a proposed book that had already been purchased for a TV miniseries. The news infuriated Dorsey; at least until a month passed and he heard that the writer had been hospitalized. ''Can you believe it?'' Dorsey said. ''After squeezing us out of the money, Hamisch sneaks a knife into his cell and carves that New York hotshot into a sliced salami.''

Chris read the story carefully. Hamisch—the same man whom Chris had left crying over his victims, pleading misunderstanding and forgiveness, the same man who had won the trust of his guards, the same man with whom Chris had been alone—had, at the first opportunity, tried killing again.

It amazed Chris. Why couldn't Chris or the guards—

people who could pick out Moment Makers on the street—stare into Hamisch's eyes and see the killer?

How had Hamisch hid it so well, and could others do the same?

"We moved here in the seventies," William Meacham said. "For fourteen years, I guess, we've been growing wheat, but on occasion we've experimented. Except the frost and winter can be hard on other crops. That's what you're here for, right? Frost?"

"Soil and frost," Chris said.

"Then you should know the biggest problem isn't the winter, it's the summer. The summers are getting long, hot and dry. More farms are losing to the heat, not the cold."

"At least during the summer you got some help," Chris said.

"I got Todd," William agreed.

"How does he manage?"

"He manages," William said. "Between school and here, he keeps busy."

They were standing at the porch, with Chris beside William and Billy off to the side, the camera perched on his shoulder. There was no reason for discretion: Chris was interviewing William. That had been part of Chris's arrangement—while shooting on his land, Chris could interview Meacham about farming. Except Chris never seemed to talk long about farming.

"I don't mean to be too personal—it just adds to the overall picture," Chris said. He looked toward the fields. "It's a cold one today."

William opened the front door. "Let's go inside and get warm."

Chris and Billy followed him into the living room, Billy still shooting. All the camera toting was beginning to annoy Meacham.

"Does he have to take that thing everywhere?" he asked Chris.

Billy lowered the camera, his expression one of exhausted

impatience. William hesitated, then led them back to the kitchen.

"I just don't want some son of a bitch seeing my home and getting ideas," William said.

"Of course not," Chris said.

"I probably shouldn't even let you in."

"I appreciate it," Chris said. "And it's going to be very helpful."

"Like I care," William said.

William went to the sink, filled a pot with water, then walked to the range.

"I do most things myself around here," William said.

"Is Mrs. Meacham sick?"

"Mrs. Meacham?" William grinned. "Hell, she might as well be dead." He walked to the door and shouted her name, but no one answered. William listened, waited, then went back to the range.

"I'd like to talk with your wife sometime," Chris said. "I'd like to get a sense of how she spends her day."

"Why does the government need to know that?"

"Like I said, it adds to the overall picture," Chris said.

William took the pot off the range, and Chris held up his cup.

"Besides," Chris said, "I can tell your family works hard. How do any of you manage to relax?"

"Well, let me ask you something," William said. "What do you do to relax?"

"Nothing special," Chris said.

"All right," William said. "So why should we be different?" He poured the coffee and settled the pot. "Why do you keep asking all these questions? What makes you think I'm so special?"

Chris reached for his cup. "You are special," he said. "You're a farmer."

Meacham considered the answer and sneered. "Nothing special about that," he murmured.

Chris smiled as if he understood. "How does your son spend his free time?"

"I don't know," Meacham said. "I can't watch over him every minute."

"So you don't keep an eye on Todd."

"I keep an eye when I need to. When he's doing things for me, then I watch him," William said.

Chris kept smiling, but the look was wearing thin. He realized it and turned to Billy. "Do you have everything?"

"I'd like some shots of the rest of the house," Billy said.

"Forget it," said William.

Billy talked to Chris. "It'll give a better sense of a farmer's life."

"That's crap," William said.

"It would help, that's all," Chris told Meacham.

"I'm helping enough," William said.

Chris waited, but William was through being host. Chris admitted as much when he stood and nodded Billy toward the door. "All right," he told Meacham. "You don't mind if I use the bathroom, do you?"

Meacham did, but he led Chris to the staircase. He watched as Chris headed up to the second-floor landing.

"First door, straight ahead," he told Chris.

Chris thanked Meacham, entering the bathroom and closing the door. He actually did need the toilet; the trip, however, was to get Billy upstairs with the camera. Chris wanted a video record of the bedrooms. Later, at the motel, they could play the film slowly and see what they uncovered—if, of course, they uncovered anything.

Chris opened the small window and looked outside. The bathroom faced away from the barn. About a foot from the window was a rotted gutter running from the roof to a ground-level rain spout. Chris reached out and picked at the long, aluminum pipe. The aluminum bent easily.

Then he went back to search the bathroom. There was a medicine cabinet, but nothing was inside. A look into the cabinet under the sink revealed only water damage from a leaky drain. In fact, the entire bathroom looked unused. He wondered if Mrs. Meacham cleaned it hourly, or if the family just pissed in bottles.

Finally, Chris sat on the edge of the tub and began

unraveling the toilet paper. He tore the sheets in clumps and dropped them in the toilet. He did this until a muck of paper had collected in the drain; they he stepped back and flushed.

The water poured over the toilet and onto the floor. Chris kept his hand on the lever so the water wouldn't stop flowing. "Damn it," he shouted.

He heard Meacham climb the stairs, and Chris threw open the door.

"The toilet's clogged," he said.

Meacham stepped to the edge of the pool and looked down. Behind him was Billy.

"Why don't you step outside," Meacham said to Chris. He looked back at Billy. "What are you doing?"

"Looking for towels," Billy said.

"I got towels here," Meacham said. "Why don't you both go downstairs."

Meacham dropped a cloth on the floor and started swabbing. "Hey," he said. Billy was still near the bedrooms.

Billy smiled and raised his arms, shrugging. The camera wasn't on his shoulder; Meacham could see that, so he controlled himself. "Will you please go downstairs?" Meacham asked.

Billy obeyed, heading back to the living room.

"How about me? Can I help?" Chris said.

"Just keep an eye on your friend," Meacham answered.

Chris also went downstairs. Billy waited for him near the door, the camera still off his shoulder, but the lens pointed straight ahead. Chris saw what he was doing. The camera was down, but Billy's finger was on the trigger.

"I think we should wait in the living room," Chris said.

Billy agreed. With Meacham upstairs, he put the camera on his shoulder and took aim. He did a slow pan about the room, then went in the living room and did the same. When Meacham still didn't come downstairs, he opened the closets and did quick shots inside. "Is there a basement?" he whispered to Chris.

Before they could check, however, Meacham again joined them. Billy took the camera off his shoulders and rested it on the floor. Chris put on his smile, apologizing again and asking if there had been any damage.

"Don't worry about it," Meacham said. "It's not your fault the toilet flooded, right?"

"Right," Chris said.

A few minutes later, he led Chris and Billy out of the house. He stood by the window and watched as the two men headed for their car.

He stood there, wondering why two men interested in soil erosion spent so little time in the fields.

While Chris and Billy visited the farm, Denny watched Todd enjoy a long, slow tour of Hayden.

The town was eight blocks long, with the center marked by two intersecting state roads. Todd started at the northernmost edge of town, then walked into the business district. There wasn't much to see, but Todd seemed to take great interest in everything. At first, Denny thought he was shopping, then she thought he was looking for someone, finally she decided he had no purpose—Todd was simply drifting according to mood. She watched as he slowed before a store, stopped, stared and kept going. Only once did the pattern change, when he approached a card shop. This time he actually entered the store, and Denny approached the window. She saw Todd resting by a counter, talking to a girl close to the age of Kathleen Donnelly. Denny paid attention to the girl's appearance. Her hair, cropped near the shoulder, black, straight, except for a slight inward curl near the neck. Her skin, almost pale. Her body, edging on heavy, but the weight added a fullness to her figure. Her face, a calming face, colored slightly with makeup.

Todd talked, the girl talked, then when Todd left the store, Denny turned and waited a moment. When it was safe, she entered the shop. The girl behind the counter smiled at Denny and Denny returned the greeting; still, Denny knew better than to approach too quickly. She walked through an aisle, picked out a birthday card, then finally approached the register. "Hi," Denny said.

"Hi," the girl answered.

While the girl checked the price, Denny dug for her wallet.

"Was that Todd Meacham I saw a minute ago?" Denny asked. "I'm Denny Fischer. I'm part of the film crew shooting on his farm."

She offered her hand and the girl shook it. "Sarah Boden," she said.

"You're a classmate of Todd's?"

"That's right."

"Maybe a little more than that, huh?" Denny said. "I saw the two of you talking through the window."

Sarah shook off the suggestion. "I'm dating someone else," she said.

"I like your town," Denny said. "Seems like a nice place to live."

"It's okay," the girl said. "You come from Hollywood?"

"That area."

"That's where I want to go," Sarah said.

"You want to get in movies?" Denny said.

"I think it'd be fun," Sarah said. She glanced around the store and said, "There's not much to do here."

"I meant to ask Todd about the area, but we keep missing each other," Denny said. "What's he like anyway?"

"Todd?" Sarah said. "Todd keeps to himself. I mean he talks, but he doesn't say much."

"Good student?"

"Average," Sarah said. "He doesn't say a lot in class. I think he's been cutting classes."

"I wanted to talk to him about the school, but maybe I should talk with someone else."

"Todd's kind of weird," Sarah said. "He's nice and all, but he doesn't have a lot of friends. He can be strange. He's kind of intense, I mean." She smiled and shook off the question. "I'm seeing someone else." She squinted and again shook her head.

By the time Denny left the store, Todd was out of sight, so she finished her town tour alone. Denny backtracked, making a second pass of the storefronts: a savings and loan, a grocer, the sheriff's office, two clothing shops, a realty office. Off the main road, she could see two diners, two bars, a V.F.W. lodge and a church.

Nothing, she thought. The place was true boredom. It was the reason scores of Midwestern kids, including herself, left home.

Later, sitting with Chris, she made a simple drawing of Hayden and gave him a finger tour of the streets. "The truth is if anything happens off the farm, you lose," she said. "It's winter, so any place Todd goes it going to be indoors, except there's no place for him to go around here, so he's going to head out of town. He can't get in the bars. The best he can do is get a friend to buy liquor, except that doesn't help you because he'll probably drink it in a van, so you can't even film that."

"I heard there's a mall," Chris said.

"It's an outdoor mall," Denny said. "Anyone with a car drives to Marsh, and anyone with a good car drives to the city."

Chris leaned back. "Where else did you go?" he asked. "Did you see the school?"

"I didn't see the school, but if you're thinking of digging out his records, forget it," she said. "I keep telling you, this place is small. You poke around and everyone knows it."

When Billy was ready, they stopped talking. Billy sat beside the VCR, Chris leaned against the bed board, and Denny moved to the edge of the bed. All eyes were on the monitor. Finally, Chris gave the go-ahead, and Billy ran the footage.

It was the film of their visit with Meacham. The first shot was outdoors, and Chris pointed at the house. "You see over there?" he said to Denny. "There's a gutter. If I get upstairs again, I can peel back the gutter stripping and drop a line. That way we can run a wire up the gutter to the second floor."

"A wire to the bathroom?" she said.

"The bathroom's next to the master bedroom," Chris said. "The wall's rotted under the sink, so if we can get a microphone into the wall and pointed at the bedroom—"

"*No*, Chris," Denny said. "Not these mikes. They barely work in the open."

"What if we get better equipment? Can you tell me what to get?"

Denny nodded.

"All right," Chris said, and ran the tape forward. He skipped to the indoor footage, then sat back and watched.

Billy got as much as he could under the circumstances, and that amounted to a quick shot inside each room. Chris inched through the tape, watching carefully as the camera tilted first through the hallway, then into the kitchen. They paid particular attention to the upstairs. These were the most difficult shots. The angle wasn't only low—at hip level—it was shaky, sometimes cockeyed.

The camera tilted its way past the bathroom and along the landing. There were two bedrooms—one at the end of the hallway, and another adjacent to the bathroom. Billy started by walking to the end of the hall and pushing in the door. Chris recognized the room immediately. It was Todd's; Chris could tell from the desk.

"Let's see that again," Chris said.

They did, rewinding, this time watching carefully. It wasn't the best of angles. The door hadn't swung completely open, so about a third of the room remained blocked from view. Still, they could see the desk, a closed closet door, a bureau, and about half the bed. On the wall were a pair of posters, and on the desk was a pile of books, probably schoolbooks.

There was also something odd about the room. Apart from the books, the place was immaculate—the bureau closed, the floor clean of dust and clothes, the bed not only made, but the bedspread smooth and tight. It was as if they had taken the camera into a freshly sanitized motel.

Billy eyed Chris, and Chris waved him on. Billy let the film run. There was a brief interruption, when Meacham caught Billy outside the bathroom, but as Meacham returned to mopping, Billy turned the camera toward the master bedroom.

"Jesus," Denny said.

Another immaculate room. This time, not a hint of activity.

Billy kept the tape running, but they saw nothing. Nothing strange, no clues, no hard or even soft evidence.

Chris finally turned off the machine. "We did all right today," he said. "We got inside. Billy did a terrific job." He rubbed his forehead. "If I broke into the place and went through the drawers, and maybe in the basement and attic—"

"*Excuse* me," Denny said, "but if you break in, I'm leaving. And once I get back to L.A. I'm going to tell Dorsey, and Billy'll be out of here too and you'll be totally alone."

"The girl was killed," Chris said. He talked slowly, more to himself than Denny. "Let's *assume* she was killed. They pulled her from the pond, they drove off with the body . . ."

"She drowned," Denny said.

"We don't know that," Chris said. "No one checked anything. Not how she died, not the woods, not the pond." Chris sat on the edge of the bed. "If no one checked anything, there could still be something out there."

"Out where?" Denny said, exasperated.

"Where they found the body," Chris said.

They were parked near the pond. Denny stood with the camera while Chris and Billy did their best to search the area. It took only a few minutes to realize the difficulty of the job. It was winter, there were several inches of snow, and whatever clues might have been left behind were long buried until spring. This was also true among the evergreens. Earlier in the winter, the branches may have protected the base; now, the snow had completely taken the hillside.

Billy walked once around the pond, then climbed back in the van. Denny stood by the camera until she saw no point and joined Billy in the van.

As for Chris, he walked by the evergreens, closing his eyes, trying to get into Todd's mind. He thought of other killers. What would Hamisch have done? Where could he have his pleasure, but still be unseen and still be this close to the pond?

Where?

It was like stepping across some far corner of that dark land of murderers and maniacs—some lost neck of woods that had become a dumping ground for corpses. It should have alerted him; instead, his imagination absorbed the fear and led Chris deeper into the forest. He was looking for some manner of turnoff from the road, and finally found a drive that led off the highway and near the trees. The entrance was chained, but there were tracks that went around the chain. During winter, Mr. Donnelly found it easier going around the posts rather than undoing the lock.

Chris stared at the tire tracks and wondered if, several days ago, he could have found tracks to match Todd's pickup.

He studied a small embankment that sloped toward the trees. That would make sense: off the road, but not so far that he'd risk being stuck in the snow. Chris walked to the embankment. If it was cold out, he probably killed her in the truck. On the other hand, if everyone thought the girl had drowned, Todd probably hadn't used a knife; he strangled her, or perhaps drowned her. Or if Todd didn't mind the cold, he might have been adventurous. He might have taken her among the trees, seducing the girl until she was submissive and—

Chris looked away from the embankment and toward a knoll.

He was absolutely sure of it. The area was a dimple in the ground: a hollow, cupped against a cluster of trees and small boulders. It was a guard against the wind. Even the snow was a light dusting. Chris bet that a week ago, the ground had been clear.

He reached the knoll and dropped on his knees, feeling and scratching at the dirt, wedging his fingers between the boulders and searching for anything within reach. A beer cap, a cigarette butt, the neck to a broken bottle . . .

He was on the ground almost ten minutes before he hiked back to the van. He climbed into the front seat and leaned into the heater, frustrated, but also thinking. While he thought, he stared outside, his attention on the pond.

The pond. The one place where Todd couldn't clean up.

"Denny," Chris said, "do you have any wool sweaters?"

"I brought two," she said.

Chris considered this. He never looked at her; he was still thinking, but now about the sense of his idea, not its wisdom. "I got another place to look."

"Where?"

"Here," he said. "But later. When it's dark." He leaned back to face his cameraman. "Billy?"

Billy looked wary.

"Billy, can you swim?"

Billy didn't understand. Chris looked again at the ice. "How are you at underwater photography?" Chris said.

TEN

I T was a bitter, clear evening. On the good side, this
meant it would be easier seeing in the dark; on the bad
side, this also meant they would be easier to see.

Billy pulled on the last of the sweaters, then a second
hood, then a fourth pair of socks, then finally the face
mask.

"No—wipe your face first, then put on the mask," Chris
said.

Billy dipped his fingers in the motor grease and started
wiping. "This is disgusting," he said.

"It's better than frostbite," said Chris. When Billy was
finished, Chris reached in a paper bag for the diver's mask
and snorkel. Neither were professional; he had found them
in a toy store at the town's mall. The mask barely fit Billy's
face, and the elastic band was stretched to its uncomfortable
limit.

"This is so fucking crazy," Billy complained.

Denny didn't say a word. She didn't have to; Chris knew
she agreed.

They were in the back of the van, a few steps from the
pond, probably parked on the very spot where the ambulance had waited for Kathleen Donnelly. The state road was
clear of traffic, which only made sense; it was close to
midnight.

"I don't even know what to look for," Billy said.

"You're looking for anything," Chris said. "Or nothing. That would be okay too."

Chris handed him a watertight flashlight—a block battery with a halogen beam—and grabbed hold of his own. Finally, he reached into a travel box.

Inside was the video camera. Foam was wrapped about its casing, and the entire unit tucked inside a sealed plastic sack. When Chris lifted the hardware, Billy sighed and shook his head. True, they had already tried it in a bathtub, but this was different. The bath water had only been cold; this water was ball twisting. Billy didn't care how much foam they wrapped about the camera; the hardware wasn't meant for this kind of abuse.

Denny turned off the inside light and nodded them out. Chris and Billy opened the rear, Chris heaving a duffel bag over a shoulder.

Thank God no one was around. At night, with his dozen layers of clothes, Billy had the shadowy image of a bear—or, more precisely, a bear wearing a snorkel and goggles. They glanced back and saw Denny near the side of the van, a video camera on her shoulder, filming the idiocy.

Chris took the lead, heading for the center of the pond and bending down. The hole was now only a yard across. He touched the edges of the ice, then opened his duffel bag and took out a small axe. While Billy kept warm, Chris hacked at the hole, chopping until he felt it was broad enough for slipping into the water.

"People are going to see this tomorrow," Billy said.

Chris brushed the chips into the water.

"How deep is it?" Billy asked.

"It's a pond," Chris answered. "Tops, I'd bet fifteen feet."

Chris reached in the duffel bag again and took out a folding measuring stick. He snapped it to the full eight feet, then lowered it into the water. The entire stick disappeared.

"This is not funny," Billy said.

Chris pulled out a rope and tied it about Billy's waist. "You're going to get wet, that's all."

"Suppose there's a body under there?"

"Then it's dead. It can't bother you."

Billy took a breath and lowered his legs into the water. "Jesus," he gasped. He sat there a moment.

"It'll get easier once you're in," Chris said. "The wool's like a wet suit. Once the wool gets wet, your body heats it up."

Billy slipped in.

"*Shit*," he said.

Chris turned on his flashlight and dipped it in the water. They could see down several feet, but soon the light became confused with shadows. "Come on," Chris said. "Let's get this over with."

Billy bit down on the snorkel. Chris went to the duffel bag a last time and retrieved the camera. Seconds later, Billy was under: the camera in one hand, his other hand holding the edge of the hole. He was filming, but just under the surface. Finally, he bobbed up.

"Jesus, it's cold," Billy said. Then he ducked under, this time letting the weight of the camera carry him down. Chris watched. In a way, it was beautiful. He saw this round halo of light drifting into the water, and the glow of the light misting beneath the ice.

Billy held his breath almost a minute, then bobbed back up.

"How is it?" Chris asked.

Billy was adjusting. He nodded, caught his breath and went down a third time. Chris waited, then he realized by cupping the water, he could see Billy more clearly. Billy had not only touched bottom; he was moving in a circle, filming his steps.

After the fifth trip, Chris caught Billy and took away the camera. "That's enough," Chris said. "Just go and check the bottom for anything that might have dropped."

"The water's getting to me," Billy said.

"Just two more trips," Chris said, and Billy, exhausted, went down.

The first time, Billy was under almost two minutes. When he came up, Billy shot through the hole, and Chris gave him a towel to cover his mouth. Billy breathed through the cloth.

"Nothing," he finally managed.

Chris nodded. "Double-check," he said. "Look all around the hole, Billy. You have to be sure."

Billy took two more breaths, then tossed the towel and ducked underwater. Chris saw him searching the ground with his flashlight, looking for a glimmer of anything. Still nothing. No lost jackets, no missing jewelry, no dead bodies. Billy had done enough, and Chris was ready to tell him, but Billy had drifted too far. He was so busy searching, he lost sight of the hole. Now, coming up, he struck his head against the floor of the ice. This not only surprised him; it made him panic. Chris saw the air burst from his mouth, and Billy lunged about, like someone had shot him with a spear.

Chris pulled on the rope until he dragged Billy back to the hole.

"Christ," Billy gasped.

"You okay?" Chris asked.

Billy kept struggling for air.

"You're doing terrific," Chris said. "I mean it, Billy. I just need one more favor."

Billy managed to look astounded. He tried crawling up onto the ice, but slipped back in the hole.

"This will be quick," Chris insisted. He untied one of his sneakers and dropped it into the water. "Go down and get that."

Billy couldn't believe it.

"Please," Chris said. "Hurry up. My foot is freezing."

"I could give a shit about your foot," Billy said.

But he went straight down, found the sneaker, then came back up. With the job finished, Chris helped him onto the ice.

"What's wrong with you?" Billy asked. "You think I'm a goddamn retriever?"

"Get back to the van," Chris said.

Billy did, leaving Chris to clean up their mess. When Chris made it back, he hobbled into the rear and pressed his foot against the car heater. In the meantime, Billy had stripped himself of clothes and was wrapped in a blanket.

Denny dropped a blanket by Chris and settled in the driver's seat. She exchanged a look with Billy, then said to Chris, "Nothing?"

Chris kept rubbing his foot. "Yeah, but there should have been something. When they pulled Kathleen Donnelly out of the water, a shoe was missing. Everyone probably figured she lost it in the water, but it's not there."

"It's there," Denny said. "It could have drifted."

"That's my whole point," Chris said. "I dropped a sneaker in there, and it dropped straight down. She had *shoes* on, which are heavier. Where is it?"

Neither answered, but it didn't matter; Chris was thinking aloud.

"The shoe didn't just drift off," he said. "If it fell in the pond, it would be directly under the hole. At least it would be *near* the hole. So if she wasn't killed, what happened? Where did she lose the shoe? How did she get to the pond?" He felt thoroughly pleased with himself. "Why isn't the shoe in the water? Where is it? In the woods? In Todd's car?"

"In the basement?" Denny said, now also thinking aloud.

Chris nodded, knowing he was no longer alone. "Where's the shoe?" he asked a last time.

Billy nodded right along.

You had to test the lines, Chris thought. *That* was the secret to success: going where other people didn't dare, keeping your eye off that horizon so it didn't scare you off. Screw boundaries. Screw it all, and then lean back, smiling.

They reached the motel after midnight. They stopped briefly outside Chris's room, Denny exhausted and Billy excited. "We got a big day later," Chris said. "I'll phone Dorsey, but even if we don't get the equipment, we have to start doing this right."

"Tomorrow," said Denny.

"Tomorrow," Chris agreed, and she left.

Billy stayed longer, following Chris into his room to see

the evening's tape. They sat together perhaps another half hour, just to see if they had filmed something Billy had overlooked with his own eye. They watched until Billy looked to Chris and said, "You hungry?"

Chris told Billy to relax and drove to the gas mart. It took only a few minutes to reach the store. Once inside, he went to a refrigerator, pulled out a sandwich, and headed back to the counter. He was near the register when he noticed two other customers in the store. A man was buying a six-pack of soda, while a woman stood by the movie rentals, bending down and thumbing across the tapes.

Thumbing across the lowest rack.

She was young, maybe in her mid-twenties, with dark hair and freckled skin. She also wore jeans, a bomber jacket and leather boots. Chris noticed all these things, but what he noticed most was her tape. It was from the special collection, and while he couldn't make out the title, he knew what it was: if not *Raw Death*, then a close copy. Or maybe one of those true blood slasher gems out of New York.

Nothing passed between the manager and the woman. When she left the store, the woman went to her car, revved the engine and angled quickly out of the lot. In seconds she was gone, racing the road like a native.

And Chris wondered: was she really from the area? If so, what was it like borrowing a bottom-rack tape from a store owner who had probably known you since childhood? Would he think any less of the woman, or was this standard, local behavior? After all, the tapes wouldn't be here for only one customer.

By the time he returned to the motel, Billy was back in his own room. Chris walked down the hall, knocked on Billy's door and left the food outside. Finally, Chris went to his own room.

It was very late now, and he figured on no more than four, maybe five hours sleep. He was thinking about this and letting the early morning slow him down, when he saw a slip of paper lying at the base of his door. Chris picked it up and discovered a phone message from the front desk. Dorsey had called, which was surprising, because the time on the message was two in the morning, which meant Al had phoned at midnight L.A. time. It not only meant there was something urgent; Dorsey had been so urgent he had woken the motel management and dragged some poor fool across the snow to Chris's room.

When he found the note, Chris was still thinking about checking into Todd's school, tracing the boy's steps, identifying his friends, doing the same with his enemies . . . It was overwhelming, but it was exciting. Everything was ready to fall together, and he couldn't wait to get started.

Then he read the message. *Come back immediately. Reservations on 8 a.m. flight.*

Best, Al.

ELEVEN

THE bomb exploded just as Dorsey was wiping his ass. That was the only reason he was alive. Dorsey had ordered out for Chinese food and something didn't sit right. Instead of heading out of the office by six, he spent an extra forty minutes on the toilet, cradling a bottle of Pepto and relieving himself of double-fried pork. He was barely flushed clean when he heard this loud pop. Then he went outside and saw it: a ton of smoke billowing past his window and blackening the sky. Parked near the curb, maybe twenty feet from the front of Dorsey's two-story office headquarters, was the burning shell of his Cadillac. The Caddy was still there when Chris arrived in L.A. "They could have towed it, but I said no way," Dorsey said. "It's a monument to free speech."

Chris rested his suitcase. "You're sure it wasn't an accident?"

"What, you think it was spontaneous combustion?"

Chris said nothing.

"It's the shmuck who thinks he's God," Dorsey answered. "It has to be him. Unless it's that pimp who's suing me for breach of contract." Dorsey shook his head, disgusted. "Just think—except for a little pink pork, I'd be dead."

Chris sat there, tired, listening, not so much worried

about Dorsey as wondering why he'd been dragged all the way back to L.A.

"You look awful," Dorsey told him.

"I could be better," Chris said, then, "Is that why you brought me back, Al? Because of the bomb?"

"You make it sound like nothing," Dorsey said, "but there's also a budget meeting tomorrow, remember? For RD-three?"

Chris still waited.

"Also, there's someone I want you to meet. I think he's going to be a big help around here, but I don't want to do anything without your approval. I mean, he's good, but when it comes to RD-three, you're the one in charge. You're the mastermind."

"Who is he?"

"First worry about the budget figures, okay? I got a backer meeting on Wednesday."

Chris knew Dorsey wanted him to go, but there was too much bullshit floating. "I'm sorry, Al, but I don't understand. You brought me back for a meeting? That was the emergency?"

"The meeting's why you're here, but the bomb was the emergency," he said. "Doesn't that sound like an emergency to you?"

Chris didn't know what to say. He was too tired for Dorsey's logic. "You haven't asked me how the film's going. You wanted proof Todd Meacham's a killer, and I got it."

He pulled the tape from his satchel. Dorsey, however, kept his hands out of reach.

"This is good work, Al," Chris said. "It's gonna make our reputations."

"I got a reputation already, thank you. If you're not happy with yours, that's your problem."

Chris left the cassette on Dorsey's desk. "You promised," he said.

Dorsey laughed.

"You promised and you owe me," Chris said.

Dorsey laughed harder. "That's how you want to play it?

Not business, not common sense? You want me to do this because of friendship?'' He shrugged, then reached out and took the tape. "All right. For your sake, I'll look at it. And for my sake, get the figures together, so we can make some money next year."

Chris headed for the door.

"And another favor. Call up your police friends. See if they can find God and take him off the streets."

Chris left. As for Dorsey, he carried his fruit juice to the window, stared down at his destroyed Caddy and wondered what else was going to explode.

Chris started by going to his apartment—the second floor of a two-story stucco home, reachable by way of its own outdoor staircase. As for the inside, it was proof Chris was truly cheap work-for-hire. He flicked a wall switch and settled in something that passed as an all-purpose living room. He had one other room—an oversized, windowless closet that was his bedroom—but he spent most of his time out here, surrounded by old furniture and old clothes.

It was a cramped, uncomfortable apartment, but the rent was less than $900, so people considered him lucky. Of course, these same people considered him lucky to have a full-time job. With the benefit of experience, Chris knew the limits of his luck.

He settled by the telephone and thought about Dorsey. Foremost he wondered if Dorsey was out to get him. After all, Dorsey had treated him like crap, and in this city you simply didn't do that unless you were prepared to cut a person from your life. It was a town of coddling, not attack. Film work, for all its pleasures, had made too many people insecure, sensitive and self-centered. If you hurt an ego, it could stay bruised for years.

So why had Dorsey tried so hard to piss him off? Was Dorsey starting to look beyond Chris?

Chris thought a moment and decided to phone Iowa. He tried Denny's room, and when no one answered he tried Billy. They were both out, which, Chris realized, was good; better to have them filming than locked in a motel room. At the same time, he would have liked to know how matters were progressing. It would help his next few phone calls.

With Dorsey still on his mind, he opened the L.A. phone book and jotted down the numbers to a half dozen production companies. He dialed all of them, leaving messages for three of the calls, getting a rejection on the fourth, a dinner date for the fifth, and a recording for the sixth, telling him the number had been disconnected.

Nonetheless, he had the dinner and that was a start. He thought briefly about Gwen, but only briefly. Then he sneaked a nap, changed clothes and decided that he should take care of Dorsey's favor. With an hour before dinner, he headed to his car and drove crosstown to the station house.

It was an odd drive. For the first time in a long time, he felt uncomfortable in the city. It wasn't so much a feeling of distance; it was more a matter of sensing something missing, and that something was Todd. Killers belonged in megacities like L.A., not in cornfield communities. People like Todd—people born to cut throats—needed someplace where the throats were bare and ready. They needed to be where the good and bad had crossbred so many times you ended up with streets of blurred and forgotten boundaries. Where no one was quite sure if you had crossed the line or not.

Chris drove until he reached Dorsey's police precinct, then went inside to the front desk. The sergeant saw him and grinned. "It's the man who's gonna make me a star," he said.

Chris walked up to the desk. The sergeant's name was Edgar Denton, and during the editing of *Raw Death* he had supplied Chris with clips from the police hold. "Hey, I heard what happened to Al," Denton said.

The sergeant talked about Dorsey like they knew each other—as if associating with one of Dorsey's flunkies was a connection to Hollywood and Beverly Hills. As if Dorsey *had* a connection to Beverly Hills.

Denton talked briefly to a clerk, and the clerk trotted off for the file. Then the sergeant said to Chris, "You missed some great action the other night. A chase with an eight-car pileup."

"Car chases are tough to film."

"Nothing's tough for you," Denton said. "You guys are really sick, you know that? I don't know why we're even talking."

"Money wouldn't have anything to do with it?" Chris said.

The sergeant waved aside the idea. "I just get a kick out of it. You movie people, it's fun seeing how low you'll go." The clerk returned and dropped the file by the sergeant. Denton glanced it over, then slid the file to Chris. "You can tell Al there's an investigation going on, but the truth is we got files on about eight guys who call themselves God and none have active addresses, except maybe Heaven. Personally," he said, grinning, "I only believe in one God."

Chris gave the file a cursory scan. Finally, he slid the file back, his obligation met.

"This guy blew up a car," Chris said. "He's going to do something again."

"Maybe not," Denton said.

"It'll happen," Chris said. "Dorsey brings out the worst in people."

The sergeant jotted down a phone number. "Give this to Al," he said. "If he spots anything, have him call me directly."

Chris took the number. "I got one other question. I'm working on this film about a teenage killer in the Midwest. What's your experience with teenagers?"

"Teenagers kill like everyone else," he said, "except usually they kill their parents."

"This kid killed his girlfriend, and I think he'll kill again, but I'm not sure who or when. Truth is, I can't stick around waiting forever."

"So?"

"So what sets them off?" Chris asked. "What makes them snap so they do things?"

"Christ, I'm not a psychologist."

"I just want your opinion," Chris said.

"I don't know," Denton said. "What do you think? Sex maybe?"

Chris thought a moment. "The kid's father beats him," he said. "I think he may have even molested him."

Denton opened his hands, as if Chris had answered his own question.

Chris glanced at his watch. The time was five-thirty, and he had twenty minutes before dinner. That was twenty minutes to figure out how to pitch for a job. He thanked Denton and headed for the restaurant.

Chris had met his dinner appointment during last year's video convention in Vegas. The producer identified himself as Wynn Strickler, handed Chris a card that read *BMD Productions* and told him that he was an admirer. The conversation ended with a handshake and an almost forgotten invitation for Chris to call him anytime.

Now, half a year since a five-minute conversation, Chris was accepting the invitation. He parked, grabbed his satchel and headed into a seafood restaurant several dollars above his range. Strickler greeted him by the bar.

"How's my favorite new filmmaker?" Strickler said.

Chris shook his hand. Strickler was in his late forties, extremely fit, with a grip that was firm, tight, secure . . . that was, simply, fitting for a man who would risk dinner on an acquaintance.

"It's about time you called," Strickler said. "How's Al doing? I heard something about a bomb."

"Hate mail from a lunatic," Chris said. "Probably overdue."

"I think it's terrific you called. I was just talking with Zabrinski, the Polish director. He's working on a film about Shakespeare's love life."

"I heard."

"We got to talking about death sequences, and I was telling him about this fabulous filmmaker I know who had taken all this raw footage about murder and put together this really special documentary."

"That's kind of you," Chris said.

"I was telling him what really impressed me was your

inventiveness. I mean, other companies have done this same thing and ended up with the usual sensationalist crap. But you gave it context. I swear, by the time I was done talking about you, I had Zabrinski running to the video store.''

"*Raw Death*'s been good,'' Chris said, ''but there are just so many limits to what I can get done with Al. I can't help wondering if there's life after R.I.P.''

"Well, nothing against Al,'' Strickler said, ''but in ten years you're not even gonna remember R.I.P. R.I.P. is gonna be one little line on a long list of credits. It's gonna be a segment in one of your death films.''

"God forbid I'm still making them,'' Chris said.

"God forbid you should ever do anything you don't want to do,'' he said, ''but don't knock yourself. I don't want to back stab Al, but I'd love to have you producing a line of *Raw Deaths* for my company.''

"The truth is I'm working on something now, except I'm not sure Dorsey's the right person for it.''

Strickler assumed the pose of a professional listener.

"It's a kind of documentary,'' Chris said.

"Documentary?'' Strickler said.

"I know this kid in the Midwest. He's already committed one murder, and he's going to do a second one soon.''

"A loose killer?'' Strickler said.

"What I'm trying to do now is put a film together that follows him right up to the next attack.''

Strickler stopped him. ''The victim—is it a man or a woman?''

"I don't know about the next person, but the last one was a teenage girl.''

Strickler looked interested.

"We got footage of her being pulled from the water,'' Chris said. ''What I'm looking for now is financial backing. It's not going to take much money—maybe fifty thousand, a hundred tops. What I need is equipment and time; another cameraman would also be good. But I have to get it together quick or else I'm going to lose the whole thing.''

"How quick?''

"Within the week,'' Chris said.

"You mean *very* quick," Strickler said. He thought a moment, then shook his head, laughing. "It's a fabulous idea, Chris. It's completely original."

Chris carefully considered what to say. He knew that completely original ideas were death to producers. "Well, it's not that original," he said. "It's structure is a murder mystery, except this time the killer and suspect are real people."

Strickler stopped him. "Now *that's* interesting," he said. "What you said right there—real people."

Chris nodded.

"Are you sure that's the right way to go?"

Chris didn't answer.

"A killer stalking a small town," Strickler said. "I see the possibilities, but a documentary . . . I can't remember the last documentary to make money. *Born Free?* Was that a documentary?"

"The point of the film is to chronicle a real murder," Chris said.

"And it's a good idea," Strickler said. "I'm just not seeing the audience." He squeezed a lime wedge into his glass of water. "What did Al say?"

"Al's hedging," Chris said. "He wants me working on the next *Raw Death*."

Strickler looked disgusted. "Al has no imagination," he said. "But he's a businessman. You have to forgive him."

"I personally think he can make a lot of money off this," Chris said. "It would also do something for the company's reputation."

Strickler laughed. "You can't save what you don't got."

Chris sipped his own water.

"Chris, I don't think your problem is with this documentary, it's with R.I.P. Now if I were you—and, of course, I'm *not*—I'd think less about new projects than repackaging the one you have. You want to find someplace that is ready to give you the support and trust and backing to really get this death thing off the ground. And then, once you start bringing in fresh dollars, you should take your chances. That's when you branch out."

Chris responded slowly, deliberately—aware he was on the verge of a turndown. "I don't have the time to wait," he said. "A chance like this comes once. If I don't get the backing now—"

"Chances come every day," Strickler said, "especially for people like you." He grabbed Chris's wrist, letting him know it was time to be earnest. "I look at you and I think, Christ, if only I had a tenth of your talent, I could own Hollywood."

"I understand," Chris said, "it's just—"

"The one thing Al and I do have in common is backers," Strickler said. "He's got his backers whacking his butt, and I got the same. As much as my heart aches for people like you, this ridiculous city is interested in just one thing, and that's collecting bundles of green paper."

Chris was again quiet.

"If I were you, I'd think about turning my skills to more steady projects," Strickler said. "Have you thought about packaging yourself? I'd really like to hear about that."

Chris talked, but no longer about his film. Later, back at his apartment, he wondered if he'd spend the next ten years clipping together hybrids of *Raw Death*. Maybe that was why Matt had killed himself; he saw the future and realized suicide was less painful.

The next morning, Chris went into Dorsey's office without the budget numbers and prepared for a furious rage. Instead, Dorsey was warm and friendly and, all and all, in a tremendous mood. Beside him, in the chair Chris usually occupied, was a stranger: a large, heavyset man with black, thinning hair and a thick, ragged moustache. "Chris, come closer," Dorsey said. "I want you to meet someone. I want you to meet your new partner."

The stranger rose from the chair and offered his hand. The grip smothered Chris's fingers.

"Know who he is?" Dorsey asked.

The stranger grinned. "I'm a big fan of yours, Mr. Thomas," the man said.

Chris studied the stranger's face.

"You saw one of my tapes, I think," the man said.

Then Chris understood. He turned to Dorsey, his own face without expression, not quite believing what was happening.

"My name's Campo," the man said. "Don Campo. I sent you my video."

Chris looked into the man's eyes. It was like staring into the eyes of Dwight Hamisch.

"It's a pleasure to be working with you, Mr. Thomas," Campo said.

TWELVE

"**I** see great things happening around here," Dorsey said. "Chris, I would have waited, but hey, Don's background is so perfect."

"It's really great meeting you, Mr. Thomas," Campo said. "Back in New York, we think a lot of your work."

"Don says that on the East Coast, they can't wait for RD-two," Dorsey said.

"This is such an honor," Campo said.

Chris listened, trying to be patient, wondering how the hell Don Campo spoke for the entire East Coast. Then, to Dorsey, he said, "I don't have the budget figures."

Dorsey showed no sign of caring, and Chris realized something: the budget meeting, probably even the car bombing, meant little to Dorsey. Campo was the reason Chris had been brought to L.A. Campo was the emergency; the sole point for his flying in from the Midwest.

To Campo, Dorsey said, "Tell Chris what you were telling me."

"Just that I had a friend with a drive-in chain. I think if we came out with a ninety-minute feature, he'd jump at the chance of showing it."

"That wouldn't be so bad," Dorsey said. "Some outdoor money before hitting the video shelves?"

Chris tried looking interested, but the situation was too ridiculous. He finally asked Campo for a moment alone with Dorsey. Campo understood. He excused himself and left to sit with the secretary. Chris waited until the door closed; then he also sat down, not even thinking of something to say, since he expected Dorsey to break right in with apologies.

Only Dorsey surprised him. Dorsey matched silence with silence, which, if Chris thought about it, only made sense, since Dorsey was always surprising him.

Chris sighed. "You know what I'm going to say," he finally said. "You saw his clips. Campo is crazy."

Dorsey started chuckling.

"I'm serious," Chris said. "I'm not just talking about what he films, I'm talking about the kind of person that makes movies about people getting tortured. Women getting cigarettes ground in their breasts? Not only does he make them, he brags about it." Chris caught his temper. He couldn't believe Dorsey was obliging him to say this. "When I'm making *Raw Death*, Al, what makes it interesting— its only saving grace—is that it takes people deeper into themselves than they've ever gone before. We're stripping them clean. But Campo . . . he's a maniac. I watched two minutes of his crap and wanted to vomit."

Dorsey finally spoke. "What you're trying to say," Dorsey said, "is that his films are pretty damn effective."

Chris was completely at a loss. Dorsey, sensing his opening, walked around the desk so they could be closer.

"Come on," Dorsey said. "With Don here, this is a perfect chance for you. You're going crazy with these films, and he would chop off a hand to do what you're doing."

"So?"

"So if Don works out, then he can take over the sequels and we can get you working on better things."

"What better things?"

"We'll work on that," Dorsey said. "But I can tell you now, I'm thinking features. Ninety minutes, two hours—"

"Soft porn?"

"Screw porn," Dorsey said. "Maybe action/adventure. Those are selling before they're even made."

"What about my movie?" Chris said. "Did you look at the tape?"

Dorsey moved away from Chris.

"Al, did you see the footage?"

"I saw it," Dorsey said. "I can't believe you got Billy to go swimming in ice water. That alone's worth the price of admission."

"Be serious," Chris said.

"I am," he said, but Chris wouldn't let him off the hook. "All right. Seriously, I think you're crazy. No, excuse me. The rest of us are crazy. You're the only sane one in the world."

"You wanted proof," Chris said.

"That's right," Dorsey said. "I wanted proof this thing would make money. I could give a crap if the kid's guilty. That's for cops, not me."

"What you're saying is you never had any intention of financing me."

"What I'm saying is, who's this movie for? Who's your audience? Is it cops? Is it French film critics? It sure as hell isn't for me, but I'm the one who's supposed to pay."

Chris stared at Dorsey. He felt completely betrayed. "You should have said this to me before," Chris said. "You've been jerking me around."

"Hey," Dorsey said, "I told you do what you want, so long as you took care of your job. I never said I'd spend money on the fucking thing."

Chris thought a moment. He left his seat, pacing the room, again making his case. "It wouldn't cost much, Al. A couple of good mikes, more cameras, maybe another cameraman. Denny wrote me up a list of what I—"

"Please," Dorsey said, begging off.

"Do it as a favor."

"Another favor . . . ," Dorsey said, exasperated.

"You do this as a favor to me, and I'll get Campo set up in L.A."

Dorsey glared at Chris. "You should do that anyway," Dorsey said. "You work for me, remember?"

Chris didn't answer. Almost instantly, Dorsey understood. "You talking quitting?" he said.

Chris remained quiet. Still, the threat was out, and it was Dorsey's turn to think. And he thought quickly. Chris *was* R.I.P. In the future, maybe it would be Campo—*maybe*—but for now he was too new, too untested, too psychotic.

"Where'd you go yesterday," Dorsey asked. "Have you been talking to someone else?"

Now Dorsey looked betrayed. He tried wringing out the guilt, but got nothing for his effort. Finally, he sat back, disgusted. "You know what you're doing, don't you? This is no way to conduct business."

"I'm committed to this, Al," Chris said. "For Christ's sake, I'm not asking for a hell of a lot. Not when you think about all the money you made off me."

Dorsey's face was tight, like he was considering a new assault and had opened Chris for a prime attack. Chris prepared, but then Dorsey's mood took a new term: the look of a tired, vanquished mogul.

"You're playing too many cards, my friend," Dorsey said.

"Just give it a chance," Chris said. "That's not asking much."

Dorsey looked totally unconvinced, but it didn't matter. He walked Chris out, acknowledging at least a first step toward agreement. Chris headed out of the office, satisfied. He was almost past the secretary when Campo touched his arm.

"Mr. Thomas?"

Chris turned.

"Excuse me, but I got the feeling Mr. Dorsey pulled a number on you," Campo said. "I thought maybe he brought me here without letting you in on the move."

Chris shrugged.

"That sucks," Campo said.

Chris waited, expecting Campo to offer his resignation, but Campo knew better than to risk that much.

"I just want you to know, Mr. Thomas, I'm gonna work my ass off. I should have made the move to L.A. years ago. This is the money town, not New York. I got the ideas, too. Did you like my clips?"

Chris looked embarrassed by the question. Campo instantly understood.

"You're right," Campo said. "Shit. Utter garbage. I shouldn't have shown them to someone as good as you."

"Al liked them," Chris said.

"Yeah, but you're the one who matters," Campo said. "You're the genius."

Campo opened the door, and together they walked outside.

"This *Raw Death* format," Campo said. "I think it can really branch out. I don't mean to shoot off my mouth, but you got yourself a cutting room?"

Chris looked confused.

"It's a big thing back East," Campo said. "You rent a place in a ghetto, make it up comfy, leave the door unlocked . . . Pretty soon, word's out there's a nice little room for doing just about any bit of shit you want. What they don't know is there's a camera in the room, catching everything on film. Or at least sometimes they don't know. Sometimes they do, and that can be half the fun."

"Cutting room?" Chris said.

"Nickname. The first guy who did it used an old editing room in a warehouse," Campo said. "Truth is, eighty percent of the stuff is garbage—sometimes a quick fuck, sometimes just a runaway looking for free bed. But that twenty percent . . . come on, you know this crap."

Chris shrugged, actually uncomfortable that he didn't.

"All you do is find the space and fix the cameras," Campo said. "Wait a week, and the psychos know that any time they want, they got a free hotel room with a peephole."

"What about the film you sent me," Chris said. "Were real people getting hurt?"

Campo looked insulted. "Hell, no. I paid those people."

Campo acted like the question had been answered. Only later would some small part of Chris wonder if being paid necessarily meant that the people in his film hadn't been hurt.

"You like it, don't you?" Campo said. "Not the clips—the idea."

Chris hesitated. "Mr. Campo—"

"I'm asking, because you got a head for good ideas," Campo said. "I bet that's how you made it to the top."

Chris stopped talking. Did Campo seriously consider working for Al Dorsey the "top"?

"Mr. Campo—"

"Don," Campo said.

"Don, you can't go setting up rooms for people to kill each other."

"But you can," Campo said. "It's easy. All you need is—"

"I mean it's not right," Chris said.

Campo quieted, perturbed. "Look," he said, "I know the idea has problems. It gets too routine, for one. The same room, cut after cut. But there's ways around that."

"That's not what I—"

"I also have this new concept in mind," Campo said. "Like a fact/fiction movie. Maybe this feature film about a city gone killer crazy, but the twist is we take a fiction movie and stick in real murder clips. You get it?"

Chris was mesmerized. He walked alongside Campo, wondering if it was safe to argue.

"I got other ideas, too," Campo said. "Want to hear them?"

Campo wrapped an arm about him and they walked to Chris's car.

THIRTEEN

H E should have talked to Denny at least once on the phone. They had called each other every day, but only managed to trade messages. Now, after flying back to the Midwest, Chris tried to imagine how things would stand. It left him in a curious position: on the one hand, he didn't want to be wishing for another murder; on the other hand, it would be proof of the pudding.

Chris sighed. Probably the worst part of all was how good he had become at these moral balancing acts.

When he left the plane, Denny met him at the gate.

"It's about time you came back," she said. Denny hugged him, then took one of his bags.

"Where's Billy?" Chris asked.

"Out with the camera," Denny said. "How'd things go with Dorsey?"

"About what you'd expect," he said.

Denny grinned. "Well, I got interesting news for you here. Things have been happening."

"Things like what?"

"Things that may change Dorsey's mind," Denny said. "Another girl's disappeared."

* * *

They were in the van, driving in the early dark, heading back to the motel.

"Billy heard about it in the police station," Denny told him. "Not the Hayden station, the one in Marsh. Billy was checking on any write-ups about Meacham when they mentioned the girl. They wanted to know if he'd seen her. They said she disappeared the night you left."

"Who is she?"

"Jessica Robie," she said. "Sixteen, high school sophomore . . ."

"Do you have her picture?"

"We got something, but it's not great," Denny said. "We're going to need better."

"What about Todd?"

"Todd's another story. That's where everything gets fucked. Billy and me planned to cover him night and day, but then he left," Denny said. "I mean he left *town*. I filmed his father putting him on the Greyhound. The same day that girl disappeared, Todd was about four hours due south, visiting an uncle."

"That can't be right," said Chris.

"We double-checked," Denny said. "Billy was able to track down Todd's address. He called and Todd was there. Billy even got him on the phone."

"Billy doesn't know Todd's voice," Chris said.

"He knows it as well as me or you."

"Besides, Todd could have still killed her," Chris said. "He could have taken the bus out there, then driven back and forth without anyone knowing."

"What would be the point? He doesn't know what we're doing."

"Maybe he does."

Denny shook her head.

"Maybe he saw Billy," Chris said.

"Or maybe Todd didn't have anything to do with this one," Denny said. "Maybe the girl really did disappear."

Chris glared at her. "Where's Billy now?" he said.

"At the farm," Denny said.

Chris asked her to keep driving and Denny headed for the

Meacham farm. When they were within a hundred yards, she turned off the headlights and stopped. "We got a signal," she said, and glanced at her watch. She waited until the time was on the hour, then slipped a cassette in the car stereo, rolled down the passenger window and turned up the volume.

"Arrowsmith," said Denny.

With the headlights on again, she drove past the Meacham farm. They traveled another hundred yards past the driveway before she turned off the stereo and pulled over.

"We spent a day working on this," Denny said. "We thought about flashlights, mirrors, honking the horn. I finally figured if you can't be discreet, be obnoxious."

Another ten minutes passed before Billy came jogging down the road. Under his arm was one of the cameras. He glanced at Chris, grunted his discomfort, then looked to Denny.

"Nothing?" Denny said.

Billy was too cold. He shook his head and pressed near the van's heater. "Not there," he finally managed.

"He means no Todd," Denny told Chris.

"No Todd?" Chris said.

"Just the parents," Billy said. "And snow."

"You're sure?" Chris said. "You were able to see upstairs? You checked all the windows?"

"I checked everywhere," Billy said.

"He could be coming in late at night," Chris said. "Did you check after midnight?"

"We've been out there as much as we can," Billy said. "I set a time exposure to cover when we're gone. It's zero out there, and if that's not good enough, fuck yourself." Billy took off his gloves and rubbed his fingers.

Chris said nothing, which was enough to keep Billy quiet. Denny turned the van and headed to the motel. When she parked, Billy grabbed his equipment and headed for his room. Denny reacted more calmly, walking Chris to his room, taking the time to give Chris some manner of good word.

"Don't worry," she said. "We just have to figure out what's going on."

Chris looked at her, wishing Denny didn't sound so indulgent. Then he closed the door and started unpacking. He was part exhaustion, part nervous energy—in short, the same mess he had become since first learning about Todd Meacham.

Had Todd left town? If so, what would it mean? Where did it leave Chris?

As always, he tried finding his answer in the film clips. He studied them all: the clip of Todd and Donnelly heading for the pond, the footage of Todd and his father, the shots in the Meacham house, the shots around the farm . . . He went frame by frame through the underwater footage; at first thinking he saw something new, then thinking he saw nothing.

Then he tried a game. Suppose Kathleen Donnelly had died accidentally? Suppose the second girl had simply run away? But then how could Chris explain the missing shoe?

He went back to that first clip. It was, after all, the reason he was staying up yet again, testing his instinct for the fatal. And he saw what he always saw—a young girl, relaxed and sitting beside someone preternaturally focused. Chris froze the image, then turned off the lights and lay in bed. The only light came from the television monitor . . . the image of Kathleen Donnelly turned toward Todd, and Todd, behind the wheel, staring in his rearview mirror.

He relaxed. The entire episode reminded him of a short story he had once read about a photographer who took a picture of a park scene, then began seeing new things in the picture every time he looked at it. When the story begins, the photographer sees nothing more than a boy in conversation with a stranger. Later, however, the same picture brings a different interpretation. By the story's end, it's of a boy being led away so a man in a nearby car can rape him.

Was that Chris's mistake: seeing the wrong story in his pictures?

He touched the remote and slowly the pickup jerked

forward. A blurring momentum. No sooner was Kathleen out of view then the footage ended.

Chris stopped the clip and moved it back, just a fraction. Todd was gone, but he could still see the side of Kathleen's head. Mostly, Chris saw the back of the truck. And, like before, he saw the front end of the following car. It was the car that had Todd's attention—the thing that had him afraid; that made Todd unnerved and preoccupied.

Chris brought the tape back a few frames. Again he stared at Todd; this time, however, he also realized something. Todd's look. He had seen it before. The fear, the absorption, the total concentration . . .

Chris got out of bed, changed cassettes and ran the tape of Todd beside his father. If William Meacham was abusing his son, by all rights he should be the boy's next victim. When Chris looked at the tape now, he could see Todd's killer look focused on his father. It was the look of the Moment Maker. The look that was making everything happen.

Except Todd hadn't killed William Meacham; instead, a second girl had died. A girl had died and Todd hadn't been in town and . . .

And Chris returned to the first tape. This time he ignored the teenagers. He was only interested in the second car. Chris would have loved an extra few seconds of footage. Once he understood, however, he didn't need them. He studied the frames long enough to memorize the few necessary details, then grabbed a flashlight and left the motel. He went downstairs, climbed in the van, turned the ignition and started driving. He didn't stop until he was the usual hundred yards from the Meacham house. Then he parked, turned off the headlights and walked quietly up the Meacham driveway.

The house was asleep. Absolute quiet, which was fine; Chris wasn't interested in the house.

He was interested in William Meacham's car.

Chris walked up to the Dodge, and for only a brief moment dared to turn on his flashlight. He swept the light across the front of the car, seeing it almost as briefly as he had seen it in the film.

Then he turned off the light, glanced once at the house and headed back for the road.

He finally understood. The look in Todd's eyes—it didn't belong to a Moment Maker; it was the look of someone who glanced in a rearview mirror and saw death staring back at him. It was the look of someone who went home at night and saw it again, every day of his life.

It was the look of someone who lived with a killer.

Chris climbed in the van and rested his head.

The day Kathleen Donnelly died—the day Todd drove her to her death—the two teenagers weren't alone. William Meacham was behind them. And William Meacham had been in town this week.

In town, while another girl disappeared.

Chris took a deep breath. Suddenly, he was seeing a whole new film.

PART THREE

FOURTEEN

WILLIAM Meacham knew better than to depend on his son. For starters, Todd was unreliable. Sometimes the boy would forget his chores; sometimes he would sneak out of the house just as William was heading upstairs for one of their "talks"; sometimes Todd even lost his temper. One of Todd's tantrums had been so bad, William Meacham didn't clean up the damage. He left the blood on the ground and the pitchfork bent so Todd would appreciate that not everything could be fixed; often when things got messy, they stayed messy. William Meacham believed in reminders.

No, he definitely didn't depend on the boy; still, Todd made matters easier. He knew the people William wanted to meet and knew how to gain their confidence. Perhaps most important, Todd had himself become one of William Meacham's reminders. Staring at Todd, even weeks after they'd been out, helped William remember, and William liked remembering.

So when would they go out again? Todd and William, father and son . . . What would be the next family project?

He thought of this because it was dinner, and with Todd away, all he had for company was his wife. As always, Helen ate without saying a word. A half hour passed before Meacham pushed from his seat and said, "I'm going out."

Mrs. Meacham refused to look up, and he knew what she was thinking.

"I'm going out, but not for that," he said. "For beer."

Mrs. Meacham still wouldn't answer. He left the table anyway, looking for his jacket, for the life of him not remembering where he had left it. Then he realized it wasn't a matter of misplacing the thing; his wife had put it away. And the problem with Helen was she didn't clean to have things orderly, she cleaned to get things out of sight, like she was hiding evidence. This meant his jacket could be anywhere.

He finally found it in Todd's room, hanging in a closet, hooked over a stained bath towel. He grabbed the jacket, left the house, headed straight to the Chevy, and somewhere between the farm and the tavern he relaxed. William was completely at home in Hayden. Helen talked to her broom and Todd to the ground, but William was a people person. When he parked and walked into the bar, everyone nodded or otherwise made him feel like the trusted neighbor. Of course, William knew impressions could change, but that was part of his pleasure—knowing that at any moment, the wrong word would scrap everything to hell.

"Meacham," someone shouted.

William looked across the tavern. A man rested against the bar counter, a 22-caliber rifle raised and leveled at Meacham's head.

"Meacham, you still owe me twenty dollars for that fan belt. When am I gonna see it, buddy? I gotta pay bills, too."

William Meacham walked closer. "I'll pay your bill when you learn to hit the side of a wall."

"Walls I can hit," the man said, "but your head's too small."

William opened a hand, and the man gave him the weapon.

"What do you think?" the man said. He used his foot to hook and drag a stool. Meacham took the seat and sat down. "I'm gonna teach my boy how to shoot, and then in the spring we're going hunting. We're gonna—" He stopped talking. Another friend had walked in the bar, and he grabbed the gun, pushed off the stool and leveled the weapon at the front door. "Hey you asshole, Fritzy. What you been doing to my wife? Who you been sleeping with?"

Howie Fritz saw the gun and grinned. "I wouldn't fuck your wife if it would save my dick."

The bartender leaned over the counter. "Boden, can you put that away before someone gets hurt?"

Boden put the gun in its box. "I'm gonna teach my kid to hunt," he told his friends.

"I don't see much pleasure in killing deer," Meacham said.

"I used to hunt," Fritz said. "Now I got a VCR."

"There's nothing like tracking an animal through the woods," Boden said. "Lining the sight, pulling the trigger, watching that fucker buck and—"

"And then you got to drag his dead ass ten miles back to the truck," Fritz said.

"It's good meat," Boden said.

Meacham shook his head. "I got other things to do."

"Like what?"

"Like what do you think?" said Fritz, grinning.

During the next half hour, they'd switch talk over a dozen times—from hunting, to sex, to football, to sex, to teenagers . . .

"I don't know how Todd's doing at school," Meacham said. "Seems like I can't get his attention these days. That's why I sent him to his uncle."

"It's his age," Fritz said. "These teenagers can't control their hormones."

"You want a girl instead of a boy," said Boden. "Sarah's got a good head."

"Sarah's how old?" said Fritz. "Seventeen?"

"Yeah," Boden said. "Another good reason to own a gun." He took the posture of a guarding soldier.

Meacham looked thoughtful. "I don't think I could bring up a girl," he said. "I don't know what I'd do with one."

"Shit, just let the mother do the work," Boden said.

"Helen doesn't do nothing," Meacham said. "I swear, if I had a girl, one of us wouldn't last long."

When they finished the next round, Meacham said his goodbyes and left the tavern. He went to the car, turned the ignition and followed the north route, going about five miles outside Hayden. He finally pulled beside a wide driveway that was wet from snow, salt and sand. It was the entrance to a drive-in theater. Directly ahead was what looked like a tollbooth, and behind the booth was the back structure to a six-story screen. A movie played: Meacham could see the projection light. He sat there, less interested in specifics than whether the place had the proper feel—if the distractions were right, if it was dark enough, if he felt relaxed in the setting. Finally, he decided to approach a tall wood fence that bordered the property. By pressing up to the fence, he could see into the drive-in. Maybe thirty cars pooled near the center of the lot, and another ten were parked about the outer loop. All had their windows sealed tight, except for small cracks that allowed for a speaker and heater.

Meacham watched until he was satisfied; then it was back to the road and home. He made one last stop before going indoors—he went to the barn and remembered the last time Todd went crazy. Meacham was willing to bet that once the weather warmed up, they'd really smell the stink of blood. For now, though, things looked clean. William entered the stall where it had happened. He bent down and rubbed one of the new calves. He brushed its hair, ran his fingers along its neck and sat there until soon he wasn't brushing a calf; he was brushing a head of hair. Long, even strokes. Strokes that started at the head, then ran the length of the body. He sat there thinking, imagining, pretending...

He sat there while above him, in the barn loft, Chris Thomas kept absolutely still.

If Meacham had made some manner of noise, Chris might have had a chance to escape, but there had been no sound of steps against floorboards, no rustling of winter clothes, none of the usual sounds when trodding through the cold. It was as if the real Meacham were somewhere else—perhaps in bed, asleep—while his image had pulled free to roam the farm.

Chris had climbed up to the loft to reset his camera. Now he was locked in a squat, with one arm tucked about the camera and a leg folded in a numbing pinch. He waited a full five minutes before daring to readjust his leg; then, just as carefully, he freed himself of the camera and slid against the wall.

At least he was comfortable; it gave him the luxury to think about Meacham. Had he seen Chris? No; if he had, Meacham would already be on him. But if he wasn't here for Chris, what else was in the barn?

Chris would have loved to find out. He considered crawling to the edge of the loft and looking down; the problem was the loft itself. The wood was old and creaking, and Chris had been lucky just untangling his body.

But he considered the possibility. He was still considering it when two things happened: first, he heard Meacham moving—a long stretch and the shuffle of feet; second, there was a groan of wood. It was a painful sound, as if a board was being bent to its limit. The sound happened once, twice, three times . . .

Chris recognized the noise. It was the steps to the ladder. William Meacham was coming up to the loft.

Chris grabbed hold of the camera and tilted it into the shadows. Another step cried, and he smothered the entire unit against his body. He acted as if he could slip into a patch of complete darkness and hide.

And then he stopped moving. William Meacham was balanced at the end of the loft, his upper body framed in the darkness. Yet even in the dark, they had fixed on each other. Chris waited for Meacham to move closer, but all Meacham did was lean forward. He stretched into the straw, slid his hands along the floor of the loft and opened his jacket. Soon afterward, he headed back down the ladder.

Chris calmed down. Meacham wasn't after him; he had come to get something. A moment later, he looked outside and saw Meacham returning to his house. Chris stayed by the window until he was absolutely certain Meacham was gone, then he crawled across the loft and ran his fingers under the straw. He was searching, just in case Meacham had left something, but all he found was an empty white envelope, weak and worn from too much use.

But it had once held a secret, Chris thought.

And later, while driving to town, he realized that every time he had crawled into that loft, he'd shuffled right over Meacham's secret. He had crawled right over—over what?

Chris reached the heart of Hayden and pulled to a stop. It would be another half hour before the bus arrived. Rather than wait in the car, he parked and crossed the street to the diner. There were a handful of customers in the place—a few in booths, a few at the counter. Chris sat at the counter, reached in a pocket and pulled out paper and a pen. He jotted down ideas—thoughts about how to keep track of Meacham, a schedule of responsibilities for Denny, Billy and himself.

He was still writing when the waitress approached him. "You want coffee?" she asked.

Chris looked up and stared at her. The waitress stood there, waiting for his answer, her smile weak from a full night's work.

"I asked if you want coffee," she said again.

"Please," said Chris.

The waitress left and Chris watched her go to the machine. She was attractive, but that wasn't why he stared. He had seen her before. The waitress was the same woman who had been at the gas mart; the one who had checked out the video.

She returned with the coffee. "You want a menu?"

Chris shook his head and looked at her name plate. "Julie," it read.

"I think we've met before, Julie," Chris said.

"Uh-huh," she said.

"I don't mean really met," Chris said, "I just mean I've seen you around town. I didn't place you with the diner."

"Well, I'm afraid I can't return the compliment," she answered, and walked off.

Chris sipped his coffee and took turns jotting notes and staring at his waitress. This was how the time passed until she visited a third time. She came up quietly, leaning over his paper and asking, "What's that?"

This time, she was very close. She looked down at the counter, her head cocked to the side, her concentration deliberately on the pages, so Chris could stare at her freely.

"I'm out here on a project," he said.

"I knew you weren't from around here," she said. "You're with the movie people."

"Yes."

"How's it going?"

"It's going all right," he said. "I'm waiting for the bus. I'm expecting some equipment."

She faced the front window. "Should be here soon," she said.

She was posing for him—first looking down, then the left, then the right. Maybe she was modeling for work. Whatever the reason, Chris paid attention, and soon he realized that he wanted to know her. This wasn't just an attractive woman; this was a *Raw Death* customer. And when he looked in her eyes he saw complete harmony, as if there was nothing at all incongruous between what she was and what she did.

"There it is," she said.

At first he didn't understand, then he saw the bus. He put down two bills and stood. "Maybe I'll see you later," he said.

Then he headed outside. When the bus came to a stop, a passenger stepped down along with the driver. Chris went up to the driver and said, "I'm expecting camera equipment. Black boxes with nylon straps." He leaned forward, helping the man pull out three long, black cartons. Chris was double-checking the labels when the passenger stepped beside him. "There's another in the back," the man said.

While the driver reached into the compartment, the man pulled out his receipts and turned to Chris. "I came with the boxes," he said. "You're Thomas, right?"

Chris nodded.

"Stan Hooper," the man said. "It's a real pleasure meeting you."

Chris wouldn't answer and Hooper grinned. "I'm not a surprise, am I? Didn't Al tell you I'm coming?"

When he realized a joke was the truth, Hooper looked apologetic. "All right, let's try again. I'm Stan Hooper. Al sent me because he wants someone to see how you're doing."

"What does that mean?" Chris said.

"It means I'm here to be Dorsey's eyes and ears."

"You're here to watch over me?"

"Al wants me to make a professional judgment on the viability of this project. He thinks it represents a potentially expensive situation."

Chris took a moment to consider this. He walked away, shook his head and rested against the car. When he came back and faced Hooper, he was still furious. "This," said Chris, "is bullshit."

Hooper said nothing.

"I know what he's doing. Al sent you to shut me down."

"Chris, if that was true, why send me at all?" Hooper extended a hand and waited, his manner friendly and patient.

Chris looked away.

"Come on," Hooper said. "I'm already here."

Chris wanted nothing to do with him.

Hooper took a long breath. "Hey, I already don't like this place. Do you want to be friendly, or do you want to start this by pissing me off?"

Hooper never lowered his arm, waiting for Chris to finish the handshake.

Chris shook his head, still in a state of disbelief.

He also shook Hooper's hand.

FIFTEEN

CHRIS didn't know Hooper personally, but he soon remembered the name. Over the years, Hooper had done over a dozen projects for Dorsey, and while he had a reputation for working on time and under budget, he was also known for saving money at the expense of quality and coherence. Since Dorsey cared little about either, Hooper provided the kind of emergency backup Dorsey needed to produce an assembly line of films.

In looks, Hooper was in his fifties and had the brittle white hair and tanned, lined skin that came from living year round in warm weather. He was a middle-aged, Sun Belt prototype and had dressed for his trip as if he were heading for a Colorado ski resort: wool ear band, red turtleneck and designer wool pants.

"Iowa," Hooper said. "I'm so used to bouncing between coasts, I forgot there's a Midwest."

Chris looked to the boxes. "Is the film equipment any good?"

"Al didn't break the piggy bank, but I did my best. By the way, Dorsey wants my costs to come out of your budget. He also wants your current and expected expenses. I'm mentioning this because I thought you rented a van, not a car."

"I needed a second rental," Chris said.

"I'm not arguing with you, I'm just mentioning that before you managed with a single van, and now you've doubled traveling expenses. These are the sort of things I'm supposed to notice."

Hooper jotted something in a notepad, while Chris pretended not to notice.

They were at the motel in fifteen minutes. The plan was for Denny and Billy to meet at Chris's room. Chris knocked on the door, Denny opened it and then stepped back.

"Stan?" She looked and sounded shocked.

"I prefer Santa Claus," he said. "I brought everyone presents." Stan pushed by her and lowered two of the boxes.

Denny couldn't quite believe he was here. Billy, meanwhile, walked up to Hooper, slapped him on the back and said, "Stan, you asshole. What's in the boxes? What kind of toys are we talking about?"

"Three cameras, four mikes, a camcorder, another pair of battery packs, magazines, stock, a few other things like mounts and balance slides and other garbage."

Billy pulled the lid off the first box and dug under the protective foam.

"You've got one hand-held thirty-five-millimeter silent Arriflex," Hooper continued, "a thirty-five-millimeter Eclair lightweight—both reflex cameras—and one sixteen-millimeter Panaflex. I brought the sixteen-millimeter because it's the quietest thing we had. With all this secret shooting I figured you could use quiet."

Billy pulled out the hand-held camera.

"Is the sixteen-millimeter super-sixteen capable?" Billy said.

"Of course," Hooper said. "I also brought stock for the sixteen."

"And mounts and remotes?"

"All that crap is in the small box," said Hooper.

Billy screwed in the shoulder rest and lodged the camera against his neck. "What kind of lenses?"

"I brought some range extenders."

Billy looked disappointed. "Oh, Stan—"

"You guys already got telephoto and zoom," said Hooper. "There's only so much I can carry."

"Yeah, but extenders are gonna make the film look like crap."

"Well, maybe next time I'll load up on lenses and forget the cameras," Hooper said. "For now, I did the best I could." He turned to Denny. "Don't you want to check your presents, little girl?"

Denny glared at him. "Stan, what are you doing here?"

"I'm supposed to check on things," Hooper said. "Christ, what's wrong with you people? You make me feel like a Nazi."

Denny turned to Chris. "You shouldn't have brought him, Chris. He's only here to screw you."

"That's not true," Hooper said.

"Of course it's true," Denny said. "I've worked with you. Your life is dedicated to fucking up other people's work."

"I only go where I'm invited, Denny," Hooper said. "Besides, it's *Al's* work."

She turned again to Chris. "If you let him stay, it'll be the worst mistake of your life."

"Excuse me,' 'Hooper said, "but I'm already here and that's what Dorsey wants."

"How's the sound equipment?" Chris asked.

Hooper was more than happy to get back to business. "For sound, I went above and beyond the call of duty. Al didn't have anything close to what you needed—I mean, what you got here isn't a typical Dorsey production—so I stopped by the rentals and picked up a few things. A cardiod, three omnis, a shotgun mike and two remotes. I also brought along a balancer, which you can use with the camcorder."

It was Denny's turn to open a box. At Chris's urging she squatted on the carpet and began examining the electronics.

"The distance on the remote is about fifty feet," Hooper said. "I know it's not as long as you'd like, but it's the best I could find for the price. I also brought along a few hundred feet of cable. Between the cable and the remote, you should be able to cover a lot of territory." Hooper looked to Chris. "Incidentally, you did get permission to shoot on this guy's farm, right? We can at least pretend it's legal?"

"He signed a paper," Chris said.

"I want to see it tonight," Hooper said. "Drop it by my room and I'll read it before going to bed." He lifted his luggage and headed for the door.

"You have a room?" Chris asked.

"I phoned ahead," Hooper said. "Don't worry about me, worry about yourself. And keep your soundwoman under control."

Hooper left and closed the door. Denny stopped examining the microphones.

"Well?" Chris asked.

"Everything's dated," she said. "None of this is top stuff."

He looked to Billy.

"It's in fair shape," Billy said.

"It's insulting," Denny said. "It's not as good as we should have."

She said goodnight and left the room. Billy did a last check of the cameras before heading for the door. As he left, he tried reassuring Chris. "What Denny said about Stan—Don't let it worry you. I've worked with him lots and he's a good guy."

"I'm glad to hear that," Chris said.

"Just don't care too much," he said. "That's what it's all about with Stan. Dorsey has a special arrangement with him. Stan gets to pocket ten percent of any money he saves from the budget."

Chris nodded along. "Thanks, Billy," he said. "That's great."

Billy also left the room.

The next morning, Chris and Hooper were again in the car, this time finishing a tour of the area.

"That's the pond," Chris said. "Did Dorsey show you the footage? We got tape of Billy going into the—"

"I saw it," Hooper said.

"We checked the surrounding woods and we checked the water. There's nothing anywhere, but that's not bad. In fact, it's—"

"I told you I saw the tape," Hooper said. "A missing shoe, right?"

"Right," Chris said.

"Then let's keep going."

Chris turned the ignition and took him back on the highway. The entrance to the Meacham farm was only a quarter mile from the pond; Chris, however, drove slowly, so Hooper could take in the landscape. Finally, Chris turned and stopped by the driveway. He leaned across Hooper and pointed toward the house.

"That's where he lives," Chris said.

Hooper looked at the farm. "So that's the Bates Motel," he said.

"We've been filming from all sides of the house, including the barn," Chris said. "So far it's been working out. He doesn't know what we're doing, so he hasn't been too protective. We've had incredible access."

"Sure you have," Hooper said. "But suppose he starts closing the curtains? What if he blocks you from the house?"

Chris said nothing. he didn't know how to answer Hooper, because there were all sorts of things that could go wrong. The point was what they would have if things went right.

"Are we through?" Hooper said.

Chris thought a moment. He tried to think if there was anything else to show him. "It depends," he said. "Do you want to go up?"

Hooper was surprised at the suggestion. "Should I?" he asked.

"Why not?" Chris said. "We're paying Meacham. He's just another Dorsey employee."

Hooper liked this logic. He grinned, and Chris turned up the driveway. A moment later, they were on the porch. Chris knocked while Hooper put on his straightest face.

Helen Meacham opened the door.

"Mrs. Meacham, I'm Chris Thomas," he said. Chris extended his hand. "I don't think we've formally met."

Helen Meacham considered what to do. She was as cautious with him as Chris had been with Hooper.

"I've been wanting to meet you," Chris said. "This is Stan Hooper. He's also working on the movie."

"My pleasure," Hooper said.

"There's also another friend of mine who'd like to meet you," Chris said. "She'd like to stop by today if it's convenient, just to ask a few questions about farm life."

"You'll have to talk with William," Mrs. Meacham said.

She walked back in the house and called for her husband. Eventually, Meacham came to the door. He was dressed in work overalls and his hands were dusty. He also looked neither surprised nor interested in his guests.

"Mr. Meacham, my soundwoman would like to interview your wife, if you don't mind," Chris said. "We need to get a few minutes on how she helps with the farm."

"We've already talked about this," Meacham said. "She cleans, that what she does. She's a goddamn cleaning machine." He studied Hooper. "This your friend?"

"His name's Stan," Chris said.

"I might make a movie out here," Hooper said.

"Yeah?" Meacham said. "You two are turning this place into a regular Hollywood."

Chris and Hooper laughed.

"I don't know if it's a good idea talking to Helen," Meacham said. "It might make her uncomfortable."

"I'm sure Denny would be careful," Chris said.

"Maybe you could think about it," Hooper said.

Meacham stared at Hooper. It was bad enough being badgered by Chris, but by a total stranger . . . Hooper, meanwhile, tried not to give an inch, as if this were a test of manhood.

"I'll think about it,' Meacham finally said.

A few minutes later, Chris and Hooper were back in the car. Neither said a word. It had been a dry encounter, and Chris was actually afraid to get Hooper's impressions.

Hooper surprised him.

"I shook hands with a killer, didn't I?" Hooper said.
He talked quickly—excited, almost breathless.

"He really is a maniac. It's so *obvious*. I mean, if you know, you can tell. He's built like a killer. He's got that strength, that menace."

Chris listened, not sure what to make of all this enthusiasm.

"I can't wait to see his kid," Hooper said. "They're probably both killers."

Chris considered what to say. Hooper was almost reacting to the wrong things.

"Who's he killing next?" Hooper asked.

"I don't know," Chris said.

"You must know something. What've you been doing out here?"

"Plenty, but it's still a matter of letting things happen."

"Like hell it is," Hooper said. "You don't have the time to wait around."

"We do if Al gives me a go," said Chris.

"Yeah, but he won't."

Chris rested on the steering wheel, caught by another blindside.

"He called me last night, just to see if I got in," Hooper said. "Did he talk with you?"

"Of course not," Chris said.

"Well there's good news and bad news. The bad news is he's made up his mind and wants everyone back in L.A. The good news is you can stay here until the end of the week."

"That's four days," Chris said.

"Yeah, but I'll talk to Al and get a full week. He'll do it as a favor."

"A week still won't do it," Chris said. "Nothing may happen. It may take two weeks, or a month, or—"

"Be real, Chris. I don't care if this guy's Richard Speck; you can't stay indefinitely. People cost money. Equipment costs money."

"A month at least," Chris said.

"You expect Al to gamble a month's budget?" Hooper said. "You definitely got yourself a killer, Chris, but a week's it." Hooper put on the thinking cap. "Now if you don't mind, can I make a suggestion? From one professional to another?"

Chris waited for the free advice.

"You can't just sit around. if you make things happen, maybe a week *can* do it. Maybe all you'll need is a couple of days. You just have to force the circumstances according to your time schedule."

"I can't force Meacham to commit a murder," Chris said.

"I'm not saying that," Hooper said. "But if he's going to kill anyway, you can provide some encouragement. You can get to know him better, figure out what he's thinking, maybe nudge the process."

"Meacham isn't the talking type," Chris said.

"Maybe not for other people," said Hooper, "but Chris Thomas, the maker of *Raw Death?* Hell, you're the goddamn Messiah of maniacs. Most of them would kill just for your autograph."

Chris shook his head.

"You'd be reaching out, that's all. Is that so wrong? Is that forcing Meacham to commit a murder?"

Chris was still uncertain. Hooper could see the problem. He leaned closer to say what needed to be said.

"You've only got a few days left, friend," Hooper said. "What else are you gonna do?"

SIXTEEN

"**M**RS. Meacham?"

Helen stared at her. It was mid-afternoon and she wasn't expecting visitors, especially someone carrying a round of cable and a nylon utility sack. Denny, however, smiled as if she'd been invited.

"We haven't met, but I work the sound for Chris Thomas. That's why I'm carrying all this equipment."

"William isn't in right now," Mrs. Meacham said.

"I know and I'm sorry," Denny said. "But I was in the area, and Chris said so many nice things about you."

Mrs. Meacham was still cautious. William had warned against guests; on the other hand, Helen had once liked company, and William was giving all sorts of warnings these days.

"I grew up on a farm," Denny said. "I was part of a corn family." She braced against the wind. "It's pretty cold outside. Sure I can't come in?"

Helen almost found the willpower. She rocked on her heels and went so far as to open the door, but she never invited Denny. She never said the words.

Yet the moment Mrs. Meacham opened the door, Denny stepped in, moving far enough indoors to oblige her hospitality.

"You have a beautiful home."

Mrs. Meacham said nothing.

"You like it here?" Denny tried again.

Mrs. Meacham nodded. She stood there, uncertain what to do, her mind on her husband.

"I don't suppose you have any coffee," Denny said.

Mrs. Meacham took the suggestion. She walked Denny to the kitchen, and soon they were sitting by the coffeepot.

"I'm from Nebraska," Denny said, "but I still can't stand this cold."

Mrs. Meacham smiled as if she understood. "I've been through Nebraska," she said.

"You have?" Denny said. She used her most encouraging voice.

"William and I used to do a lot of traveling, but that's a while ago."

"Where'd you go?"

"Everywhere," Helen said. She seemed to relax. "That's back when William wanted to keep moving. Talk to him about it. He likes remembering the past, but I don't. As far I'm concerned, all that matters is here."

"Chris says your family is very close," Denny said.

"It's a special family," she said. "Maybe not the best, and it can be hard, sometimes. But it's special." She sipped her coffee. "And this is such a big house."

"If you don't mind, I'd like to see it," Denny said.

Denny again encouraged her, and Mrs. Meacham left the table. "Do you want a full-fledged tour?"

"From bottom to top," Denny said. "I like old houses."

Mrs. Meacham headed for the living room, and Denny followed. "This is the oldest part of the house," Helen said. "The dining room was added, the kitchen and porch were added. Originally, everything was done in this room. It's the same story with most of these farmhouses."

Denny walked slowly about the living room. When she passed the fireplace mantel, she bent closer and looked at a photograph. "Is this Todd?"

"Todd at eight years."

Denny studied the photograph. It was one of those class pictures, with the boy's hair neatly combed and his collar buttoned for a clip tie. Even at that young an age, the boy was as tightly groomed as the house. Denny set the picture aside and turned to another one—a picture of William and Helen. It was also several years old, and showed the two of them in front of a motel. It was another oddly tight picture, with only William smiling. As for Helen Meacham, what most impressed Denny was her youth. Today Mrs. Meacham had surrendered to motherhood, but in this photograph, she was more than young; she was a child. And standing beside Meacham, she seemed a child bride. They stood together, with William's arm wrapping and smothering the girl. It didn't seem like a wedding photograph at all; it struck Denny more like a picture of a kidnapping.

And then Denny looked at Helen Meacham and noticed something.

Helen didn't wear a ring.

"That must be getting heavy," Helen Meacham said.

Denny put aside the photograph.

"I meant the wire on your shoulder."

"I'm so used to it," Denny said. "I hate to be a bother, but could I use the bathroom?"

Mrs. Meacham walked Denny up the stairs and to the bathroom. Denny was heading inside when they heard something—a knock on the front door.

Mrs. Meacham tightened.

"It's all right," Denny said. "It's just Billy. He was going to pick me up."

Mrs. Meacham stood there, once again uncertain what to do.

"Could you just tell him I'll be a few minutes?" Denny said.

Mrs. Meacham headed downstairs, and Denny closed the bathroom door. She lifted the window, leaned out and immediately saw what Chris meant; the gutter had rusted and could be opened with a finger. Denny did this and started feeding her cable. Then she reached in a pocket, pulled out a roll of gaffer's tape and secured the cable to the gutter. Finally, she opened her nylon pack and found the transmitter. She connected the transmitter to the cable, used plastic wrap to make the connection watertight and taped the transmitter to the outside of the windowpane. Then she closed the window and again reached in her sack.

She pulled out her three cordless microphones.

What she had in mind was an improvement on Chris's idea. Chris wanted to run a cable into the house; Denny, however, simply wanted to get the transmitter in range of the second story. By taping it just outside of the bathroom window, she could now place the omnis anywhere in the house and, most important, be assured of a strong signal for the key second-floor bedrooms.

And where would she place the microphones?

She opened the door and peeked out. Billy and Mrs. Meacham had gone to the kitchen, and Denny used the moment to tiptoe into the master bedroom. She knew the room; before coming here, she'd studied Billy's film. She went to the post bed and taped one of the cordless microphones to the back of the headboard. Then she walked just as quietly to Todd's room.

Todd's room was more difficult. His bed didn't have a headboard, and Denny decided to take her chances on a night table. She sat on the edge of the bed, leaned down, tore off a piece of tape and strapped the microphone to the bottom board. The microphone, with wire, was about six inches, but it was also thin and light. For anyone to see it, he'd have to lie on the floor and slide under the table.

There, she thought. Business finished.

But then something caught her eye. The room, of course, was immaculate, but Mrs. Meacham hadn't quite closed the closet door. Denny crossed the room and opened it a bit farther. She saw it hanging there—William Meacham's belt. Two inches wide, a brass buckle at one end, a sharp, tapered cut at the tip. It hung off a hook, beside a worn and stained bath towel.

She examined the belt. It was no longer a clothes item; someone had tailored the belt for pain. The studs were filed to points, and even the leather felt sharpened, like the edge of crisp paper.

She stared, stepped back and again sat on the edge of the

bed. And then, while trying to calm down, she felt something hard. It was something with a stiff, sharp edge, hidden beneath the blankets. Denny ran her hand over the bedspread, and soon she had made out a shape—something oblong; firm, yet flexing with her weight.

Mrs. Meacham was growing impatient; Denny could hear it. She was trying to leave the kitchen, but Billy kept trying to keep her busy, now asking questions about Todd. Soon they'd be in the living room.

But what was in the bed? What was Todd hiding?

Denny pulled back the bedspread.

And what she found was so ridiculous, she could have laughed. A Playboy. Not even a recent issue.

She could have laughed and should have, except for something else.

The Playboy was between a set of dirty sheets—not only dirty, but filthy with stains. The same type of stains that were on the towel.

Denny finished pulling back the bedspread.

It was all over the bed. Some areas had been bleached, others looked recent, but it made no difference; the stains were everywhere. No matter how much Helen Meacham had scrubbed, they had become as much a part of the bed as the mattress. The remnants of pain and torture.

Bedsheets and pads, dirty and caked in dried blood.

A moment later, Denny walked downstairs. Mrs. Meacham was clearly upset, but so was Denny.

"You were upstairs a long time," Mrs. Meacham said.

"I just wanted to look at the rooms," Denny said. "That's not a problem, is it?"

Mrs. Meacham didn't answer.

"I was wondering," Denny said. "Do you think we could go downstairs?"

"We are downstairs," Mrs. Meacham said.

"I mean the cellar," Denny said. "I have an interest in cellars."

Mrs. Meacham hardened. She seemed to realize, all at once, the visit had been a mistake. "You'll have to talk to William," she said.

"Just a quick look," Denny said. "It would be—"

"There's nothing in the cellar except boxes and a furnace," Mrs. Meacham said.

Denny nodded. "Of course," she said.

Mrs. Meacham opened the front door.

"I'm sorry if I imposed," Denny said. "I enjoyed meeting you."

"My pleasure," Mrs. Meacham said.

"Perhaps we can meet again?"

"Perhaps," Mrs. Meacham said.

Denny and Billy left the house—Billy going to the car, Denny stopping at the doorway. "Give me a call," Denny said to Mrs. Meacham, "if ever you want to talk."

Mrs. Meacham looked annoyed, afraid. "And what would we have to talk about?" she said.

Denny stared at her.

Helen Meacham closed the door.

Meacham looked to his side. He was in Hayden, waiting by the bus stop and reading the newspaper, and now he had a visitor.

"I was just going to get something warm to drink," Chris said. "What are you doing in town?"

Meacham folded his paper. "I'm picking up my boy," he said.

"Cold weather to be outside," Chris said. "You want to join me in the diner?"

"No, thanks," Meacham said.

"Come on," Chris said. "I guarantee it'll interest you." He nodded toward the coffee shop, and Meacham decided to give him a few minutes. They took a table near the front window, so Meacham could keep an eye out for the bus. While a waitress brought menus, Chris rested his shoulder bag.

"I figure I'll be here another two weeks, then it's back to L.A.," Chris said. "I got a whole new project waiting for me."

Meacham looked to the waitress, raised two fingers and again regarded Chris.

"You really like it in Hayden?" Chris asked.

"What sort of question's that?" Meacham said.

"You just strike me as someone who wouldn't be satisfied in a place this small."

"Is that so?" Meacham said. "And since when did you start developing opinions about me?"

Chris shrugged.

Meacham was at first annoyed, but he relaxed and sat back. "I've been around," he said. "I met Helen on the road. I've been as far south as Mexico."

"Ever visit L.A.?"

"Why should I? Los Angeles is no big deal."

"I just think you'd like it, that's all," Chris said. "There's more happening in a city."

"There's plenty happening here," Meacham said. "Is this what you wanted to know? My travel history?"

"No," Chris said. "I thought you might like to hear a little about me. Once I'm through here, I'm getting to work on another project. In case you hadn't guessed, agriculture isn't my specialty."

"I wouldn't call that a secret," Meacham said, grinning.

"My specialty is . . ." Chris struggled for the right words. "I guess you could call me a specialist in true-life drama."

"True-life drama," said Meacham, testing the phrase.

"I put out a video earlier this year," Chris said. "Maybe you've heard of it. *Raw Death?*"

Meacham didn't answer, but there was no look of recognition.

"That's why I'm heading back to L.A.," Chris said. "To start work on the sequel."

"So?" Meacham said.

"So I've got something for you." Meacham watched as Chris reached in his shoulder bag and pulled out a video cassette. "It's a copy of my movie."

Meacham took the cassette and turned it in various directions, as if handling some strange object.

"I thought you might like to see it," Chris said. "I'd value your opinion."

Meacham still said nothing.

"Do you have a VCR?" Chris said.

"I can borrow one," Meacham said. He kept turning the cassette. "You really want my opinion?"

Chris nodded.

"*Raw Death*, huh?" Meacham said. He considered the request. "I'll tell you right now, the name sucks."

Chris said nothing. Clearly, there was something more to this, but Meacham let him have his mystery. When the bus arrived, he slipped the cassette in a coat pocket, pushed from the table and headed for the door.

"I'll talk to you later," Chris called. "I hope you like it."

Meacham left the diner. Chris stayed at the table and watched him meet the bus. He was still watching as the father and son went through their reunion—Meacham hovering over Todd, Todd staring into his father's eyes.

Chris sat alone until they had gone, then Stan Hooper left the van and entered the coffee shop. Hooper took Meacham's seat and said, "Perfect."

Chris glared at Hooper. "You sound like a director."

"I just meant the sound was perfect," Hooper said. "And it was smart sitting by the window. I was able to shoot the whole thing."

Chris finished his coffee. Hooper looked relaxed, but Chris was feeling uncertain about what he'd done. "I don't know about this," he said.

"Don't worry," Hooper said. "You had to do something. Don't forget that."

"I just don't know how he'll react," Chris said. "I don't know if I can handle the situation."

"Hey," Hooper said, "at least you'll have a situation."

It was a stupid remark, but Chris didn't let Hooper sucker him into an argument. Instead, he stood and left the coffee shop. And when he was outside, he ran down the sidewalk, chasing someone until he reached out, touched her on the arm and said, "Hey."

The woman stopped and turned.

"I didn't tell you my name before," Chris said. "I'm Chris Thomas."

Julie looked as if she needed help remembering him. "You're the movie man," she said.

"Right," Chris said. "Your name is Julie. I got that much from the name tag."

He smiled, but she held back. It was one matter talking to strangers in the coffee shop—that was work—but outdoors, in the cold . . .

Chris knew this, too. "I don't mean to bother you," he said. "I don't know many people around town. It's nice saying hello to someone who's not a complete stranger."

"Right," she said, and turned away. Chris stood there, watching, wondering what to do, when Julie glanced back and nodded him alongside.

Chris trotted up to her.

"I remember you," Julie said. "You were flirting with me."

"You were flirting with me," Chris said.

"I flirt with everyone," she said. "You're not so good at it, though."

She was joking with him, and Chris knew it. "I'm still no good at it," he said.

"No kidding," she said. "So what do you want? Conversation? A date? Dinner?"

"I'd like us to spend some time together," he said.

"A little time or a lot?"

"A little, but it'd be quality time," he said.

She smiled. "I think we're on different tracks here," she said. "The only thing I know about you is you're from out of town. Granted, that's a point in your favor, but it doesn't make you my fantasy man."

"What exactly is your fantasy man?" Chris said.

"Someone with a good sense of humor," she said. "I like good jokes, good brains, good passion and clean hands." She looked down at him. "How're your hands?"

Julie turned his hands, rubbing the skin with the tips of her fingers.

He grinned. "You're not making this easy," he said.

"Of course not," she said. "You made up your mind about me, but I haven't made up my mind about you."

"I just think we've got a lot in common."

"Oh, do we?" she said.

"I know we do," he said. "We share the same interests."

"Like what?"

"I told you; I've seen you around town. I've got an idea of what you like."

Now she looked intrigued. "Where've you seen me?" she asked.

He didn't answer. Why should he? He had her hooked. "Maybe first you can tell me your phone number," Chris said.

While the Meachams ate dinner, Denny walked quietly across the snow and approached the back of the house. With each step she unraveled more cord, while behind her Chris covered the wire with snow. When they reached the rain spout, Denny took off a glove and reached up the gutter. It was awful wedging her fingers into the metal shell—the cold cramped her hand and the edge of the aluminum cut her fingertips. Denny struggled almost a minute before tucking her hand back in the glove. She shook her head, and Chris took his turn at the job. When he also failed, he tried changing angles and lay flat on his back. His hand squeezed an extra inch into the gutter and he felt it—the tip of the second wire. He squeezed the tip between two fingers and gently brought it down, then stepped aside, warming his hand while Denny went to work. She screwed together the connection, and suddenly they had one continuous wire running from behind the tool shed to the second-story transmitter.

They hurried back to the sound mixer. Denny took the headset off Hooper and settled in front of the console. She played with the dials, rechecked her connectors and touched a switch.

"Wow," she whispered.

"Wow what?" Chris said, expecting the worst.

"I think it works."

"Of course it works," Hooper said. "You people are so fucking paranoid."

"No," she said. "I just..." She shrugged, still surprised. "I haven't done anything like this before."

Chris looked to Hooper. "Where's Billy?"

"He went off to find a shot," Hooper said.

"I can't believe this," Denny kept saying.

"I'm going to find Billy," Chris said, heading off for one of their shoot locations. He figured Billy would be near the front of the house, but it took time to get there; Chris had to avoid the light from the windows. He also tried keeping on packed snow, to make the footsteps less visible. The trail led him around a thorn bush, past a woodpile, up and over a tree stump...

"Slow down," Hooper whispered.

Chris stopped and turned. Hooper skidded across the ice and caught up with him.

"I want to see in the window," Hooper said.

Chris was annoyed, but he kept walking and Hooper followed.

"This takes a lot of guts, Chris. I hope you know that."

"Walking through the snow?" Chris said.

"You know what I mean," Hooper said. "If Meacham's really a maniac, there's no telling what he'll do."

"We're not in danger now," Chris said.

"Yeah," Hooper said. "Not right now."

They found Billy behind the woodpile. He turned his eye only briefly from the camera, then was back to work.

"How's it going?" Chris said.

Billy didn't bother answering.

"What do you see?" Hooper said.

Chris squatted beside him. "Denny's got the sound working. If we can keep him in view, we can match it."

Hooper was dying to get closer. He moved forward until he almost leaned into the light.

Inside the house, Todd was doing a lot of talking while William listened and Helen Meacham watched the food. It looked like Todd was lecturing his father. And William sat there, almost respectful, listening to every word. "Look at that," Hooper said. "Look at how he's gripping the knife."

Chris watched the scene more carefully. Todd was talking

and Meacham was still listening, but Chris didn't see a knife. Both of Meacham's hands were on the table, locked in a single fist.

Hooper glanced at Chris and pointed it out. "Not the father. The kid. He's got it tight."

Now Chris saw it. Todd was pointing at his father with one hand, but his other was kept to his side, and a steak knife was indeed tight in his grip. Granted, they had been using knives for dinner, but Todd didn't hold it for eating; he held it for protection.

"Are you filming that, Billy?" Hooper asked. "You zooming on—"

"I got it, Stan," Billy said.

Hooper was still excited. He stared at Todd as if the boy had been his discovery. "I think you got it all wrong, Chris."

Chris faced him, but Hooper was fixed on Todd Meacham.

"It's him," Hooper said.

"No, it's the father," Chris said.

"Look at how he's holding the knife," Hooper said. "And what you told me before about that girl . . . You can just see it all over him."

"No," Chris said again. "I made the same mistake. Todd helped, but it's the father."

Hooper said nothing at first. Then he said, "I think the kid could use some checking out."

Chris sat so he could give Hooper all his attention. He knew what was happening; This small discussion had all the importance of a project meeting. It was about judgment and control. "I seem to remember you saying we only had a week for filming," Chris said. "I thought that was why I'm pushing Meacham."

"I'm just saying we should also push the kid," Hooper said. "Maybe they're both killers."

"We don't have the time or resources," Chris said.

"I can do it myself," Hooper said.

"I said forget it," Chris said again. "Let's stick to what we got."

Billy glared at both of them. "Can't you guys shut up?"

Chris pulled Hooper aside.

"You know I'm right," Hooper whispered.

"Bullshit," Chris said.

"Don't bullshit me," Hooper said. "Your way only works if you can get close to Meacham, and when are you going to do that?"

Chris didn't know the answer. He again watched the dinner scene. Todd said a last word, dropped the knife by his plate and left the room. Meacham sat there and watched Todd leave. As for Helen Meacham, with dinner over, she began cleaning the table.

Chris waited. For a moment, he thought Meacham was going to follow his son upstairs. Maybe it was again time to bloody the sheets.

Instead, Meacham left the table and turned on his television. Then he went to a bureau and picked up a black video cartridge—Chris's cartridge.

They watched as William Meacham hooked up a VCR, turned down the lights and hit the play button. The title of the video flashed on, and soon they were all being welcomed into the world of *Raw Death*.

In the freezing, bitter cold, Hooper, Billy and Chris watched as William Meacham was introduced to his fellow murderers and maniacs. They watched as the first footage began and Meacham leaned back, relaxing.

Hooper moved closer to Chris. "What do you think?" he whispered.

Chris wasn't certain what to make of it. Meacham was obviously comfortable, but it was more than that. Chris had never seen anyone so thoroughly at ease with the video. It was as if Meacham were watching a favorite, familiar TV show—maybe even watching home movies.

"I think you're in luck," Hooper said. "He likes it."

Chris nodded.

Maybe he was luckier than anyone realized.

Midnight at the tavern.

When Chris entered, Meacham was already in the bar,

which was perfect. Indeed, Meacham was the only reason he had come to the bar.

He took his place beside Meacham. For a moment, nothing was said. Then, finally, "Did you see the film?"

Meacham thought before nodding.

Chris again waited, his face without expression. Meacham revealed nothing until a grin sneaked up on him. He turned and lifted a hand. "Two beers, Mike."

The drafts were brought and Meacham hesitated a last time. Finally, he slid one of the beers to Chris and lifted his own mug.

"It's an interesting bit of work," Meacham said.

Chris listened and followed Meacham to a table.

"You got some strange things in that movie," Meacham said, "but I know worse."

"Worse?" Chris said.

Meacham sipped his beer and gave a slow nod.

"Worse how?" Chris said.

Meacham started talking.

And they were still talking at three in the morning.

SEVENTEEN

IT was six in the evening, and for a change Chris had been invited to the Meacham house. Chris stood in the foyer and presented Mrs. Meacham with a bottle of red wine. Chris had wanted to bring white wine, but Denny thought the Meachams would prefer something blood colored.

He was there just a moment when William leaned out of the living room. "Chris, come here."

Chris joined him by the television. Meacham was once again watching *Raw Death*—this time a segment on robberies. In the tape, a holdup goes wrong and the thief is shot point blank by a plainclothes officer.

"People do send this in, right?" Meacham said. "Helen wouldn't believe me."

"Sometimes people send it in, sometimes I collect it, sometimes I film it."

"That last one," Meacham said. "That's the part which sounds interesting."

Helen Meacham announced dinner, and they converged around the dining table. William, Helen, Todd and Chris.

"Sit to my side," William said.

Chris was being offered Todd's seat. Chris hesitated, not only worried about the boy—there was the camera angle to consider. By bumping him, Todd would have his back to the window.

"Sit," William insisted.

Chris obeyed.

"You remember my boy," William said to Chris.

"Of course."

Todd barely looked at him. William nudged Chris. "Todd's been moody," he said. He talked as if he was confiding, but his voice carried for the whole table. "We normally try to spend time together, but things haven't quite worked out lately." Meacham took a bite of food. "How much longer you gonna be in town?"

"Just a week or so," Chris said.

Meacham nodded. He took another bite, then leaned toward his son. "Todd, there's a videotape in the living room, but I don't want you looking at it. Not until you're eighteen." Meacham turned to Chris. "That's what the package says, right?"

"Right," said Chris.

William again turned to Todd. "Chris is a big movie maker," he said. "You should ask him all about Hollywood."

Todd looked at Chris. He thought a moment and said, "You know any stars?"

"Not personally," Chris said. "I've seen one or two."

"He's more in the star-making business," Meacham said. "People get in his movies and become big news."

"Most of the people in my films are already big news," Chris said. He looked to Helen Meacham. "This is delicious."

Mrs. Meacham accepted the compliment. It was hard wrestling with old habits, and she couldn't quite bring herself to talk at the table.

"It's nice having a home-cooked meal," Chris said.

"Chris lives alone," William said to his wife. "Chris is single. Me, I just feel single."

"My social life leaves something to be desired," Chris said.

"Not the lady killer?" William said.

"I have a problem with relationships," Chris said.

"'Relationships,'" Meacham mimicked.

"The women I go out with complain I don't involve myself."

"You sure you don't just suck in bed?" Meacham said.

There was a sound at the far end of the table. Chris looked in the direction of the noise, as did William. The noise came from Helen. She was smothering a laugh.

This surprised even William. He ran with the moment. "You need a good, noisy bed," Meacham said. "Nothing gets a woman going like the sound of a good workout."

Todd glanced at both his parents. He was more surprised than anyone. He looked to Chris, at once embarrassed by his parents, but in a good way. A few seconds passed with William, Todd and Helen actually enjoying each other.

"Of course," William said, "there's other ways to work out a woman."

Helen Meacham slowly stopped laughing. Meacham looked at his wife.

"I just can't seem to make a relationship last," Chris said.

Meacham threw down his napkin. The moment had definitely passed. Todd also knew it. It was once again just Meacham and Chris.

"So," Meacham said, "I've seen the tape and we've talked about it. You still haven't said why you gave it to me."

"I wanted your opinion," Chris said.

"My opinion's worth bullshit," Meacham said.

"Not to me," said Chris.

"Why?" said Meacham. "Hell, you show that to a stranger, most people'd throw up after five minutes."

"You didn't," Chris said.

"No, I didn't," Meacham said. "Does that mean something to you?"

He stared at Meacham and could see that maybe it was all right to say too much. Indeed, that was exactly what Meacham wanted: someone to talk with and share a secret. "It means something because when I watch *Raw Death*, I don't throw up."

"And?" Meacham said.

"And I've got an eye for people."

"And?"

"And you strike me as the sort of person who lives by his own tastes and own rules."

"I strike you like that, do I?" Meacham said. "Helen, is that the kind of man I am?"

Helen Meacham had closed off the conversation. She sat with her attention dead on her plate.

Meacham looked at his son. "Does he know me?"

Todd glared at his father and left the table. Meacham returned the look, but with a guest in the house, he couldn't do a damn thing. It nettled him, and Meacham faced his wife.

"You two are making me feel real alone," he said.

"It's not my fault," Helen Meacham said.

"Never is, is it?" William said.

This time, Helen Meacham did leave the table. Meacham and Chris stayed in their seats. Meacham was in a struggle. He wasn't used to having company in his house, and at the moment he didn't like it at all.

Meacham wiped his hands a last time and stood up.

"You through eating?" Meacham asked Chris.

"Yes," Chris said. "It was delicious. I wanted to tell your wife that—"

"Why don't you go home," Meacham said.

Chris dropped his napkin.

"I got things to do," Meacham said, "but we can meet later."

"Sure," Chris said.

"If you want, I'll meet you at the tavern."

"I'll be there," Chris said. He took his coat and walked to the door.

"Fucking family," Meacham said.

Chris heard, but didn't answer. "Tonight at the tavern," he repeated.

Meacham grunted and led Chris outside. The door closed, and Chris glanced at his watch.

Only forty minutes had passed from the time he entered the Meacham house to the time he left. Forty minutes, and he had eaten dinner, revealed some secrets, seen the Meachams happy, seen them angry, seen them sad . . . It was as if life had accelerated, and perhaps this made sense. With only a few days left, Chris was pushing for all the speed he could muster. Chris was making things happen without even realizing it, literally setting the pace.

Later, back at the motel, Chris lifted his arms while Denny ran adhesive tape across his chest. The microphone wasn't made to be hidden—it wasn't the kind of miniaturized bug the police used when wiring an undercover cop—but it could still be kept a secret, so long as the wires and the mike could be hidden in the tucks of his winter clothes.

While Denny finished taping, Billy checked the charges on the battery pack and Hooper tuned the monitor.

"I went over last night's take," Hooper said. He turned a dial, and the tavern focused on the screen. This wasn't the master cassette; it was an editing job Hooper had spliced together as part of his contribution for the day. It started with a broad outdoor shot of the bar, then clipped closer so the camera had an extreme focus on the front door. The tavern had no windows, so this was the only way Billy could capture glimpses into the place, at least without going inside and asking permission to film.

Still, it was interesting. The camera shot nothing more than a hardwood door, but the microphone had worked perfectly, and you could hear the bar talk between Chris and Meacham. Occasionally, when the door opened long enough, you could see the two of them talking.

CHRIS: *So you liked the film.*
MEACHAM: *I watched it. It reminded me of some people.*
CHRIS: *What kind of people?*
MEACHAM: *I know people who've killed people. People down south. Some friends.*
[The door swings open, and Meacham is leaning forward, his mug cradled near his lips, his eyes dead on Chris. Chris sits with his back to the camera, his mug down and his attention dead on Meacham.]
MEACHAM: *I don't talk about it much, because most people wouldn't understand. I mean, these aren't close friends; they're people I know. But they're okay, that's my point.*

CHRIS: *I don't know them.*

MEACHAM: *Yeah, but just the idea of them killing someone would turn off most. These friends . . . I bumped into them even before I met Helen. They just traveled all over the goddamn place, doing whatever the hell they liked, and if they liked you they treated you like gold, but when they didn't like you, that's when the trouble started.*

CHRIS: *This was a gang?*

MEACHAM: *Just a pair. Sometimes just one . . . You ever know anyone who killed someone?*

CHRIS: *I've talked to a few.*

MEACHAM: *They all got one thing in common. Mean tempers. They can all throw a tantrum like you've never imagined.*

CHRIS: *So these friends were serial killers?*

MEACHAM: *Killing and taking. Mostly women. And one kind of retired and took off. That's what I heard.*

CHRIS: *They don't sound too friendly.*

MEACHAM: *You just had to know them. I don't think anyone's all bad. What time is it?*

CHRIS: *Two-thirty.*

MEACHAM: *I don't think anyone's all bad. At the same time, who says what's right and wrong?*

CHRIS: *You still talk to them?*

MEACHAM: *I hear about them now and then, through friends of friends. I swear, back then they'd go from town to town, doing some good things, doing bad . . . hurt a lot of women. Younger the better. Used to just pluck them off the road and take them traveling. They'd keep them until these girls thought they were part of something. These are the same bitches that were crying and whining the first time they got plucked.*

[The door again swings open. Meacham is laughing; Chris is forcing a smile. Meacham leans back and looks to the bartender.]

MEACHAM: *So what about you?*

CHRIS: *(chuckling)*

MEACHAM: *You ever kill anyone? You ever think about killing anyone?*

CHRIS: *I've thought about it.*

MEACHAM: *But you haven't done it.*

CHRIS: *I don't know if I could.*

MEACHAM: *You mean you don't have the stomach.*

CHRIS: *I don't know what I mean.*

MEACHAM: *But you wouldn't rule it out.*

CHRIS: *No.*

MEACHAM: *I wouldn't think so. Not after that film.*

CHRIS: *It just doesn't look that hard.*

MEACHAM: *Hell, it's the easiest thing on earth. You just can't get too used to it, that's all. I mean, it's like eating candy and never getting a cavity. Do what the fuck you want—like those friends of mine—fuck who you want, fuck over who you want, then do them with a knife and you got no one to worry about.*

[The door opens again. Meacham and Chris are starting fresh beers. Meacham has one arm resting over the back of Chris's chair. Chris leans closer to Meacham.]

CHRIS: *I don't think I've ever been angry enough to kill someone.*

MEACHAM: *Well, it's not really about anger, is it?*

Hooper turned off the editor.

"You had a long night yesterday," he said to Chris. "You sure you can do this again?"

Chris said nothing. Denny had stopped taping the microphone. They had all stopped to watch the monitor. Now Chris was the first to move. He ripped the tape and made sure the microphone was set. He pulled on his shirt and pulled a sweater over the shirt.

"How do I look?" Chris asked.

No one answered. They stared at Chris as if he was something strange, as if no matter what he wore, he had already transformed into a different creature.

"It looks good," Denny finally said.

"Good," Chris said. "And you're all going to be in the van?"

"Not quite," said Hooper. "I've got some other things to do."

Chris sensed trouble, but he didn't have time to talk. He clapped his hands and said, "All right, let's go." He sounded like he was leading a pep rally.

Denny simply lifted her satchel. In a few minutes, they were in the van. A half hour later, Chris was once again at a table with William Meacham. Only this time, the conversation went differently. This time, Meacham sat beside Chris and in no time flat leaned close to him and said, "How'd you like to kill someone?"

Chris looked Meacham in the eye and listened.

EIGHTEEN

C HRIS had anticipated something like this; he just didn't know if Meacham meant it or was kidding. Certainly Meacham had every reason in the world to feel murderous. He was completely alienated from his family, and worse, his family had come apart in front of a virtual stranger. William probably wasn't only angry; he'd be embarrassed and frustrated and whatever else churns inside someone before they snap into action.

So Chris listened, but he didn't give an answer. He waited because he knew Meacham would say more. Meacham needed a friend.

"You think it's tough, but it's not that tough," Meacham said. "I've seen a murder or two."

"You watched your friends, you mean," Chris said.

"That's right," Meacham said. "It's easy. It's easy and it's safe."

"I didn't say it was hard," Chris said, "I just don't think I could go through with it."

"Shit," Meacham said, "you don't have to go through with it. I'm just talking for the fun of it. Just for the game."

"You mean *almost* kill someone?"

"Sure," Meacham said. "You could 'almost' kill, couldn't you? Anyone can do that."

Chris looked agreeable. "I could do that," he said. "There's just no one out here that I almost want to kill."

"No one?" Meacham said. "Hell, I know plenty of people I'd almost kill. A few I could."

"You live here," Chris said.

"I haven't always lived here," Meacham said. "Besides, I'll probably move soon. Then I'll be like you. I'll have to pick my friends and enemies quick." Meacham smiled and patted Chris on the back. "Can't think of anyone, huh?"

"One person maybe," Chris said. "Maybe Tom Rawlings."

Meacham looked amused. "You mean *Sheriff* Tom Rawlings?"

"He made me some trouble a few weeks ago," Chris said. "I told him a few things, and he treated me like an idiot."

"So because someone treats you like an idiot, you're gonna kill him?"

"I'm gonna *almost* kill him," Chris said. "Just so long as he doesn't find out and no one gets hurt."

Meacham grinned. "All right," he said. "So let me ask you again, Chris Thomas. You want to go out tonight and almost kill someone? You want to go out and almost kill a sheriff?"

Chris also grinned, leaning forward, feeling the microphone press between his chest and the edge of the table. "Why not?" he said.

They parked outside the sheriff's office. It was close to midnight, and Rawlings should have been at home asleep, but he was there, resting in a chair, sipping coffee with the receptionist. During the late hours, the only person who manned the sheriff's office was the receptionist; Rawlings, however, had apparently stayed for some work, or perhaps had stopped by the office on his way home.

Whatever the reason, Sheriff Rawlings was there, and he was a marked man. Sometime before morning, Rawlings would be almost dead.

"Now, of course I'm not talking from experience," Meacham said, "but one of the big things about killing is what it does for the different parties. These friends of mine got particular that way. I mean, sometimes you'd just do it for the hell of it, but a lot of times you had a mood, and everything had to match that mood.''

They were in Meacham's pickup, with Meacham behind the wheel and Chris beside him. Chris knew the van had to be somewhere in the area, but that wasn't on his mind. For the moment, he was interested in seeing this through and also in making sure this was really a game. It was this second doubt that kept him on guard. Before, when they had talked, it had been in the bar or at the house or near other people. But now they were alone, and even though they had discussed the ground rules, Chris worried about the rules changing. After all, they were in Meacham's car, playing Meacham's game, doing something Chris had never before considered. Meacham was in command, and this was the first time Chris had allowed such a thing.

"How would you kill him?" Meacham said.

"I'd try shooting him right now," Chris said.

"To hell with that," Meacham answered. "Besides, at this distance you'd miss."

"I'd shoot him when he came out the door."

They watched as the sheriff said his goodbyes and headed outside. He lifted his collar, walked around the building and headed into an alley.

"This might not be a bad time," Meacham said. "Alone, behind the building."

"Then I'd do it now," Chris said.

"Except he's also got a gun," Meacham said. "If he heard you coming up, he'd kill you."

Now they saw headlights and after a moment, the sheriff's car turned onto the street. Meacham gave him about fifty yards, then started to follow.

"This is more cops and robbers than you'd normally do," Meacham said, "but most people don't go killing sheriffs."

"*Almost* killing," Chris said again.

Meacham didn't answer.

"He's probably got a shotgun too," Chris said. "I wouldn't try killing him on the road."

"It would be extra dangerous," Meacham agreed.

"I probably shouldn't kill him in the first place," Chris said.

"You cunt," Meacham said, but he said it with humor.

They followed the car onto the highway and drove about ten miles out of town. The entire time, Meacham followed with his lights off, playing the game to its fullest, relying on some sixth sense to stay on the road. They were still driving when Meacham reached across Chris and opened the glove compartment.

Meacham dug into a mess of papers and came out with a handgun.

Chris said nothing, and Meacham glanced at him. He wanted to see if Chris was losing his nerve. Chris, meanwhile, stopped watching the road. His attention was fixed on the gun. In the dark it should have been hard to see, but it wasn't. Even in Meacham's lap, the moonlight touched the blue metal and gave it a shadow of shape. Meacham drove with one hand, and with the other he rolled the gun's cylinder. He finally used his leg to hold the steering wheel and lifted the gun to check its chamber. Satisfied, he again rested the weapon.

"Ever use a gun?" Meacham asked.

Chris said no.

"It's real easy," Meacham said. "All you do is aim and pull the trigger."

"Why do I need a gun?" Chris said.

"So you can almost kill him."

The sheriff turned onto a driveway. Meacham slowed and then stopped, a safe and quiet distance from the house.

Rawlings was home. With the car parked, he flicked off the headlights and went into his house. There was another car already in the driveway; Chris had seen that much before Rawlings killed the headlights. Now, Meacham and Chris waited as Rawlings moved about his house, turning on and off lights, apparently going to the kitchen. He finally ended up in the front of the house. They knew this because they could see the glow of a television set. Rawlings was home and relaxing.

Outside the house, Meacham reached across Chris and opened the passenger door.

"Let's get closer," Meacham said.

Chris obeyed. It wasn't just a matter of Meacham holding

the gun; this was also Meacham's situation. Chris left the car while Meacham led the way toward the house. Just as in the barn, Meacham could have been floating across the snow. Meanwhile, each of Chris's steps broke the crusted snow and echoed into eternity. They walked until Meacham was beside the living room window. There was the sheriff . . . slouched on the sofa, sipping a glass of milk and watching the tube. His gun was off and resting on the coffee table. Elsewhere he'd taken off his shoes, and his hat had been left on a recliner.

The sheriff watched television perhaps ten minutes, then finished his milk and turned off the set. He gave one long stretch and headed upstairs, and the moment he went upstairs Meacham grabbed Chris. He pulled him back and they looked toward the second-floor windows.

A bathroom light flicked on and water began running.

"All right," Meacham said. "Let's go in."

He went to the front door, but it was locked. Meacham, however, simply hopped off the front steps and started for the back of the house. He was almost around the corner of the house when he stopped.

Chris hadn't moved. He was still standing in the front yard, staring at the bathroom window.

"Come on," Meacham whispered. "You can't kill him out here."

Chris slowly followed. He walked as though each step was painful, and when Meacham turned around the corner of the house, Chris considered running for the road. Hell, the van should be somewhere. How far would Chris have to run before crossing paths with Billy and Denny?

Meacham came back and slapped Chris's arm. "Come on," he insisted. "Here. Take the gun."

Meacham handed Chris the revolver and again led the way. Holding the gun made a difference for Chris. He slipped his finger about the trigger and followed Meacham. At least now he had a semblance of control. If Meacham went too far, Chris could just pocket the gun, say no and walk away.

"We're going inside and upstairs," Meacham said. "We'll

get into the bathroom, then you put the gun up to his head and pull the trigger.''

''You want me to shoot him?'' Chris said.

''Christ, the thing's not loaded,'' Meacham said.

Chris held the gun to the house light and turned the cylinder. Meacham was telling the truth; there were no bullets.

Meacham tried the kitchen door.

Unlocked.

He winked to Chris and led the way into the house. Meacham was still the silent giant, but Chris was doing fairly well. Neither made a sound crossing the kitchen, and when they reached the living room, Meacham leaned close to his ear and said, ''Be extra quiet. His wife might wake up.''

Chris froze, but Meacham nudged him, and Chris started the climb upstairs. He stepped slowly, doing his best not to make a sound. With each step, he felt more like someone doing a fraternity prank than performing a murder. Maybe that was Meacham's joke: get Chris upstairs, then make a loud noise and get him caught in the bathroom, alone with a naked sheriff. It wouldn't be a bad joke.

Chris moved onto the landing. There was a change in the water, and they could hear the shower spraying. Of course, the bathroom door wasn't locked. It wasn't even properly closed. Chris walked up to it, glanced once toward the bedroom door and looked behind to Meacham. If Chris was going to join the club, he wanted to be sure he did everything right. Meacham pointed at the sheriff's head and pulled a phantom trigger. Chris nodded, then pushed at the door.

He was in the bathroom.

He could see the shadow of the sheriff—a thin, blackened, blurred image that wavered against the shower curtain. As far as Chris could tell, the sheriff had no idea he was in the room. Chris took it slow. He leveled the gun at the sheriff's shadow, started to pull back the trigger . . .

And stopped. The hammer would make a noise, wouldn't it?

He turned to remind Meacham. He wanted to silently explain that he couldn't pull the trigger without bringing down the house.

He turned and found Meacham at the doorway. Meacham was holding the sheriff's gun, and the weapon was leveled at Chris's head.

Chris didn't move. He stared at Meacham, his own weapon dead at his side. Behind him, Sheriff Rawlings was slapping soap under his arms. He was actually starting to sing.

Chris opened his mouth, wanting badly to scream.

Then Meacham stepped forward. He slid the gun past Chris's cheek and pressed it to the shower curtain. He made sure it was level with the top of Rawlings's shadow . . . level with that singing head. And then Meacham took a deep breath and leaned so his mouth was near Chris's ear. He whispered one word:

"Pow."

Meacham backed out of the bathroom.

Chris still couldn't move. In fact, Meacham had to wave him out. They walked downstairs, and Meacham slipped the sheriff's revolver back in its holster. He also took back his own gun, and led Chris through the kitchen and out of the house.

"Hot shit," Meacham said.

Chris wandered in no direction. Meacham walked beside him and led him toward the pickup.

"Pretty fucking exciting, huh?" Meacham said. "Welcome to the party. You almost killed a man."

Chris looked at Meacham. Meacham wasn't just enjoying himself; he was proud. "I thought you were really going to do it," Chris said.

"Kill Rawlings?" Meacham said. "Hell, I like Tom. Why would I kill him?"

They walked a few more steps toward the car.

"I thought you were going to kill me," Chris said.

Meacham put his arm over Chris's shoulder. "Now you tell me," Meacham said, "why would I want to do a thing like that?"

NINETEEN

"I'M looking for my shoes," she called. "Sure you don't want a drink?"

It was the night after his game with Meacham, and Chris was in Julie's house—one in a row of cramped homes that lined a back road of the county. He stood in the living room, thumbing across a library of books, keeping his body in motion while thinking solely of what had happened during his last evening out: the drive in the car, how Meacham and he had parked and crossed the snow, of the moment Chris had pointed a gun at the head of the naked, singing sheriff and then turned to see a loaded gun pointed at his own head.

"You hear me, Chris?" she called. "Chris?"

Meacham had terrorized him. Within a few hours, he had taken Chris as close to the brink as anyone could go, then left him with more adrenaline and fear than he could bear. And as Meacham drove off, he had given Chris one parting gift, a kind of unstated promise that maybe next time Meacham would hold on to him.

Maybe next time, hand in hand, they would go over the brink.

"Chris, are you listening to me?"

Chris turned and met Julie as she came out of the bedroom. She was dressed in jeans, a denim shirt and leather boots.

"We should get going," she said. "They don't take reservations, and the lines can be awful."

"All right," he said, and a moment later they left the house.

While Chris drove, Julie made herself comfortable in the passenger seat. "Head south about three miles, then make a left and go another two," she said. Julie talked easily, ready to enjoy the evening. "It's called Rudy's. You ever been there?"

Chris shook his head.

"It's a steak house," she said. "It's about the only good place around."

"I don't know a lot about the area," he said. "Just certain parts."

"You probably know more than you need." Julie leaned against the side door and relaxed. "So, are you ready to tell me?"

Chris glanced at her.

"Where you first saw me?" she said. "That's why you asked me out isn't it? You said you saw me somewhere in town and decided we should spend some time together. Tell me where it was."

"Later," he said. "Let's start with something else."

"All right," she said. "Tell me about California."

"All right," he said. "Have you ever been there?"

"Not that far west," she said. "What's it like?"

Chris thought a moment. It was odd talking to Julie. After Meacham, a part of him had grown used to cocked guns and dead-eye stares. "Dry," he told her. "I probably wouldn't live there if I had a choice, but I don't. It's where you have to be to make films."

"What kind of movies do you make?"

"Nonfiction videos," Chris said, resorting to Dorsey's description. "You wouldn't have heard of them."

For the moment she accepted the answer. "And what kind of work are you doing?"

"Directing, producing, editing," he said. "Depends what has to be done."

"And you make money at it?"

"I make other people money."

"That's good," she said. "If you're making money, you must be talented."

"That's the Hollywood way of thinking," he said.

"Hey, I took business classes," she said. "I don't care what you're doing—if you're a success, that takes talent."

Chris grinned.

"I'm serious," she said. "You're making nonfiction videos, right? People are buying your product? That means you not only know how to make a film, you can make something that's popular. You can provide what people want." Julie patted his hand. "I bet you've got talent, I bet you've got drive, and I bet one other thing." Julie turned so she faced him completely. "I bet you have a real feel for people."

Chris was driving, but he returned the stare as long as he could. He was studying Julie carefully. He was trying to tell if she was joking.

When they reached the restaurant, Julie gave their names to a hostess and they waited in an alcove. "Just a few minutes," she told Chris. "Okay?"

"Okay," he said.

"You sure?" she said. "You don't look okay."

Chris again assured her. He was fine, but he was also uncomfortable. It wasn't just being on a date; it was being public and vulnerable. The overhead lamps reminded him of camera lights, and feeling the lights, and seeing no place to avoid them, was like being forced before the camera of someone else's film. He could even imagine a lens focused on his face, every turn of his head, every movement of his eyes being recorded.

"I think we can go in," Julie said.

The hostess led them to a table. They weaved through the restaurant, with Julie almost routinely nodding to friends and acquaintances. Chris supposed it made sense; considering her job, she would be familiar with most people in the area. And if Chris had felt a spotlight in the alcove, Julie was now in the light, entering a restaurant with a stranger to the town. A man from Hollywood, California; someone who, if not a celebrity, was a curiosity.

"Julie," the waiter said.

"Frank," Julie answered. She turned and introduced him, and Frank handed out the menus. When the waiter left, Julie said, "I know him from school."

"You probably know half the people in the restaurant," Chris said.

"Frank's gonna get me a job here," she said. "I don't like being a waitress, but if I'm gonna do it I should make more money." She scanned the menu, running her finger down the card. "You want me to order? I've tried it all."

Julie waved Frank back to the table. When he arrived, he was carrying a bottle of wine. He opened the wine, poured, took their orders and left. Finally, Julie lifted her glass and said, "To your latest movie."

Chris also lifted his glass and they sipped their drinks.

"Tell me about yourself," he said. "Do you like working at the diner?"

Julie grinned. "Are you kidding?"

"Then why work there?"

"There aren't a lot of choices in town."

"You could work on a farm."

"Not this time of year."

"You could move someplace where you have choices," he said.

"I've been around some," she said. "I worked in Minnesota. After that I went to state college for two years, and after that I came back. My parents used to live about five miles from town. They moved to Florida when I was at school."

"You mean your family was gone, but you still came back?"

Julie understood what he meant. She grinned and said, "I know. I can't explain it. I don't even have a lot of friends here."

"But you like living in Hayden," he said.

"*Like* is too strong a word," she said. "I'm comfortable in Hayden, and I like being alone. I may not be here forever, but if I'm going to leave, I should have someplace better to go. I've got roots."

Chris shook his head. "I never felt any roots to my home town," he said. "I have roots in L.A., but it's all professional. If the business moved, I'd move with it."

"People around here wouldn't move short of an atomic bomb," she said.

"People can sometimes fool you," he said. Chris thought a moment, then asked, "You know the Meachams?"

"I know who they are," she said. "Mr. Meacham comes by the diner."

"What's your impression?"

"Bad tipper," she said. "But if you're serious, I don't know him well. I didn't go to school with Todd, and when Mr. Meacham comes by, all I do is take his order."

"He comes by regularly?"

"Not really."

"I'm asking because I've spent some time with him lately," Chris said. "He's got roots, but they're short ones. In California we have these palm trees that can stretch four stories up, but they have almost no roots under the ground. A good wind can bring them down. I think a good push could get Meacham in motion."

"But the Meachams moved here," Julie said. "It's different when you don't come from the area. Everything's a little more disposable."

"Disposable," Chris said, considering the word. "That's good." He sipped his wine. He was willing to guess much of Meacham's life fit that explanation. "Meacham's an interesting man. I've never met anyone like him. Not up close."

"Yeah?" she said. "I think I could throw a rock in any direction and hit a dozen like him."

The dinner finally arrived, and they continued talking— sometimes about Chris, sometimes about Julie.

"I don't have any family now, but I grew up in the east," said Chris. "You have brothers or sisters?"

"One brother," she said. "He's down in Texas."

"Sometimes I wish I had a brother or sister," Chris said.

"Looking back, I don't think I came close to having a normal childhood."

"I don't know anyone who has," she said.

"Are you kidding?" Chris said. "Hayden's about as normal as this country gets."

"There's nothing normal about this place," she said. "What's normal about living a hundred miles from anyone else? We're probably all crazy." She rested her hand over his. "Have you gone back to your hometown?"

"Not since my mother's funeral," he said. "Before that, I went back for my father's funeral." He grinned. "Death has an interesting role in my life. It's kind of a running theme."

Julie looked confused. Chris moved closer.

"Let me ask you this," he said. "What do you think people are most curious about in life?"

Julie carefully considered the question. "I don't know," she finally said. "People are most curious about people, I suppose."

"That's too easy," he said. "What are you most curious about?" Chris leaned so she could confide in him. "What do you want to know most? Something you keep secret from people. Something that makes you feel guilty as hell."

"You mean sex?" Julie said.

"I mean something else," Chris said.

She shook her head. Chris tried helping her.

"Try this," Chris said. "Is curiosity healthy?"

"Of course," she said.

"Even if you end up experiencing things you aren't meant to experience?"

"I don't believe that," she said. "I think a person should feel and experience everything."

"Really?" he said. "No matter what you may see?"

"Absolutely," she said. "Everything that happens is part of life. You can't hide from life." She regarded him more cautiously. "So why are we talking like this?"

Chris grinned. "I could be wrong, but I'm convinced the thing people are most curious about in life," he told her, "is death."

Julie stared at him.

"People try hard to keep it a secret," he said, "but look in the bookstores. Look at what sells in the movies. People will spend hours in the dark watching a film just to see how other people die."

Julie looked uncertain, but Chris knew she was following him.

"Most won't admit it," he said, "but some do, and they're willing to take more risks. They'll do it with anything. If it's sex, they'll explore it, sometimes alone, and sometimes through other people. And when it's death, they'll look for answers in the movies, in the newspapers, even in a video store. I don't mean the usual videos; I mean the videos you can't find in most stores. The kind they hide on the bottom rack. The kind," he said, "that shows you everything."

Chris waited. Her hand was still on his, but there was no grip. As for her attention, her focus was off to his side, locked on nothing. It took almost a minute before she would talk. When she did, it was a struggle.

"Chris," she said. "I think I know where you saw me."

Chris turned his hand so he could cover her fingers. "Don't be embarrassed," he said.

Her face was flushing.

"Don't," he said. "People are trained to hate themselves for certain things. Just remember, other people made those tapes. Perfectly normal people."

Julie kept shaking her head.

"See," he said, "when I saw you buying the video—"

"Chris—"

"I got curious," he said. "I guess you can say I got curious about your curiosity. Violence, death, sex . . . I've seen all of it twisted about. As a person—as a customer— you're about as close to normal as I've ever met. That means something to me."

Chris kept pressing her hand.

"I've been involved with some strange film projects," Chris told her. "I've had to go through clips that I couldn't stand watching. For the last year, I've made a living at this sort of thing.''

"You mean nonfiction videos," she said. There was a tone to her voice, and Chris heard it.

"It sounds awful," he said, "but I think you're right about what you said. People have to open themselves up to experiences. Sometimes that means doing or watching things that go beyond the normal. It means accepting people for what they are, and letting them do what they need to do in order to face themselves. No one's about to kill himself, but maybe by watching other people experience it, a person can understand himself a little better. It's okay to be curious. And you're proof, because there's nothing strange about you, and I've seen you at the store. I saw you pick up a tape, I saw you buying it—"

"It was a rental," Julie said.

"My point is it's all right," Chris said. "I just want to talk about it, that's all. I'd like to know what you thought you'd see. I'd like to know how you felt after seeing it."

Julie listened, then nodded, at last fully understanding. "Is this why you took me out?" she said. "You wanted to see what kind of person rents that kind of garbage?"

Chris waited. He stared at Julie, wishing she would understand, sensing what was going to happen.

"Not just that," he said. "I wanted to be with you."

Julie thought a moment, then stood. Her attention was focused far from Chris.

"I think," she said, "I want to go home."

Chris watched as she turned and left the restaurant.

By the time he paid the check, she was gone. He looked once in the car, walked around the restaurant, went back inside... He was looking a last time when Frank, the waiter, approached him. Chris thought he was bringing him change; instead, Frank handed him a note.

"She got a ride home," Frank told him.

Chris returned to the car, turned onto the road and drove back to the motel. He didn't look at the note until he was back in his room, alone and with the door locked; then he opened the piece of paper.

He knew what it would say. There was almost no point in reading it. Still, he felt an obligation. Slowly, carefully, he flattened the note on his leg.

They were simple words, but they were familiar ones.

He read the message again, then went to a drawer, found a roll of adhesive, and taped the note to his bathroom mirror. He wanted to look at the note the next time he faced his reflection and begged his image for a little understanding. At last, there would be something to answer him when he told himself he was basically a normal, sane, good human being.

The answer was there in pencil.

Chris, Julie had written, *Please keep out of my life. You are scum.*

Todd was feeling watched.

Of course, the feeling wasn't unusual. Every day he felt the presence of his father, either staring at him or calling after him or even just thinking of him. In Todd's life, William Meacham was an everlasting presence.

This time, however, it was a different. This time, he felt as if the world was watching him. He'd look about, and even if he saw no one, he felt something. It was a new kind of invasion; as if he was being hunted. As if, for a change, Todd was to be a victim. And Todd didn't like the feeling.

He didn't tell his father. For one, William Meacham wouldn't believe him. More importantly, though, he didn't know how his father would behave. Todd had never before felt so threatened; maybe it would also be new for William Meacham. Was it worth the risk of making his father upset?

Which was worse: being nervous or being punished?

It was late afternoon, a few hours before Chris's date, and Todd was parked in front of a hardware store. That was one of the reasons he'd come to town. The other reason was Sarah Boden. On the weekends, she worked at a card shop, and after Todd bought his supplies, he walked down the street to visit the shop. He had already turned the knob when he looked through the store window and saw someone he didn't want to see: Eric Copley, Sarah's steady.

Copley was talking to Sarah, actually touching her hand, while Todd stood outside. Todd sneaked away before anyone could see him, but that didn't change the situation. For weeks he had told Copley to back off, and Copley hadn't listened to him. Copley was still bothering Sarah.

That would have to change.

Todd kept out of sight until Copley was gone, then, with controlled temper, he entered the card shop. He walked up to the cash register, nodded to the owner and looked to Sarah.

"I was just walking by," Todd said. Sarah regarded him curtly and Todd made a motion toward the door. "Are you still going with Eric?"

"I already told you, Todd..."

"You should try going out with me," he said. "Come on. We could go out tonight."

"I've got plans."

"Then tomorrow."

"No," she said.

"Then—"

"I told you," she said. "You're nice, but I can't date two guys."

"Not even if your plans change?"

"I'm sorry," she said.

Todd walked to the door. "At least think about it?"

"Sure, I'll think about it, but I won't do it," she said.

Todd said goodbye and left the store. Everything was fine; he didn't need to date Sarah anyway, at least not this weekend. Hell, at the moment, with everything going on, his father was almost leaving him alone. But that would change once the movie people left.

Next weekend, he thought. Then things would happen.

Todd strolled about town. There was nothing else, except to avoid going home. He did this as long as he could—walking about, trying to find anything to do. But it never took long to walk through Hayden. Of course, he could go to the coffee shop, except that meant sitting down at the counter. Todd preferred being alone. Besides, if he was being watched, it was better to keep moving.

He reached his car and dug in a pocket for the keys. He was still digging when someone touched his arm.

"Excuse me, but could you help me?"

Todd looked at her. The woman was a stranger several years older than him, with makeup on her lips and cheeks.

"I'm sorry, but I'm freezing out here and I really could use a ride."

Todd regarded her more carefully. He'd guess she was twenty-five. Blonde curly hair, with lined eyes. Her skin was blemished, and there was a kind of ghostly quality to her; still, she carried herself with confidence. Indeed, when Todd stared at her, she seemed to know exactly what he was thinking.

"I'm visiting some friends down the road, heading west," she said. "If you're going that way, I'd really appreciate the help. At least as far as you're going."

Todd opened the passenger door to the pickup. She climbed in and Todd took his place behind the steering wheel. He turned the ignition and flicked on the headlights.

"This is very nice of you," she said.

Todd smiled at her. It was getting dark outside, but even in the shadows, the woman was good company. This helped Todd relax. He checked the mirror and started through town.

"Actually," she said. "I'm surprising them."

Todd said nothing.

"My friends, I mean," she said. "They don't know I'm coming. No one does."

Todd nodded as if he understood. She smiled and offered her hand.

"My name's Molly."

"I'm Todd."

"I'm very glad to meet you, Todd," she said. "You're a real lifesaver."

Todd looked pleased.

"You're a good-looking boy," Molly said. "Are all the boys here good looking?"

"I'm one of a kind," Todd said. He again smiled and looked at her.

She was staring right at him.

"I'm not just saying that," she said. "You're a real turn-on."

Todd turned onto the route and drove out of town.

"I kind of know this area," she said. "You got lots of farms out here, don't you?"

Todd chuckled.

"Is that funny?" she said.

"Farming's the main business," Todd said.

"Stupid me," she said. "I still think I've been out here before."

"Maybe you have," Todd said. "Who're you visiting?"

"Friends," she said.

"Who?" Todd said.

Molly didn't answer. Instead, she looked out the window. "Some of this looks familiar." She touched Todd's shoulder and reached across him, pointing. "Do me a favor, will you? Pull over there."

Todd hesitated and Molly squeezed his arm. "Come on, Todd. I think I know that spot. I've been there."

Todd did what he was told and turned onto the chained driveway.

"Where're we at?" she asked.

"We're on a farm," he said.

"Whose farm?"

"The Donnellys'," Todd said.

"And that belongs to them?" she said. "That pond straight ahead?"

Todd nodded.

"Do me one more favor, Todd. Please?"

Todd listened.

"Turn off the motor."

Todd obeyed. It was the right thing, obeying. She had been giving orders from the start, and throughout he had complied. It was like listening to his father, when William Meacham really wanted something done. Todd could fight, but in the end William Meacham gave the order, and Todd did what he was told.

With the lights off, she rested a hand on his thigh and let

her fingers slide to the inside of his leg. She gave a gentle squeeze.

"Can I tell you something, Todd?"

Todd listened.

"Todd, I meant it when I said you were attractive."

She moved so her breasts pressed against his arm. Her fingers moved ever so lightly up his leg.

"The truth is, I really don't need a ride. I've been making everything up just because I wanted to be with you. When I saw you walking down the sidewalk, it made me start thinking things. It made me want to do things."

She brought her hand all the way up his thigh and cupped him. Todd tightened—closing his eyes, biting hard on his lower lip.

He also hardened.

Molly felt it. She kissed his ear and started rubbing him. While Todd sat there, she unclasped his belt buckle.

"This is a romantic little spot," she said. "A woman could really lose her head out here."

Todd barely moved, but Molly knew what she was up against. Todd was half passion and half nerves. She was using one to overcome the other.

"I really got a thing for you, Todd," she said. "You want to know another secret? I'm wet. You can reach down and feel me."

She picked up his hand and rested it on her own crotch. When she did this, she took a deep breath, as if his dead hand had made her more excited.

As for Todd, she had undone his belt and opened his pants.

Todd looked down. He was exposed.

"That's really something," she said. "You're big, Todd. You know that? You really got me going."

She rubbed him up and down.

"You like that?" she asked.

Todd didn't answer, and she again pressed her lips to his ear.

"Talk to me, sweetheart," she said. "Come on, honey.

We're alone. We can do what we want. You like what I'm doing, don't you?''

She kissed his neck and then his lips. Todd sat there, taking what he was given, feeling, breathing, staring . . .

Staring at the pond.

"Just tell me, Todd. Anything you want me to do, anything you want to do for me. Anything, Todd . . . out here, in the woods, by the water . . . Isn't there something you want?''

She kissed him a last time and lowered her head. She wet her lips. She opened them.

And Todd screamed.

Not even Molly expected this. She lurched back, but Todd was already shoving her. It was a weak, open-fisted attack, not so much directed at Molly than the passenger door. Finally, he found the door handle. In the same frenzy, he turned the handle and swung Molly out of her seat.

"Hey," she shouted.

Todd slammed the door and locked it. He turned the ignition and back-wheeled onto the road. If there had been any other traffic, he would have had a pileup; instead, he spinned the car straight, leaving Molly alone in the snow.

It took only a few minutes before he was back on the farm. He skidded up the drive, and luckily for Todd, only his mother was home. He parked the car around the side of the house, then closed his pants, turned on the cab light and looked for any sign of the woman's company. The whole time he was shaking. He was still shaking when he left the pickup and ran the distance to his house.

"Todd?" his mother called. "Todd, it's dinnertime."

Todd went straight to his room. His mother was used to this; Todd, however, knew this was different than the other times. Just as the watching was different.

Someone had touched him. An absolute stranger had pulled down his pants and gone to work on his body, like her whole purpose was to drive him to a frenzy.

All in sight of the pond.

All in sight of something else.

The feeling of being watched. It was there in town, it was there at the pond . . .

Todd locked the door to his room.

He was terrified, and he knew why. After all he'd done, God was going to get him. God was looking down at him steady, and Todd was feeling it, and the eyes of heaven were going to destroy him. The only thing to do was keep out of sight, but what could he do? Where could he hide?

He pulled down the shade and turned off the lights.

He didn't normally feel safe in his room, but in the dark, with the door locked, he felt like nothing could see or reach him. He went to the door and pressed his ear against the wood, just to be certain his mother was leaving him alone. Not a sound.

He crawled across the floor, pulled back a corner of the shade and looked outside. Again, nothing. Complete quiet. He was alone, high above the ground, safe and secure. With the blinds closed, even God couldn't find him. All he had to do was lay low, and maybe in a few days, the eyes would look elsewhere. Hell, there were worse people than Todd walking the earth. Not even Heaven could spend eternity staring at him. And the night looked like it was already relaxing. The sky was clear, and the snow was smooth, and there was a kind of pleasant chill to the winter. A numbing draft had slipped through the windowsill. Todd pressed his cheek to the breeze and looked outside, loving the cold and nosing into it like someone stealing the freshest breaths of air and . . .

And eyes.

Todd didn't move. It was there, in the second story of the barn. A glimmer, like someone tilting a jar in the moonlight.

Todd dropped away from the window. It had come and gone in an instant, but Jesus Christ . . . Was it real? Was it still there? Todd peeked out again and waited and waited and—

There. *Again.*

He was being watched. There *were* eyes.

Todd rushed out of his room and ran downstairs.

"Todd?" he heard, this time his father.

Todd ran onto the porch. He wasn't wearing a coat, but it didn't matter. He didn't feel the cold; he only felt the terror. He leaped off the porch and rushed across the snow. When he reached the barn, he stopped at the open gate doors and looked all about.

"Who's there?" he shouted.

He walked inside. The place was dark, the only sound coming from the animals.

Todd moved slowly through the barn. He tried looking everywhere, but mostly he watched the loft. He walked until he reached the tool wall, then armed himself with the pitchfork.

"I said who's there?"

He kept the pitchfork in front of himself. Up there, he thought. That's where he'd find the eyes.

"I swear to God I'm gonna kill you."

He started up the ladder.

"Whoever the hell you are, you messed with the wrong man," Todd said. "I'm gonna cut you up, buddy. I'm gonna tear you to shreds."

He went higher, the steps crying from his weight.

"You following me?" Todd said. "You watching me around town? I'm gonna kill you. I'm—"

Todd fell backward. One second he had reached the end of the loft, the next moment something struck him. He dropped ten feet and landed hard on his back. He was still lying there when a shadow dropped beside him and ran out of the barn.

"Oh, God," he moaned. He started rolling, but jerked away. The pitchfork. He had almost landed on top of it.

Todd managed to stand. He got on his feet, then bent down and picked up his weapon.

It was all true; there had been someone after him. He went to the barn door and looked out, but whoever it was had gone. Todd turned around and walked back into the barn.

Everything was starting to come apart.

He went into the center of the barn, looked about, then opened one of the stall doors.

And then, with the animals before him, Todd screamed. He screamed and fell on his knees and started stabbing, and brought the weapon down again and again. Soon Todd was completely lost in his rampage.

And even sooner, the barn was once again wet with blood.

William Meacham heard his son. He was outside and at the barn in less than a minute, but not before Todd had done his damage. Not before Todd had bent another prong on the pitchfork.

"Todd?"

Meacham talked quietly. It was the only way to talk when Todd went delirious.

Todd either ignored William Meacham or didn't hear him; he just kept plunging the pitchfork. William Meacham walked carefully behind Todd and at the right moment grabbed him. He pulled the boy out of the stall, slapped aside the pitchfork, then slammed him against a far wall.

"You calm down," William Meacham said. "You're acting like a lunatic."

Todd slumped to the ground. He was breathing hard. "Someone was watching me," he managed.

"You're having more nightmares," William said.

"Someone was here," Todd said. "He hit me." He looked beyond Meacham and to the loft. "He was up there."

Meacham looked up. Carefully, he stepped up the ladder. He went up, saw nothing, saw no one . . .

Then he saw it.

The hay had been moved. He knew, because he'd been up here just a few days before to collect his travel money. He moved through the hay until he found something else.

A lens cap.

"Someone was watching me," Todd kept saying. "They're following me."

Meacham came down the ladder. Todd reached up for his father, and Meacham lifted his son and wrapped him in his arms.

"Let's get you back in the house," Meacham said.

Todd pressed against his father and let himself be led out of the barn.

"Don't you worry about a thing," Meacham said. "I'm gonna take care of everything, all right? I'm gonna take care of it."

Todd nodded, and on the way to the house, William Meacham looked toward the main road. He saw a car suddenly turn on its lights—a car already on the road. It was as if the driver had driven in the dark simply to get past the Meacham house.

Very strange, he thought.

But then again, maybe it made sense.

TWENTY

WILLIAM Meacham stared at Chris as if a sacred trust had been broken. And perhaps it was true, because Chris avoided the stare. Even though they sat directly opposite each other, Chris did everything possible to avoid eye contact. But that wasn't enough to stop Meacham from talking.

"You really took me for a fool," Meacham said. "You haven't been filming my land. You've been peeking through the windows."

"This is just a misunderstanding," Chris said.

"The fuck it is," Meacham said. "Either you or one of your friends beat up my son last night. Todd almost got killed and I found pieces of your camera all over the goddamn floor."

"I wasn't at the barn," Chris said. "If Billy or Denny was there, I'm sure there was a logical reason for—"

"Stop the bullshit," Meacham said. "You're spying on my family and I want it stopped." Meacham turned and faced the sheriff. "Are you gonna tell him to keep away?"

Sheriff Rawlings sat to their side, his hands folded, acting more like a mediator than an officer of the law. It was morning, and they were in his office, sitting around a plain wood table. Rawlings listened to what Meacham said, then listened to Chris Thomas, and between the talk, he'd throw in remarks. "Now Chris, are you aware of anyone going on Williams' property at night or filming any member of his family without consent?" "William, now it seems to me you signed an agreement allowing Chris on your property."

They talked, argued, listened and talked again. At one point, Meacham reached across the table and tore up the letter of agreement he had signed. Rawlings only shook his head. "William, that doesn't mean a thing," he said. "You just can't tear up a contract."

Rawlings turned back to Chris. "At the same time, you can't hold a person to this type of thing if he didn't understand it."

Chris listened, but it was difficult. Whenever he looked at Rawlings, he remembered putting a gun within inches of his showered head. And having Meacham in the room made it tougher, although Chris was the only one struggling with the situation. Meacham carried on as if nothing in the world had happened, between any of them. From Meacham's behavior, they could have been meeting for the first time.

"Sheriff Rawlings," Chris said, "I haven't talked to my coworkers today. I don't know if anyone was at his farm last night. But we sure as hell wouldn't hurt anyone. If something did happen, it was an accident."

"Bullshit," Meacham said again. To Rawlings: "Bring them in. Let me talk to each one of them." To Chris: "You're a fucking back stabber. I'll bet you've been doing this for weeks." Something rang true for Meacham. He stared at Chris and shook his head. "Man, you got no idea who you're fucking with."

Chris tried returning the anger. "We signed an agreement," he said. "Anytime you want to give back the five hundred dollars, you can call it a deal."

Chris wanted to show Meacham he could go head-to-head. It was probably the stupidest thing he could do. Even Rawlings knew it.

"William," the sheriff said, "can you leave Chris and me alone a minute?"

Meacham didn't want to leave. His attention was fixed on

Chris. There was something much more going on between them—things not even Chris could comprehend.

"Come on, William," Rawlings insisted, and Meacham slowly stood up. Rawlings walked him out of the office, then came back into the room and closed the door. They both relaxed some.

"I've been getting a lot of abuse lately," Chris said.

Rawlings settled opposite Chris. "Chris," he said, "am I supposed to believe that of all the farms where you could've shot your damn movie, you just happened to pick the home of some kid you suspect of murder?"

Chris looked away.

"Absolutely incredible," Rawlings said.

"Sheriff—"

"You just completely ignored me, didn't you? You got something in your head and that was the end of it. You even got William to sign some crap document, just to film his boy."

"No," Chris said. "It's not Todd. It's him."

"Him what?" the sheriff said. "Now William's a killer?"

"I've got proof," Chris said. "I've—"

"You got crap," the sheriff said. "I know it's crap because you're crap."

The sheriff stood up and opened the office door. William Meacham was standing at the doorway.

"Come in, William," Rawlings said. Meacham obeyed, and for the moment Rawlings was in control of his office. He paced the room, collecting his thoughts. "William has lodged a complaint against you, Chris, saying that you're bothering his family and trespassing on his land. Your document gives you the right to cross onto that land, and you paid for those rights, and William took the money. But I don't think those rights are good forever. They sure as hell don't give you the right to harass and endanger anybody's family."

Chris looked anxious to argue, but Rawlings raised a hand.

"We've all been patient and courteous to you and your friends. I'm not at all sure you've shown us the same respect. What I do know is I'm not about to let some stranger come into my town and start acting like he owns the damn place. So I am ordering you to keep off the Meacham farm, and I am ordering you to keep away from him and his family, and I am ordering you to listen to what I'm saying, because if you don't I'm going to make life very difficult for you."

The sheriff stood in front of Chris, trying to tower over him, making Chris understand that he meant his threat.

"What you're telling me to do," Chris answered, "you don't have the authority to tell me."

"You're free to take it up with the county court," the sheriff said. "Call the ACLU. In the meantime, I am the law, Mr. Thomas. So find yourself another farm and finish your business. Do you understand me?"

Rawlings had finished. He waited for Chris to again be a smart-ass, expecting at least some manner of last-minute fight.

What he got was a handshake and an apology. "I'm sorry," Chris said. He looked to Meacham. "You're both right. Not that I was spying, but that I shouldn't be forcing myself on anyone. This whole thing's nothing but a lot of misunderstandings, but if I'm not wanted somewhere, I know enough to get up and leave."

"Good," said Rawlings. "Does that satisfy you, William?"

"Do I keep the money?" William said.

"It's yours," Chris said.

"Then I'm satisfied," William said. "Just keep off the land and keep away from my family."

"Of course," Chris said. "I'm sorry to have caused any trouble."

Meacham shook hands with the sheriff and left. Rawlings made a point of walking Chris to the door. "If you still got some filming to do, I'd be happy to find another farm," the sheriff said. "Just so long as the ground rules are clear from the start."

"Thanks," Chris said.

"In the meantime, keep away from the Meachams. Give

them some breathing room. I really don't want any trouble from all this.''

Chris agreed and left. He headed outside and walked down the sidewalk, fully expecting Meacham to jump out of nowhere, grab him by the collar and really teach the lesson.

But he was wrong. For now, there was no warning. That would come later, when it was dark.

It would come when Chris was truly alone.

''It was a good idea,'' Hooper said, ''it just didn't work out.''

They were all in the motel room. Hooper, Chris, Billy, Denny... It was a half hour after Chris's visit to the sheriff's office, and ten hours after Hooper and Billy had come running into Chris's room, still terrified over how close they'd come to being caught.

Chris should have seen it coming. Ever since meeting Todd, Hooper had been undercutting Chris. And, in a way, Hooper had been destined to undercut him. That's what people often did in the movie business. While feigning support—while pretending to stand behind you—they spent the time looking for flaws and digging your grave. With a little luck, they gained control of your project.

But this... Shipping in a whore to entice Todd into a sexual, murderous frenzy. Sending Billy up to the loft and nearly getting caught. Screwing up *everything* after Chris had tried so hard to make Meacham his friend. After surviving the initiation, and maybe being on the verge of something much, much more.

''I still think it's Todd,'' Hooper said.

Chris didn't know what to say. Hooper hadn't apologized or explained himself. He really hadn't done much of anything except bring it all to a crashing end.

''Hooper—'' Chris started.

''*Hey*, don't start,'' Hooper said. ''I got you closer to Meacham than anyone else. I made things happen, and if it didn't go perfect, what does? Who the hell are you to complain? Without me, you'd still be sitting on your ass.''

''At least I'd have a film,'' Chris said.

"All you'd have is more of nothing," Hooper said, and with that he left the room.

Chris turned. Billy was on the bed, cleaning the cameras. "What about you?" Chris said.

Billy shrugged.

"Come on, Billy. How could you let him screw things up?"

Billy looked up at Chris. With an absolutely straight face, he said, "Because I've known Stan longer than I've known you."

Denny led Chris away from him. "It doesn't matter anymore," she said. "Whether we can go on the farm or not, he's not going to do anything."

"Not if he thinks we're off his case," Chris said.

"Chris—"

"I said I'd leave him alone," he said. "I promised in front of the sheriff. He may believe that."

"Would you believe it?"

"But Meacham's different," Chris said. "He isn't someone who can control his temper."

Denny shook her head. She wanted to be sympathetic, but not if it meant being a fool.

"We're going to be pulled out of here anyway," Chris said. "It can't hurt." Chris returned to Billy. "You're still on Dorsey's salary, right?"

"I was on Dorsey's salary when I did the job for Stan," he said.

Chris grabbed him. He wanted to be obeyed. "Spend the day in your room, then meet me in the van at dusk. And if Hooper asks you to do anything, tell him no. Tell him you don't want your nose broken."

"My nose, huh?" Billy said.

Chris picked up one of Billy's cameras and threw it into the wall.

"You have no idea who you're fucking with," Chris told him.

Billy straightened. As for Chris, he turned and left the room.

* * *

Meacham left his house at ten P.M.

Denny was the first to see him go. She was again plugged into the house and she heard Meacham ask for his coat. She finished recording, unplugged the cable, wrapped up the wire and ran behind the bushes. She kept low to the ground while Meacham left the house and settled in his car.

When he drove off, she began hiking across the field. For Denny, the evening was finished.

As for Billy and Chris, they tailed Meacham into town and watched him enter the tavern. They waited over two hours before Meacham returned to his car. Then, instead of heading home, he drove west. They were heading in the direction of the sheriff's house, that much Chris knew, but Meacham made several turns, and soon Chris had no idea where they were, except that it was a dirt road.

There were trees all about. Maybe they were in a state park, or a patch of undeveloped land. Whichever, it was a problem. If Meacham knew he was being followed, Chris was being set up. If Meacham didn't know, Chris was caught blocking what was probably the only road out of the forest.

When he saw the road fork, he pulled off and parked away from the junction.

"We'll follow on foot," Chris said.

They took the cameras and started walking up the road. They did this even though the road could have gone on for miles, and there was no guarantee Meacham had stopped.

But they walked only a quarter mile before seeing Meacham's pickup. It was parked in the center of the road and the headlights were off; still, Meacham was there. They stopped, they watched, they waited, and finally Meacham opened the side door. He started into the woods. In one of his hands was a flashlight, in the other was a shovel.

Chris nudged Billy, and when Meacham was far enough ahead, they began following him. It was easy tracking Meacham. There was the flashlight, there was the path through the snow...A few times they stumbled, but that was all right; Meacham never stopped moving. He went around a boulder, and Chris knew the hike was finished.

While they couldn't see Meacham, the beam held steady, which meant he had rested the flashlight. They was something going on behind the boulder, only they couldn't see it.

"I think I hear digging," Billy whispered.

Chris listened. "We have to see what he's doing," he said. "We have to head off the trail."

"Which way?" Billy said.

"We got two cameras," Chris said. "You left, me right."

Billy agreed and they separated.

And almost immediately, Chris knew he'd made a mistake, because you never wander alone in the woods, especially when you're stalking a killer. Chris made a broad arc through the forest, and he hoped Billy did the same. With their zooms, they didn't need to be that close to Meacham; all they needed was a clearing. In the winter, with the leaves off the trees, that wasn't asking too much. In fact, Chris easily found what he needed. He put the camera to his eye, focused, zoomed in . . .

And Meacham was doing nothing. He was sitting on a boulder, the flashlight on his lap, the shovel between his legs. Occasionally he slapped down at the snow, but other than that, he made no sign of action. It made no sense to Chris. He sat in the snow, and Meacham sat on the rock, and Chris could only guess what Billy was doing. Almost five minutes passed before Meacham so much as lifted a hand. When he did, things became more confusing.

He touched the switch on his flashlight and turned it off. Total dark.

Chris lowered the camera. He looked for Meacham, but he couldn't see him. Then he tried listening for Meacham's footsteps. Chris stood there with his head cocked before remembering—you didn't hear Meacham walk. He was the silent giant.

And here was Chris, alone in the woods without a flashlight or weapon; alone and trying to get a close-up of someone he couldn't hear and couldn't see.

Alone with a homicidal maniac.

He thought of Billy. He wondered whether he should

shout, but suppose Meacham didn't know they were in the woods? Or suppose he couldn't find them?

Chris stepped backward, only it was so much harder without light. And he had to be careful, because even if he survived Meacham, he could get lost in the woods.

He tripped and his foot sank into a snow drift. Already he was fucking up; instead of following his own tracks, he was backing into fresh snow. He stumbled to his starting point, then searched for his prints. He found them not so much from sight as from feel—tapping with his lead foot, feeling for the gaps and sink holes.

He heard something. He heard pain, just the softest cry.

Billy. Jesus Christ, what was Meacham doing to him?

"Billy?" he called.

Nothing.

Chris quickened his steps. He was now completely off his track, but maybe that wasn't bad. Meacham had probably found Chris's trail and was following him now. Moving patiently, in completely control.

My God, Chris thought. No one even knows we're here.

He tried running. He sloshed through the snow and fell face forward, then started getting up . . .

The camera shattered.

Chris was surprised. The camera had been jerked from his hand. Then he saw something long and powerful swing down and Chris rolled over to cover himself.

The shovel struck him flat against the side of his head.

"You're a real genius, aren't you?" said the voice.

Chris tried crawling away, but again the shovel came down on him. Chris's arms collapsed and he went face-deep in the snow.

"I heard you and that fucked-up excuse for a sheriff," said the voice. "I was standing right by the door. You think I'm deaf?"

Chris tried moving, but a foot pressed on his spine, just below the neck. Chris no longer struggled. He was there to be controlled, just like before.

Just like everyone in Meacham's life.

The foot lifted, and Chris still didn't move. He lay there while his attacker straddled him.

"You're way out of your league," the voice said. "You're so far gone I don't think you're ever gonna make it home."

He grabbed hole of Chris's hair and pulled back.

"Don't you have anything to say for yourself?" he asked.

Chris fought for the strength to talk. He opened his mouth and struggled for a breath.

"I'm not here alone," Chris managed.

"Yeah, but you're alone now." Chris's head was pulled back even further, and he felt a breath near his ear. "I know what you're doing," the voice whispered, "and I know what you want me to do. But it's not gonna happen, understand? Nothing's gonna happen. *Nothing*. So do me a favor and get the hell out of my life."

The shadow leaned closer. Chris thought he saw a gun.

It came closer. It pressed to his head. Chris felt the tip and closed his eyes. It was going to happen. He didn't move until he heard the sound.

"Pow," the voice said.

Moments later, Chris was alone in the snow.

TWENTY-ONE

IT was beautiful in L.A., just as it had been for two weeks. Days, sunny and warm; nights, clear and cool. Quite simply, if you didn't like wonderful weather, winter in L.A. wasn't for you.

Which was why Chris baffled Dorsey. Granted, Chris had wanted to make a movie, and granted, Dorsey had pulled the plug and brought everyone home, but at least Chris was back in a place where the most you needed in January was a pullover sweater. Surely that was good for something?

Chris, however, acted like a zombie. Shell shock, Dorsey figured, and when he heard all the stories from Denny and Billy shell shock made sense.

"I don't know what happened," Billy said. "The light went out, and I went running back to the car, but Chris wasn't anywhere. I stayed about three hours before he came stumbling out of the woods."

"Is that what happened?" Dorsey said. Then, to Chris, "Is that what happened?"

Chris rested. He was too tired of the story and too tired of Dorsey. "I don't know," he finally said. "I thought Billy was in trouble. I heard him scream, so I called his name."

"I tripped, that's all," Billy said. "It wasn't my fault. Don't make it sound like it was."

Dorsey fixed again on Chris. "But the guy," he said. "He tried to kill you?"

Chris shook his head. "I don't think that was the idea."

"Then what was?"

"I think," Chris said, "he wanted to almost kill me."

Dorsey stared at him. Chris talked as if he had made sense. Dorsey looked to Billy for an explanation, but explanations weren't one of Billy's strong points. As for Denny, she stared at Chris with concern.

"It sounds to me like I couldn't have ended this jerk-off game too soon," Dorsey said. He pushed his intercom button. "Bring Stan in here."

Hooper walked in. It had been one day since their return and Hooper couldn't have looked happier. Once again in his native clothes, he walked into the office, warm, smiling and fresh from a health bar. "Al," he greeted.

"You look toasty already," Dorsey said. "I hope all of you thanked Stan."

"They were terrific, Al," Stan said. "And they did the best job they could."

"I'm sure," Dorsey said.

"It's just not movie material, that's all," Stan said. "But if anyone could have pulled it off, it's Chris. He's ahead of his time."

"Yeah, a real visionary," Dorsey said. "Maybe he can use some of that vision on RD-three."

"That would be something," Stan said.

Chris walked to the window. He looked outside and realized something was missing. The car, he thought. Dorsey's monument to free speech had been towed.

Chris turned and faced Dorsey. "No more bombs, Al?" he asked.

Dorsey was confused. He had no idea what Chris was talking about. Then, once he understood, he had no idea why Chris had brought it up.

"Can you stay on the subject, Chris?" Dorsey asked. "I just want to be sure I understand. Someone put a gun to your head, right? He pulled the trigger and nothing happened, but there you were, on the ground, rolled tight in a ball and watching your life flash before your eyes. That's what happened? That's why you're such a mess?"

Chris remembered it all too clearly. "Yes," he said.

Dorsey thought carefully. He wanted to be certain he comprehended the scenario. A minute passed before he gave his verdict. "I've got three words for you, Chris," he said. "Big. Fucking. Deal."

Chris stood there.

"I'm not saying it wasn't bad," Dorsey said. "But bad is bad. Everybody has bad days."

"Al . . ." Chris never knew what to say when they were this far apart. "Al, whatever my problem, it has nothing to do with the movie. I said I'd track a killer and I did. Even Stan thinks I did. And if you'd given me a few more weeks, and if you'd shown a little faith, I'd have delivered."

"You think," Dorsey said.

"It was worth the gamble," Chris said. "It still is."

Still? Dorsey tried looking nauseous. "Chris, you didn't say that. Please tell me you didn't."

"We've already got ninety percent of the movie filmed," Chris said. "All we need is the last ten percent."

"Ten percent my ass," Dorsey said. "Listen to you. That ten percent could take all year."

Hooper walked for the door. "Al, are we done?"

Dorsey pointed at him. "Next week, Stan," he said. "Bob's movie needs work."

Hooper left and for another long moment, nothing was said.

"Al—" Chris tried again, but Dorsey cut him off.

"Billy," Dorsey said, "go talk to Ruth. She's got directions down to High Wire Productions. We're doing a coproduction and they need a cameraman."

"Right," Billy said. "Thanks, Al."

Dorsey turned to Denny. "You. I need help on Bob's film. The sound's okay, but what it really needs is some quality control. How'd you like a crack at assistant producer?"

"Me?" Denny said.

"Of course, you," Dorsey said. "You got a brain, right?"

"Al, I'm not sure that—"

"We're talking a major credit here," Dorsey said. "Take off for the afternoon and think about it, okay?"

Denny hesitated. "Okay," she said.

"Good," Dorsey said. "Good for both of you. Now let me talk alone with Chris."

Billy headed straight out the door, but Denny moved more slowly. She waited for Chris's okay, which he gave by nodding her out. With Denny and Billy gone, Dorsey walked to his refrigerator, pulled out a cherry spritzer, then closed the office door.

"Chris," he began. The name was delivered with a long sigh. Dorsey looked as if the mere sight of Chris was exhausting. "You got no intention of doing another *Raw Death*, do you?"

"It wouldn't be my first choice," Chris said.

"You're not even gonna stick around and help me keep R.I.P. sailing."

"I have other ideas," Chris told him.

"Right," Dorsey said. "The problem, of course, is I don't want what you want."

"You're making a mistake," Chris said.

"Hey, I don't have a corner on that, pal," Dorsey said. He began pacing the office—hands behind his back, head down and shaking. Chris wasn't sure, but he thought Dorsey was genuinely angry. "Suppose you're wrong—" Dorsey said, but he stopped himself. "No, suppose you're *right*. Suppose this farmer's a real hatchet man and he's out to rid the world of teenagers. Okay?"

"Okay," said Chris.

"Now is this the kind of person you really want to be pissing off?" He stopped pacing and jabbed Chris. "Do you really want to start a personal vendetta with someone who's sole enjoyment in life is cutting down the nation's high school enrollment?"

"If that's all he wants to do, I should be safe," Chris said.

"You're a fucking moron," Dorsey said. "Chris, I care about you, but you're going way too far this time, and I can't deal with it." He stared long and hard at Chris, trying to decide if there was anything else to discuss. Finally, he waved him toward the door. "Think over your options. Take a week, then get back to me."

Chris said okay.

"You should be ashamed of yourself," Dorsey said. "Letting some dumb-ass farmer outsmart you."

Chris left and closed the door. Dorsey's secretary looked up at him with her sad dog eyes. Meanwhile, Denny was on the street, waiting for him.

"What did he say?" Denny asked.

"The usual," Chris said.

Denny nodded, knowing what that meant. "Give me a call tonight," she said. "Let's talk it over. You've got credentials now, Chris. You don't have to rely on him."

"Sure," Chris said. "Thanks."

They headed in different directions—Denny down the street, Chris to his car.

He was uncertain what to do. He had a job, but he felt out of work; he had a movie, but it wasn't going to be made. About the most reliable thing in his life was his girlfriend, and by the end of dinner, that was gone.

Gwen met him at the usual restaurant, arriving twenty minutes late and looking like she'd only last another ten. They kissed and she sat down. She looked at him with a forced smile. "Sorry I took so long," she said. "I'm really busy right now."

"You got a job?"

"I got a *terrific* job. Remember what you told me about Doug Beyer? He had a slot open for chief editor. We hit it off, and I've been up to my ears in film clips."

"That's great," Chris said.

"Yeah," Gwen said. "The thing is, Chris, we really hit it off. I don't just mean professionally. We've been seeing a lot of each other."

Gwen reached out to comfort Chris, but Chris didn't need it. This wasn't merely par for the course; it was the only possible conclusion to what was a thoroughly disastrous week.

"Things weren't working out anyway, right?" she said.

"I know," Chris said.

"We didn't have the time for each other. That's what I

need right now in a relationship. Someone who can give me quality time. Someone who can commit to me.''

Chris listened. It was the opposite of what she had once told him, but Chris supposed a person's needs depended on the person he or she was seeing.

"You never wanted that anyway, did you?" she said. "I just don't see you in any kind of long-term relationship.''

"No," he said.

"Maybe in the future," she said. "Maybe if it was someone who could really take over your life. Someone who can absorb you. Anyway, I don't want dinner—I just wanted us to sit for a minute and clear this up." She glanced at her watch. "How did things go with you in Iowa?"

"I almost got killed," Chris said.

"That's awful," Gwen said. She stood up. "Chris, I'm really sorry. About everything.''

Gwen squeezed his hand, kissed his cheek and left the restaurant.

As for Chris, he opened the menu and decided on dinner. All things considered, he ate quite well. But then again, he had fewer worries. Not only was he free of a relationship, he finally realized what he had to do.

That alone made everything easier to swallow, from Dorsey to the food.

He left the restaurant at seven o'clock, which gave him three hours before the office would be empty. So Chris did the natural thing in his profession; he went to a movie. He sat in the theater, ate his popcorn, drank his soda, watched some forgettable something, and when it was after ten he went back to his car and drove crosstown.

The building was locked, but he was still a valued employee at Dorsey Productions, which meant he had all the keys. He unlocked the front door, went into the building, headed to the second-floor editing rooms and unlocked another door. He rubbed his hand against the wall and flicked on the overhead fluorescents, then he walked to a wooden desk. Inside a drawer was a knob key. Chris carried the key to a rear closet, unlocked this door and pulled a light chain. A bulb lit and Chris moved forward. In front of him were several shelves of 35mm and video equipment. On his left, hanging on nails, were battery packs, and to his right were tripods, balance blocks and other accessories.

Chris pulled out a video camera and a hand-held 35mm. He also selected a battery pack, a headset and a sound mixer. He pulled out everything he needed, then closed the door and went to a hall closet. He loaded a cardboard box with film stock and video cartridges, then dragged it all to the front door. That was almost everything; to finish his theft, Chris needed the Iowa footage. Dorsey had taken it, not because he planned to use the film, but because he had paid for it. "Company property," Dorsey had declared. Chris prayed Dorsey hadn't used the film to start a fire.

He searched the second floor, then tried the downstairs storage rooms. Finally, he pulled another spare key and went to the third floor. He turned the lock, opened the door and turned on the light.

He was standing in the alcove of Dorsey's office.

Chris walked through the secretary's station and to the back, where he flicked on another light. Before him was Dorsey's private office. Chris gave the room a long, sweeping look, then started his search. He looked under the desk, poked in the closet, checked behind the sofa, opened the file drawers. A thought crossed his mind. Suppose Dorsey had taken the footage home? Suppose he really had used it for kindling?

Chris looked in and around everything. He was even searching Dorsey's jackets when there was a knock on the open office door.

Chris looked up. He didn't say a word. He didn't have to.

"Try the refrigerator," Don Campo said.

Chris said. He went to the kitchen, squatted down and pulled the handle.

There it was: the footage, squeezed between two six-packs of spritzers.

"As long as you're down there," Campo said, "why don't you get us something to drink?"

TWENTY-TWO

"I came by to pick up some things and I saw the light," Campo said. Then, after a moment's thought, "That's a lie. When I heard what happened, I figured you'd come here."

"What did Al tell you?" Chris said.

"Not much," Campo said. "Not about you, I mean. A few things about me, like maybe I'd be doing a lot more work at R.I.P." Campo shook his head. "I should be jumping at this, but Al's nuts. There's no way me or anyone else can do the kind of job you do."

Chris finished pulling out his film, then he went to Dorsey's desk for some strapping tape. He bundled his cartridges, taped them together and headed for the door.

Campo stepped aside so Chris could leave. When Chris started downstairs, he picked up the equipment boxes and followed. "I heard what you did," Campo said. "Filming a killer and all that. I thought it was brilliant." They reached the car and Chris loaded the trunk. "I saw one of the tapes. The one with Meacham talking about those killer friends of his? I figured you were out in the middle of nowhere and couldn't do it, so I did a little digging, and there were some problems about ten years ago. Teenage girls, primarily. I mean, there's always problems somewhere, but it seemed to fit what he was saying—the general areas and how the girls kind of snapped up and out.''

"Did you tell Dorsey?" Chris said.

"Sure, but he'd already written you off." Campo reached down and helped Chris with the last of the boxes. "You know what you got yourself, don't you? You got a killing machine who's feeling rusty. You got a retired serial killer all set to come out of retirement." He grinned and slammed down the trunk hood. "I am so fucking jealous."

Chris walked to the front of the car and Campo followed.

"You're heading back tonight?"

"I've got a two A.M. flight," Chris said.

"That's soon," Campo said. "How about I keep you company?"

Chris couldn't say no, and Campo joined him in the front seat.

"I think you're doing the right thing," Campo said. "The way you guys left, there's no way he'll plan on a second visit."

Chris turned the ignition.

"It's just a question of timing, that's all," Campo said. "You gotta hope he hasn't finished business. Plus you gotta keep out of sight. Plus, if he does see you, you'll have to keep out of reach."

Chris shifted and turned onto the street. "What's Al got you doing?" he asked.

"Like I said, he's grooming me," Campo said. "But I've been doing my own stuff. I've almost got it set up, too. You wanna see? You got time?"

Campo pointed Chris off to the left, then had him drive west. They drove until they were near the Hollywood strip; then Campo had him turn down an alley and park.

"First lemme see if anyone's upstairs," Campo said.

Campo left the car and squeezed his way past a line of garbage cans. It looked like Campo was going to walk into a wall, but Chris soon saw where he was going. Behind the cans, in the shadows, was a steel door. Campo opened the door and stepped into a short, low hallway. There was some manner of dim lighting in the building. Campo leaned forward and peered up a staircase. Chris looked up the side of the building, but there were no windows. The building was a concrete bunker.

Campo waved to him. "Come on in," he called.

Chris left the car and met Campo in the lobby. The place was more than a hole in the wall; it had real holes. Campo reached inside one and hooked his finger on a low voltage wire. The wire was spliced to a tiny bulb. "When someone's in, the light's on," Campo said. "That way I know I shouldn't go up."

Even with the explanation it didn't make sense, but Chris said nothing. They walked upstairs and reached the second floor. This was the top of the building, and the stairway ended at two doors. One was old and bracketed with a padlock, but the other had been freshly painted. Indeed, it looked inviting.

Campo pushed it open and turned on a light.

The room was a film set. There were bright overhead lights and some well-meaning but cheap board furniture, including a bed, a table and a few chairs. As for the room itself, it was a shell of thin movable wallboards: the sort of material that could be stacked and stored within hours.

Chris looked around the room. Yes, it was definitely a film set. The one thing it lacked was space for a camera. Most sets were stages; this set, however, was enclosed.

Campo knew what he was wondering. "There's three of them," he said. "One at the far end of the room, one near the door and one over the bed."

Chris walked around. If you knew where to look, you could find them. At the far end of the room, its lens beside a cabinet, was one camera. Near the door, protected by a cage, was a second camera. And the third camera . . . Chris had a harder time finding that one. He searched the ceiling.

"Beside the light," Campo said.

Chris lay on the bed and guarded his eyes. The camera was right beside an overhead light. Chris noticed something else, too. The camera was running.

"Everything starts automatically," Campo said. "Anytime anyone comes in, it starts filming."

"I don't get it," Chris said.

"Come on," Campo said. "This is what I told you about. This is a cutting room."

Now Chris understood. He took a closer look at the details. The carpets, the bedsheets . . .

"If you're looking for blood, forget it," Campo said. "We haven't had that kind of luck yet. Just some late-night S and M, some other craziness. Word's getting out, though. A little while, you won't wanna be near this place."

Chris looked down. There was a trunk at the foot of the bed.

"There's a whip, handcuffs, some other things," Campo said. "Mostly it's what people leave behind."

"And the cameras really work?"

"Sure," Campo said. "Hey, you wanna see some tape? Some of this S and M stuff's not bad. I mean, it's no *Raw Death,* but maybe we could put out a *Raw Sex*?"

Chris couldn't believe the suggestion. He also knew what would happen the moment Dorsey heard it. "You're going to be a big success, Don," he said. "Al's gonna love you."

"You think so?" Campo said. "The biggest problem is the room. It's the same place, clip after clip. That's why everything's movable, so I can change the looks and get the cameras in different spots.

"I got one tape you'll like," Campo continued. "Remember Al's mad bomber? I tracked him down. I mean, we knew the area where he lived—we had the postage meter. But then I figured, if I was God, where would I hang out?" Chris listened, while Campo waited for a guess. "*Churches,*" he said. "So I go around to a bunch, put up notices about anyone interested in doing a number on Al and wait a few days. God contacts me, I contact God, and after one or two get-togethers, he agrees to join me on a midnight attack of R.I.P. headquarters." Campo grinned. "Except I have no intention of meeting him. I just tell him to come late and to come here, during the psycho hour." Campo reached in a pocket for his own set of keys and unlocked the second room. This was Campo's storage room. It was also where he kept the tapes. He left the room carrying a cartridge.

"You gotta take a look at this. I guarantee you, he'll never blow up cars again."

Chris refused the offer, even when Campo insisted. Instead, he left the room and turned off the light.

When they were back in the car, Chris faced his supposed protégé. "Listen to me," Chris said. "You're a nice guy, Don, but I told you once and I'll say it again—what you've got here is wrong."

"But I—"

"*Listen*," Chris said. "People are going to be hurt because of what you're doing. Can you understand that? This is wrong, this is illegal, and this is dangerous. This is very, very dangerous."

Campo stared back at Chris. He looked confused, wondering what was wrong. "So?" he said. "I figured that's why you'd like it."

Sunrise, driving to Hayden.

He was all too familiar with the route, but never before had it seemed quite so long, or so quiet and alone. At first Chris thought it was the early hour. In the winter and with the snow, there was only so much work that could be done on a farm. Without men in the fields and traffic on the road, the land seemed uninhabited—a road that sloped over deserts of cold and nothing else.

This could have been the reason, but it may have been the circumstances of his trip. Sneaking off with Dorsey's equipment, taking the trip in a near-empty plane, not telling anyone—aside from Campo—what he planned to do. He even tried some of the usual deep-cover tricks, like renting a beaten wreck and doing other small things to hide his identity.

His mood could have been due to the hour, or the circumstances, or both. Chris, however, suspected it was due to Meacham.

Whatever had happened before, matters had now been stripped down to the two of them. During the last trip, the two had become friends. Indeed, they had become more than friends—it had been a pact. And when Meacham had beaten him senseless in the forest, the pact had been made with real blood.

Meacham ended the friendship with a simple message: keep away. But Chris wasn't simply answering a challenge; Meacham had taken him to the brink and Chris had lived. While it had been terrifying, it had also made him feel invulnerable.

"Just watch yourself out there," Campo had warned. "If he really thinks you're out of town, things are going to happen fast."

Chris understood. Indeed, he wouldn't even stay in Hayden. He drove until he reached the Marsh township, then he stopped at a guest house and checked in, paying with cash and using a false name.

Once in his room, Chris closed the door, unpacked, then slept. He would need this sleep, because he'd probably be awake all night. He stayed indoors until mid-afternoon, then did a last check of his equipment. He loaded the camera, checked the battery pack and finally loaded the car, heading for the farm.

It was odd driving through Hayden. He hadn't been gone long enough to lose a sense of the town; on the other hand, he had never really been a part of Hayden and whatever notion of place he'd felt had disappeared. In just a matter of days, Hayden had been reduced, at least emotionally, to little more than a shoot location. The difference, Chris supposed, was the film.

He left Hayden and continued to the farm.

Chris parked behind one of the fields. Then, with the sun almost down, he followed a foot path that led across the Donnelly property and to the Meacham house—climbing a fence, banking up a hill, bringing Chris back and around the house. Finally, he crouched low and rested, not from fear, but to be certain no one had seen him and no one was outdoors. It was dark now, which made it colder but safer. Chris took one more minute to gain composure, then opened his coat. Inside was the sound mixer, the headset and wiring. He prayed everything was still in place, then dug his fingers into the snow. It took only a moment to find the cable. He pulled it free—in fact, almost pulled it too hard. The cable snapped out of the snow, and Chris thought immediately of the second-floor transmitter. But the gaffer's tape held. With greater care, he screwed in the connectors, turned on the power and put on the headset.

Inside the house, William Meacham told his wife to stop bothering him. There was, after all, no more time for small talk. Soon Todd would be home and then Meacham would be going out for the evening.

TWENTY-THREE

AT about three in the afternoon, Eric Copley left his weekend job, put on his gloves, crossed the parking lot, then stopped. Someone had smashed his front windshield. In fact, the brick was lying on the hood. As he picked at the glass, he was struck across the head. Instead of heading home, he lay on the parking lot pavement, unconscious and bleeding.

As for Todd, he wondered if one pass was enough. But the purpose wasn't to kill Copley, just hurt him. With the job done, he drove to a pay phone and made the first of his calls.

"I'd like to speak with Sarah please," he said. Then, "Sarah, this is Todd. I was wondering how your evening was shaping up? . . . Well, maybe if your plans change we can get together. Would that be okay? . . . No? I understand . . . Okay, I'll try a little later. If you're in, you're in."

Todd hung up and headed home. He drove slowly, because on days like this, he always felt like he was looking at things for the last time. He even made a point of pulling off the road and visiting the Donnelly pond. By now, the ice was again solid. If ever the pond had been a sinkhole to oblivion, it had once again been capped and sealed. Now a new hole would have to open, and Todd could only guess where. In another pond? On a dark street? At a knoll in the woods?

At the drive-in?

"Todd?" Meacham called.

Todd was home now. He heard his father but ignored him, going up to his room and dropping on the bed.

"Todd," Meacham said. He stood at the doorway and watched his son. "Did you take care of business, Todd?"

Todd couldn't look at him, but he nodded. When Meacham saw this, he entered the room and closed the door.

"And what else have you been doing today?" Meacham asked. He reached in the closet for his belt.

Todd didn't answer. There was no need; all of this was too familiar.

"We're going out tonight," Meacham said. "You know that."

Yes. Todd knew.

"You hate the hell out of me for this, don't you? You hate me for whipping you and taking you out at night and about a million other things. You wish your own father was dead."

Todd simply listened.

"All right," Meacham said. He closed the bedroom door, crossed the room and pulled the curtains. "Let's get out your anger."

Meacham pulled back the blankets on Todd's bed. Todd stared at the camouflage of stains. He was still staring when his father threw down the belt and said, "Take it. Let's see how much of a man you are."

Meacham unbuttoned his shirt and laid down. His back was sliced with scars.

"Go on," said Meacham. "Get to work."

Todd picked up the belt, moved beside his father, knotted the leather in a grip, weighed the buckle in a gentle, easy swing . . .

"I said do it," Meacham ordered.

Todd obeyed. He did hate his father, and he did have the rage, and he swung around and lashed at Meacham, trying as hard as he could to get that buckle into the skin. He struck again and again, and when he saw blood, he got even wilder. But it didn't mean anything unless he heard his father cry. Todd needed to hear the sound of pain. A gasp, a scream . . .

A long wound opened and Todd struck only at this scar. It made a mess, but Todd was winning. For the first time ever, he saw his father flinch. Todd was getting older and stronger now. In a few more years, he could overpower William Meacham. If he found the strength, Todd might do it now. Whip and tear at the spine until he cut the nerves and his father was paralyzed. They'd be stuck in the house forever. Todd, and his father and his mother.

William Meacham grunted. Todd heard it. Todd hammered down and his father again grunted, and then gasped. His breath quickened, and . . .

And Todd slid down on his knees, exhausted. The belt slipped from his hands.

His father lay on the bed for almost a full minute—something else new. He lay there, almost in shock, then managed to lift himself. With great care, he reached the sitting position. Then, with a long, careful flexing, he regained his composure. He looked at Todd, who was still on the floor.

"You're feeling good now?" Meacham asked.

Todd wouldn't look up. When Meacham reached out and touched him, Todd flinched. The boy expected to be hurt.

"Hold still," Meacham said.

Todd obeyed.

Meacham stretched a bit further and brushed Todd's hair. He was gentle, fatherly.

"You're getting stronger, Todd," Meacham said. "I don't know how much longer we can do this."

Todd was crying. He looked up and held onto his father's hand.

"Remember when your mother and I first found you?" Meacham said. "I don't think you were seven."

Todd nodded.

"Helen and I were traveling all the time then," Meacham said. "We could have picked anyone, but we picked you.

That's because I knew you were meant to be my son. Just like Helen was meant to be your mother.''

Todd said nothing.

''We're special that way, Todd,'' Meacham said. ''That's why we do so much for each other.'' Meacham touched Todd's cheek. ''You think maybe you can do your father one more favor? Think you can do that much for him?''

Todd wiped his eyes. Meacham went back to the closet and took the towel. He started wiping his back, but the cuts were too deep and long. He struggled for a moment, doing his best to rub the towel over his spine.

Then Todd took the towel and wiped Meacham's back.

Later, in the kitchen, the boy made his second phone call. ''Sarah, this is Todd again . . . I know, I heard. Sounds lucky he's alive . . . No, I understand. But I just thought you might want to go out anyway. . . All right . . . No, I understand. I said I understand, but maybe if you're feeling better . . .''

After a few minutes, the conversation ended. ''She doesn't want to go out,'' Todd told his father.

''Let's go to the car,'' Meacham said.

They walked to the front door. Helen Meacham was in the living room, watching television. ''We're leaving,'' Meacham told her.

The words meant nothing to her. Meacham and Todd headed outside. Meacham kept quiet until Todd was in his pickup; then he waited for Todd to roll down his side window. Meacham leaned inside and talked in a low voice.

''Go to her house,'' Meacham said.

''But—''

''You're going to go up to her door and demand she go out with you. And she will, I guarantee it. That's what these girls want, Todd. They want you to take charge.''

''Yes, sir,'' Todd said.

''Other than that, things stay the same,'' Meacham said. ''All except for one thing. I'll tell you that later.''

Todd nodded.

''And Todd?'' Meacham said.

He stared at his father.

"You're a good son," Meacham said.

Todd rolled up the window.

There was only so much Chris could hear and for only so long. He heard the conversation in Todd's room, and he heard the whipping, but the episode only confused him. The sounds didn't quite match what he imagined. In short, this would be one of many times he'd wish Billy or Denny could have been filming. Still, no matter how confusing things seemed, the basic message was clear—Meacham and Todd were heading out tonight.

As soon as Todd and Meacham headed downstairs, Chris unplugged his equipment and ran across the field. He should have already been at the car, but Chris had made his first mistake: letting himself get absorbed by the conversation. Now he tried making up for lost time by running along the foot trail, but it was so damn hard in all that snow. After forty feet, he had to slow down, rest and catch his breath. The air just choked him, because the cold went straight into his lungs.

Chris finally reached the car. He turned the ignition and angled onto the main road. He drove until Meacham's driveway was just within sight, then again pulled off. He was on the side of the road that led away from town. His gamble was that Meacham would start the evening heading into Hayden; this way, as Meacham pulled out, Chris could simply pick up the rear.

He was right. Meacham slowed, turned and headed for Hayden. Chris should have felt in control of the situation and he almost was.

He just wasn't prepared for Todd and Meacham to be in separate vehicles.

Of course when Kathleen Donnelly died, the two had also traveled separately, but Chris had forgotten this. Now, alone, he wondered how to handle the situation. He was still wondering when Meacham's car blinked a right turn and Todd's car blinked for the left.

Chris's instinct was to follow Todd, but common sense said stick with Meacham. William, after all, was the key player. No matter what Todd did, in the end, Meacham would spill the blood.

Chris made his decision; when he reached the intersection, he followed the father.

They drove through Hayden, and Meacham headed onto the north route. They traveled several miles from town before Meacham signaled another right and veered into a driveway.

Chris passed the road. Meacham had entered a drive-in theater.

Chris drove back and paid his way into the place. There were perhaps forty cars in the lot. Chris spotted Meacham, then parked several rows back. In another half hour, the movie would begin. The question now was whether Meacham was here to waste time, or if there was a reason for the detour.

Chris found out before the start of the movie. Traffic was still entering the lot, and Chris saw Todd's pickup turn toward an aisle. It didn't stop near Meacham; instead, Todd followed the flow of traffic, finally parking at the far end of the lot, near the exit driveway. Chris was to the front and side of Todd, and he turned to face him.

Todd wasn't alone. Beside him, in the passenger seat, was a teenage girl. Chris stared until he remembered to keep an eye on Meacham. Fortunately, Meacham hadn't moved. He stayed in his car, his attention on the screen, not paying attention to his son or anyone else. When the movie started, Meacham reached for the sound box and heater, but that was it. Chris did the same, and a fierce, chilling wind rushed in his car. He'd remember the wind later, and how everyone huddled in the cold, turning into anonymous bundles of clothes. For now, he rolled the window up and turned the heater on high.

For the next two hours, Chris watched the Meachams, while the Meachams watched the movie. Chris spent the entire time waiting for them to make a move, but nothing happened—at least until intermission. Then people raised their collars and braved the cold. Some went to the food stand while others headed to the restrooms located at the base of the movie screen.

When William Meacham left his car, he went to the restrooms.

He turned up the collar of his coat and pulled on a dark knit cap. Like everyone else, he was an anonymous, lumbering hulk heading for the toilets, and he was barely in line when another lumbering figure approached. This time it was Todd. He also entered the restroom, and Chris stayed in his car, filming the whole thing, wondering what was happening. Were they exchanging information? Was Todd giving him something, or was the reverse true? Or was this just some trick—a chance to duck out of the lot and do their damage elsewhere?

Perhaps five minutes passed, and then Meacham left the restroom. He rushed back to his car, his head against the wind, his body huddled forward, as if there was something smothered in his arms.

As if he was hiding something, Chris thought. Indeed, he was so intent on protecting his prize, all Chris saw was the top of Meacham's cap.

Then came Todd. He just caught a glimpse of the boy's coat. He saw Todd as he squeezed past some other men and turned his back to the wind. Like Meacham, Todd had his head down and his arms locked, but Chris still couldn't imagine what they carried. Weapons? Something else?

He turned his attention back to William Meacham. In fact, he was still watching the father when Chris heard the start of an engine. He turned and saw Todd's pickup turning for the exit. Chris sat up, glancing back and forth. Todd was leaving, so who did he follow this time: did he stay with William or tail Todd?

Chris was struggling when Meacham left his car—again bent forward, this time weaving his way toward the concessions. Chris had to make up his mind: go or stay?

He glanced back. Todd and the girl had left the theater lot.

He looked ahead. Meacham had stopped by another car. Inside the car were two young girls.

Chris decided to stay.

Meacham made conversation, and Chris picked up the camera and filmed. It was frustrating because he couldn't get an angle on him, but he could film the girls. Meacham talked for a minute, then continued toward the food stand. He bought something, went into the building, exited out a far door and disappeared into a playground. Chris waited a moment, then finally decided to follow him. He opened the door, and as the wind rushed at him, Chris turned and back-stepped to the concession stand. He walked about the building, trying to approach the playground from its rear. There was only a footpath about the backside—the building was almost pressed against the lot fence. Chris thought Meacham may have actually gone over the fence and left the lot. Maybe his game was to get some witnesses to say he'd been at the theater, then sneak out, do his murder.

It made sense. He wasn't behind the building and he wasn't in the playground. Chris had made a complete circle of the place and there was no sight of him, at least until he looked back at Meacham's car. There were two people in it. The headlights turned on and so did the ignition.

Chris glanced at the car with the girls. There was now only one, sitting alone.

Meacham turned his vehicle and headed for the exit. As for Chris, he ran to his car, freed the speaker, started the engine, shifted and headed out of the lot. He reached the main road in time to see Meacham heading north, away from Hayden and toward the open farmland. Chris followed, keeping as much distance as he could, all the time remembering one thing—the last time he had followed Meacham into the open farmlands, Meacham had taken him to the woods.

The last time, Chris had almost been killed.

Meacham slowed, made a turn and headed onto the back road of a farm. Chris pulled over and watched the car bank over a hill.

This was it, Chris thought. This was death time.

Chris sat there, mesmerized. He thought he'd be ready for this. After weeks of tracking and waiting—after leading Meacham into this moment—he should have been prepared.

Chris should have driven up the road with a kind of single-minded dedication.

But he hesitated. All of a sudden, he realized he wasn't ready. He never had been. Meacham was a killer; Chris was nothing—a camera-carrying shithead. For Meacham, this was life; for Chris . . . what—an obsession? He had never before killed; he couldn't now, even in self-defense. Meanwhile, up and over the hill, that was the land of killers. That was the place where Meacham had gone, and now Chris would have to go.

Chris stared at the road.

He should have saved her at the drive-in. He should have stopped all this when he had a chance.

But he took a breath, turned off his headlights and turned onto the road. A moment later, he was up and over the hill.

And when he reached the top of the hill, he stopped.

About a half mile ahead was the car—the engine idling, the doors open, the indoor lights on. The car was empty, but that wasn't what surprised Chris.

What surprised Chris was the house.

Meacham and the girl were at the front of a home. They stayed until the front door of the house opened and a person appeared in the doorway. Words were exchanged, the girl went inside, the door closed . . .

Nothing. Meacham stepped from the door and went back to his car.

Chris didn't understand. What had he done? What had happened?

They were good questions, but not for the moment; Chris had to turn his car and get back to the main road. He tried once, but it was dangerous. There was a better chance of getting stuck in the snow than making the turn. Instead, he drove backward, weaving until he slapped into the snowbanks.

He could see the headlights from Meacham's car. The light topped the hill, and soon Meacham would also be at the crest. Chris turned the steering wheel and pressed the accelerator. The final stretch was almost straight, but the road itself was patched with ice. Chris skidded into another snowbank and . . .

Meacham was over the top. Chris saw the car bank and start the last half of the road.

Chris took his chances. He shifted forward, cut hard and tried to turn. The front tires again caught ice, but this time it worked for him, making the turn tighter, once more slamming him in the snow, but at least the car pointed for the main road. He accelerated, because with the car in the right direction, he could still make it out before Meacham saw him. He shifted and pressed the pedal.

The car wouldn't move.

Chris rocked the car. He leaned forward, slamming his fist against the dashboard, using all his weight to get in motion.

Behind him, the light became stronger. Meacham had reached the straight stretch. A few more seconds, and there would be no more secrets.

Chris hit hard in reverse. It felt like he was going to climb the snow. He thought, with a little extra heave, he could make it.

Then the lights were on him.

First the lights flashed against the back of his car, and then they reflected off the mirrors. He guarded his eyes and sank deep in his seat. This is going to be it, he thought. Meacham had caught him.

The car slowed. By the time he reached Chris, Meacham was driving at a crawl. Chris lay low, his head to the seat, but all Meacham had to do was lean and he'd see him. And Meacham was doing exactly that. Chris felt it. He listened, expecting the car to stop, waiting for Meacham to finish him.

Meacham never stopped.

Chris raised his head and saw Meacham turn on the main road. He was heading back toward town.

Chris opened the door and threw his coat in front of one of the tires. Once more he accelerated . . . gently . . . gently . . .

At last, he rocked onto the road.

As for Meacham, he was still in sight. Chris wasted no time closing the distance. If Meacham knew about him, fine. If not, fine. The only thing that mattered now was finishing the evening. And if Meacham was in control, what else was new? Meacham had been in control since the first murder.

They drove through town and made a left, heading back toward the Meacham farm. And, in fact, this was their destination. When Meacham turned up the driveway, Chris pulled off the road, grabbed his camera and followed on foot. Maybe the darkness would keep him out of sight, but it didn't matter. Meacham was putting on a show. Chris saw the man leave his car, open the front door and go inside the house. Chris staggered the final few steps to the house. He walked past the windows and looked for a clear view into the house. He stopped near the living room window. Inside was Mrs. Meacham, still by the television. Meacham was brushing himself off. He walked into the room, turned down his collar and took off his cap.

Chris stared.

He was following the wrong Meacham.

Todd unbuttoned his father's coat. He unraveled the scarf, tossed the hat on a chair and sat beside his mother. He bent close to her ear, whispering to her, touching her hand.

Mrs. Meacham nodded and took his hand. She kissed it.

Todd stood and headed upstairs.

Chris backed away from the window. He slipped, fell hard on the ice, but managed to protect the camera. Once on his feet, Chris ran for the barn. He stumbled for the ladder, climbed to the loft and fell beside the upper window. He pressed his eye to the view finder and zoomed in.

The curtains were down—left that way by the boy's father. Todd, however, soon fixed this. After turning on the lights, Todd's shadow grew against the blinds, and then they were raised. Todd lifted the window and looked up at the sky. He held this position for a long moment before turning back to his room and sitting at his desk. He took out a sheet of paper and began writing. Chris tried zooming, but the note was out of view. Instead, he focused on Todd.

Todd was calm. He finished his note, put down the pen, left the room and within a minute returned. Todd closed the door and walked to the window.

In his hand was William Meacham's gun.

Todd put the gun in his mouth and pulled back the hammer.

He was staring straight into the camera.

He stared at Chris.

Chris could see the boy relaxing. He saw his face smooth and saw the mouth struggle for a smile.

Chris dropped the camera. He scrambled for the ladder, hopped down two of the rungs and fell the remaining eight feet. He was on his feet and heading for the house when he heard the gun fire. He slammed open the front door and made it to Todd's room.

The boy was on the floor, his head tilted back, the blood pooled under his head.

He was on the floor, flipped completely about, and his eyes were still focused on Chris.

TWENTY-FOUR

THE deputy sat by the dining table, listening to Chris and taking notes.

"I tried telling you," Chris said. "I told Rawlings that Todd was in trouble, that Meacham was a killer, that the whole family was crazy."

The deputy kept writing. He had already made his phone calls—not only for the ambulance, but to the state police. As for Todd's mother, the deputy had tried talking to her, but it was impossible. She said nothing and apparently heard nothing.

He made the calls and, after radioing for help, put out a report for the father. The deputy still had only the vaguest notion of the evening, and so far no one knew who Meacham had kidnapped—assuming he *had* kidnapped someone—but they knew what kind of car he was driving, and they knew his license plate. That would be enough. There simply weren't that many roads Meacham could travel.

"I ran for the house the moment I saw Todd had a gun," Chris said. "I didn't want him dying. That wasn't the idea."

The deputy went to the window and looked at his patrol car. He wondered if Meacham really was a murdering maniac. He also wondered if he should take the rifle from the trunk.

"I've got film," Chris said. "I've got film and sound tape. We heard a lot. We had microphones all over the house."

The deputy turned and faced him. "Microphones?"

Chris led him upstairs and located the transmitter. The deputy handled the device while Chris found one of the wireless omnis.

"Are you out of your mind?" the deputy asked him.

"That's what the sheriff said," Chris answered, "and where the hell is he?"

"He'll be here soon," the deputy said.

He wasn't, but it didn't matter; once the state police arrived, it was out of the deputy's hands. Todd and Helen Meacham were taken out of the house, and while Chris repeated his story, the deputy showed a trooper the message he had found on the desk. "Look in the bushes," it read. One of the troopers asked if he had searched the bushes.

"Are you kidding?" the deputy said. "Go out there alone?"

Another hour passed, and even more police arrived. So had some locals. No one had sighted Meacham, but there was a report on a missing girl: Sarah Boden, last seen with Todd Meacham.

Chris was in the kitchen, drinking a glass of water, when he noticed the cellar door. He stared at it, then finally tapped an officer and pointed. "Can you open that?"

The trooper checked with a superior, and soon there was a crowd in the kitchen. No one wasted time with a key. One man kicked at the lock and the door frame shattered. In a moment, they were all downstairs.

Boxes. Mrs. Meacham had been telling the truth; nothing but boxes and an old furnace.

But Chris knew why Meacham had kept the door padlocked. When the police opened the cardboard flaps, they found old clothes, old photographs . . .

They found memories, Chris thought. Down here, stored and locked away, was the family history. Meacham had loved recalling his nightmares, and these were all the reminders he'd ever need. How he found Todd. How he found Helen. What he had done before kidnapping them. To whom he had done it . . .

Two hours later, someone shouted from the hillside.

Chris joined the long walk across the field. The man on the hill met them halfway, then brought everyone to the bushes. He pulled back the branches and pointed to the ground. The ground had been dug out, and there was a shovel beside a hole. Several of the men lowered their flashlights.

They discovered the top of a head. Someone picked up the shovel and carefully dug out more of the dirt.

They uncovered the body of a young boy.

"Who is it?" an officer asked. "Anyone recognize him?" He looked to Chris.

Chris shook his head.

"Do you know anything about this?" the officer asked.

Chris took a closer look at the child. He bent down, just to be sure they had been right . . . that it was a boy. He brushed back the hair and stared at the face. The child couldn't have been more than eight.

"It doesn't make sense," he said. "Meacham killed teenagers." Chris brushed dirt off the boy's cheek. He was almost tender in his touch. "He killed young girls."

Soon, while the others kept digging, Chris was again in the house.

Two more hours . . . sunrise.

"The second girl Todd picked up was just a friend," one of the men said. "She wanted to go home and Todd obliged. Nothing else."

Chris listened.

"A lot of what happened last night seems to have been for your benefit," the trooper said.

"How did they know I was here?" Chris said.

The trooper shrugged. "He must've seen you."

"I don't think so," Chris said.

"He must've," the trooper said. "Unless someone told him."

Chris thought about this. Had someone warned Meacham? A friend might have seen Chris at the airport or at the guest house. Someone like that could have warned him, except the connection between Chris and Meacham had never been clear to anyone.

So maybe no one had warned Meacham. Or maybe, instead of trying to protect Meacham, someone was out to get Chris? But apart from the Meachams, Chris had no enemies. He hadn't taken anyone else's picture; he hadn't robbed anyone. And even if there was bad blood, the bottom line was no one knew he had returned to Hayden.

Or rather, no one *here* knew.

Chris sat on the patio steps and watched the sun come over the eastern farmlands. He sat there and watched the colors, and wondered when the sun would rise over L.A.

He thought of all this, and he wondered one last time if he knew anyone who was angry. Was there someone Chris had pissed off? Someone who could guess where Chris was going? Someone Chris had annoyed and robbed, and who didn't normally like spending money, but could spare the change for one long-distance phone call, especially if it meant screwing Chris's chances at a movie?

Someone who could do all this, without even thinking twice of what it might mean to a teenage girl and a suicidal boy?

He stopped wondering. The answer had become too obvious.

Amazing, Chris thought. Once again, Dorsey had surprised him.

It was now early morning. Chris explained he had been up all night. He begged the police for a chance to go back to his room and rest, promising not to run off, more than happy to have an escort.

The promise was unnecessary. He was a witness to the bloodshed, not a suspect, and they simply asked him to come by headquarters later in the morning. Chris already intended to do so, wanting to know what happened to Meacham and the girl. After nine hours, they still hadn't been found.

He walked down the driveway and to his car. He settled in the seat, made a U-turn and headed back toward town. As he made the bend, he passed the Donnelly pond. By afternoon, that would also be surrounded by people. Police would be breaking the shell of ice and searching the water, just in case there were any clues Billy may have missed in his midnight dive. Chris headed into Hayden, made the turn and passed the diner. He wondered what stories were starting to pass through town? He thought of Julie and wondered what she would think of him after all this—would she consider him a hero or villain? And what about Meacham? How many people would be surprised? How many wouldn't?

Finally, thirty minutes after leaving the farm, he reached the guest house. The hours were catching up on him. He left the camera equipment in the car and entered through the back of the house. He had one of the ground-floor rooms, which was fortunate; he was too tired for stairs. He opened the door, went inside, turned on the light . . .

And he stopped. He stared, backed away, and finally, he screamed.

The place was a wreck. Whatever Chris had left in the room was destroyed. His clothes had been torn apart, and as for the film cartridges, some had been set on fire, but most appeared to have been stolen.

That was all terrible, but the scream was for the bed.

On the mattress, his body stretched out, his wrists handcuffed to the bedpost, his ankles tied with Chris's celluloid film, was Tom Rawlings. There was a bullet hole in his forehead, and above the sheriff, scrawled in blood across the wall, was what had become a password between Chris and Meacham. A single word.

"Pow."

PART FOUR

TWENTY-FIVE

"I don't know what you're talking about, Chris. Me, phone a fucking farmer? That's too crazy for an answer. But even if I did . . . *You* ran off with *my* equipment, *you* rob me of *my* property . . . Which is more of a crime, smart guy? What would a court say?"

This was the conversation Chris *didn't* have with Al Dorsey. It might have happened if Chris had gone to the office; instead, he phoned and left a message on the answering machine. "Al, I just wanted you to know that because of what you did, a girl is probably dead and a boy killed himself."

He hung up. Chris doubted it would mean much to Dorsey, but at least it had been said, and at least it brought a semiofficial end to Chris's days at R.I.P. Now, he had time for other matters—like thinking about survival and figuring out when Meacham would kill him.

Try to kill him, Chris corrected.

Something was certain to happen. That had been the point of Rawlings's murder—to tease Chris and give him a hint of things to come. And while the police suggested other reasons for Rawlings's death—in particular, the idea Meacham was only trying to set him up to look like a killer—any hope had disappeared the moment Chris realized Meacham had found Chris's checkbook and torn away the top of a single check. Chris understood immediately. Of all the things he could have taken, Meacham had left the room with a tiny bit of knowledge. He had left with Chris's address.

Now back in L.A.—without a job, without his film, without anything, except a death threat—Chris remembered the night he followed Todd over a hill and worried about getting stranded in the land of the dead. At last, Chris understood: he had entered that land long ago. And now, to get out, he had to first get past Meacham.

Friends tried to help. Edgar Denton pulled a few strings and had a patrol car make regular passes by his house. Occasionally, an officer would come to his door and ask if Chris had seen anything, but if he had, wouldn't it be a little late for help? Someone once explained the visits weren't for him; they were for Meacham—a show of cops to scare him off. Well, maybe. But a better possibility was catching Meacham before he reached L.A. Or, if he reached L.A. catching Meacham on the street. Denton had distributed his picture. A stranger in a strange city, Meacham could easily get lost, or catch the attention of a patrolman, or get short on cash and screw up a robbery, or . . .

Chris stopped himself. All the possibilities were right and wrong at the same time. They were right for someone else, but wrong for Meacham. Meacham wasn't the stranger in a strange land; the stranger was Chris. Chris had blundered into Meacham's territory.

Denny visited at lunchtime. She knocked, and after looking through the peephole, Chris opened the door. She came inside and regarded his apartment less like a place to live than avoid. Chris had only been back a few days, and already his home was turning into shadowland.

"How're you doing?" Denny asked.

"I talked with Denton today," Chris said. "He's getting me a gun permit."

Denny wasn't thrilled with that development. For her, guns weren't the solution; the solution was moving. As she understood matters, Chris could leave California without a forwarding address and Meacham could spend a lifetime trying to find him. It was so simple, but Chris acted like

L.A. was worth a battle. He talked like a fight was inevitable, and that Meacham wasn't just a killer, but a demon god who could sniff and snuff him out, no matter where he traveled.

"Want to go outside with me?" asked Denny. "I was thinking of going for a walk."

Chris agreed and got prepared. He went to his bedroom, pulled off his shirt, put on a t-shirt, then walked back into the living room with one of Denton's presents—a bulletproof vest. She couldn't believe he was in possession of such a thing. Chris saw the look. He put the vest on and reached for a fresh shirt.

"Denton's been great," Chris said. "If I live through this, I'm going to owe him big."

"You'll live through this," Denny said.

They left the apartment. At least Chris lived on the second floor; this spared him worrying about Meacham breaking through a window. Also, with the staircase outside the house, Meacham couldn't hide by the door without being seen from the street.

They walked to the main boulevard, and Denny tried to relax him. She held his arm, led him to an open air café, sat him down and made him face the sun. She was charming, concerned, sisterly . . . She was, in short, everything one could ask of a friend.

Chris wouldn't give her a chance. His concentration was always to her left or right . . . in all directions, really. And the more he looked about, the more he frustrated Denny. Chris as good as ignored her. Denny wondered if this had been the story with his girlfriends.

"You think he's going to kill you in broad daylight?" Denny finally asked.

Chris didn't know. If Chris had *any* idea what Meacham would do, he would have a chance.

"If you aren't going to leave L.A., then you've got to come up with another plan," Denny said. "You can't spend forever locked in that apartment."

"It's not forever," Chris said.

"Chris, you don't *know* that."

"He'll show up," Chris said. "I've been right about everything else."

"Maybe this time you're wrong," Denny said. "Maybe he's still in Iowa. Maybe he's hiding out with his brother."

Chris eyed her, curious. "Brother?"

"Didn't Todd visit an uncle?" Denny said.

Now Chris understood. "That wasn't an uncle," he said. "It was an old friend of Meacham's. Someone he used to go traveling with." He paused a moment, remembering Meacham's stories. "He's gone now anyway."

Denny didn't care. "That's just one possibility," she said. "The bottom line is if you don't get yourself a life, he doesn't have to show up. You're already good as dead."

Chris laughed at her. "Believe me, there's a difference." He dropped his napkin on the table. Denny paid for the meal and followed him out of the café. They walked less than a block before Chris stopped.

"Wait one minute," Chris said, and ducked into a store. They were at a novelty shop. Among the post cards and t-shirts was a night stick, a collection of Ninja stars and other weapon paraphernalia. She waited almost ten minutes before he came out with a full bag.

"You want to kill Meacham with a Ninja star?" Denny said. "God, isn't there something else we can do?"

"I wouldn't mind stopping by the hardware store," Chris said.

"For a chainsaw?" Denny said.

"For a deadbolt," he said.

They went to the store and Chris bought what he needed. Afterward, Denny made a last effort to relax Chris; she hooked his arm and led him to a movie. But sitting in the dark among strangers wasn't the best idea. Halfway through the film, Chris excused himself. Denny waited twenty minutes before looking for him. She found Chris sitting on the loge stairs, his back to the wall, his hands tight on one of the Ninja stars.

Denny was exhausted. "Maybe we should go home," she said.

When they reached the apartment, she refused to go

inside; the place was too dark and deadly. She kissed his cheek and said, "You don't need anything else?"

"Not today," he said.

"You have my phone number?"

"I think I can remember it."

"Write it down."

"No," Chris said. "I don't want him knowing my friends."

Denny stared at him. "You got rid of your address book?"

"I bought a new one," Chris said.

"Does the new one have any numbers?"

"Just one," Chris said. "Dorsey's."

Denny could almost smile. She squeezed his hand and left. When she turned down the street, Chris looked past her and to a police car. The driver rolled down the window and waved at him. Chris waved back.

Then he closed the door. He spent the next hour installing his new deadbolt.

It would be more than a month before Meacham arrived.

During that time, the police visits stopped and the visits and calls from friends almost stopped. Occasionally he made a trip to the store; otherwise, it was safer inside the apartment.

Most of his time was spent in the living room. Since this was the only room with a door and window, it was also the only room that needed guarding. He kept the gun on the coffee table, and in case Meacham caught him away from the gun, Chris left weapons elsewhere. A baseball bat beside the door, a hunting knife in the bathroom, a crowbar in the kitchen . . .

Campo had tried arguing against this strategy. "You place that shit around the house and you're asking for trouble," he warned.

Campo was the only one of his "friends" who showed regularly. Chris liked to think it was concern, but Campo was more fascinated than caring.

"When Meacham breaks in, he's going to have as good a

chance as you at that stuff. Anytime you reach for a weapon, he can get there first. You're setting yourself up, Chris. Better off carrying one thing and throwing away the rest.''

''You're wrong,'' Chris said. ''When Meacham breaks in, he's going to catch me off guard. I'll probably be in the shower or changing my clothes.''

''So shower with your gun,'' Campo said. ''Never take it off, not even in the shower. When Meacham breaks in, you can pop him.''

''Suppose I forget to carry it?'' Chris said. ''Besides, once Meacham's inside, he's not going to care about my crap. He'll have his own.''

They argued back and forth, their opinions formed by different theories, always agreeing on one thing: no matter what the precautions, Meacham was coming, and Meacham would break in. That was absolutely certain.

Still, Campo helped him set up a best defense—a video camera braced over the front door and wired to the TV. As the new head of R.I.P. Productions, Campo had taken the liberty of borrowing the necessary equipment. Campo had also wired the staircase. Now anytime a visitor climbed the stairs, a buzzer went off in the living room. And when the guest reached the front door, Chris could turn on the tube and see the face.

''Incidentally, I know a kid who'll do your shopping,'' Campo said. ''For ten bucks a trip, he'll get your groceries. That way you can cut down on the risks.''

''Does he carry a weapon?''

''Hey, he's gonna buy your groceries, not be your bodyguard,'' Campo said. ''Why? Do you want a bodyguard?''

''I don't think so,'' Chris said.

''I don't think so either. Meacham would just wait until your money dried up, then he'd break in.''

Campo's last visit was three days before the big event. He brought over a deck of cards, tried getting Chris to play poker and ended up playing solitaire. Weeks had gone by, and despite Campo's invitations, Chris stayed on his couch, stretched out, his eyes focused absolutely nowhere. Campo flipped over his cards and took turns playing his game and staring at Chris. "You're nowhere near your gun," Campo warned him. "What if he came in right now? What would you do?"

Chris said nothing. Campo couldn't tell if he was thinking or sleeping or dead.

"He's wearing you down," Campo said. "That guy knows what he's doing. You gotta keep yourself in shape, Chris. You gotta stay awake."

"I am awake," Chris said.

"No, you're not. You're drifting off. He's burying you before you've stopped breathing."

"I'm okay," Chris said.

"You're *dead*."

"I'm okay," Chris said again.

Campo stayed a little longer, then collected his cards and left the apartment. Once outside, he closed the door. The two deadbolts automatically locked. Campo looked up; the camera was automatically filming his face. He walked down the steps; an electric eye automatically set off a buzzer.

It was all automatic—everything set up to take care of a comatose patient.

Campo had to hand it to Meacham. Meacham had waited, and now Chris was his for the taking. Campo looked out toward the street, as if he would find Meacham in the shadows. Campo would have loved finding him. He would have loved asking Meacham a simple question: why was Meacham even bothering with Chris?

What was the pleasure in killing a corpse?

TWENTY-SIX

THE buzzer went off about midnight.

Chris was awake when it happened. He was lying on the sofa, not quite asleep, not quite awake, in the same hibernation that had become a lifestyle. Perhaps for an hour or two, he managed real sleep; the rest of the time, his mind was in a vague and shifting world. Indeed, everything was so unsteady that Chris didn't quite believe the buzzer. He didn't even trust the image on his television. Finally, however, he understood.

Meacham, he thought. He's here.

In fact, he was outside the door, his hands working on the knob. Chris heard the scratching. He sat up and looked away from the television and to his door.

He saw the steel tip of a screwdriver jammed into the doorframe.

Chris moved. He slid to his feet, reached for the gun and aimed. He fired dead center in the wood, then broadened his angle to a circle. He fired until the gun clicked dead. Then he waited to see what would happen. He watched until he remembered the television, then turned and faced the screen.

The staircase was empty—no sign of Meacham, no sign of anything.

Chris decided to collect his weapons. He wanted them all. He walked about the house and loaded up, carrying the bat in one hand, a knife in the other. He slipped a straight-edge razor into a breast pocket, wrapped a chain over his shoulder... He armed himself with anything he could find, until he once again looked at the monitor.

Meacham was back at the door.

The motion was stronger now; more certain, more secure. Chris was mesmerized by the television. He watched and saw Meacham twist and pull and slam his palm against the knob.

Chris heard a jolt. He turned to face the door.

He saw the doorframe splinter.

That was enough, and he quickly reached for the phone. The police number was stored in the memory, and he hit the button.

Dead, of course. Meacham had cut the wires.

But Chris was ready for that. In the bedroom was a car phone. Campo had even hooked it to a car battery, just in case Meacham cut the electricity. Chris pressed the buttons and heard the line open.

"This is Chris Thomas. He's here. He's breaking in right now and he's trying to kill me. I need someone to—"

The front door began shaking. The screwdriver was gone; now Meacham was applying his strength. Chris saw the doorframe begin to split.

"I need someone *now*," Chris said.

The door shattered, and Meacham was in the room. He stepped forward, looked about, then stared at Chris. That was all he did.

Chris slammed shut the bedroom door and locked it, then looked for a place to escape. Nothing. Not even a window. Only four walls and a door, with the door leading to Meacham.

Meacham tried the knob.

There was a bureau in the room. Chris used it to block the door, and for a moment it did some good. After two strong hits, Meacham rested. Chris listened, and he could hear Meacham catching his breath.

Chris was still resting when he also heard a whisper.

"I'm making it next time," Meacham said. He said it almost beside Chris's ear.

Chris stepped back.

He walked around the room and pressed his hands to the wall, acting as if there was a secret passage out the apartment. Finally, he turned again to the bureau. Chris stepped behind it, leaned his back against its side and braced his feet. In the living room, Meacham was again on the move, probably searching for a way to break the door. In the bedroom, Chris glanced at the far wall, then put all his weight behind the bureau. He pushed as hard as he could, taking one step, two... the bureau picked up momentum. Chris was almost at jogging speed...

The bureau slammed into the wall.

The plasterboard split, exposing the outer wall. Chris slid the bureau back across the room for another try. He braced for a best effort while Meacham made his own discovery.

Chris saw the crowbar jam into the door.

Chris leaned into the bureau. In two steps, he was jogging; in four, it was the start of a run.

The bureau slammed into the outer wall of the adobe and smashed open the outside shell of the house. The bureau slid out the wall, dropping to the rear yard. Chris fell face down on the floor. He was still lying there when the bedroom door burst open.

Chris crawled to the edge of his hole. He looked down and saw a fifteen-foot drop. Behind him was Meacham.

He didn't think twice; Chris threw himself off the landing. He hit the grass, rolled over, looked toward the second floor.

Meacham wasn't there.

But he was close. Chris heard him coming down the stairs.

Chris got up and started stumbling across the yard. Meacham was coming down the staircase, so Chris would have to go around the other side of the house. He kept in motion, knowing if he could only make it out to the open boulevard, he'd be safe. Chris staggered toward the sidewalk. He hesitated once, thinking that maybe Meacham was waiting to jump him, but Chris didn't hear a thing. Then again, Meacham rarely made a noise. Chris decided to go for it. He took a breath and started running for the street.

"God," he screamed.

He fell flat on his face and twisted about. Meacham had him by the ankle. And now he was dragging Chris into the bushes—hand-over-hand, gripping his clothes . . .

Chris screamed, but Meacham took him by the throat. Soon he could barely breathe, and Meacham hauled him to his feet.

"You're making too much noise," Meacham whispered. "How about we go someplace quiet?"

TWENTY-SEVEN

"You know something, Chris? I like Los Angeles. I never thought I would, but I do."

He dragged Chris by the back of the collar and took long, loping steps, probably to keep Chris off-balance. It was an unnecessary precaution; Chris was ready to be controlled. In fact, the only thing keeping him up was Meacham's grip.

Meacham led him across the boulevard and to the side streets. They passed a number of people, but it was late, and no one interfered. Perhaps they thought Meacham was making a citizen's arrest, or that he was an undercover cop. Or maybe they simply didn't care. Whatever, Chris was marched forward and Meacham never even broke stride.

"Yeah," Meacham said. "This is definitely my kind of place."

He swung Chris around and they were again in an alley. When Chris tripped and dropped to his knees, Meacham held tight and kept going. Chris was dragged until he could stumble back to his feet.

Meacham turned out of the alley.

"It took me about five days to travel out here," Meacham said. "It was fun traveling. I should've gone back on the road long ago."

Chris tried looking at Meacham, but Meacham wouldn't allow it.

"Why don't you reach for one of your weapons?" Meacham said. He patted Chris's pockets and came up with a hunting knife. "Some knife," he said. "Why didn't you use it?"

"I forgot I had it," Chris said.

Meacham sneered. Chris not only felt helpless; he *was* helpless.

"Can I ask you something?" Chris said.

Meacham said nothing, so Chris presumed he could talk.

"What happened to the girl?" Chris said.

Meacham still said nothing; Chris realized he had to be more specific.

"Sarah Boden," Chris said.

"Sarah . . ." Meacham thought a moment. "I left her in Texas."

"Alive or dead?" Chris said.

"I don't remember," Meacham said. "What do you care, after what you did to my son."

Chris wondered what to say. Was there anything that could calm Meacham? "He wasn't my fault," Chris said.

"No," Meacham said. "Of course not. You're just the fucking cameraman."

Meacham twisted and turned him down another street.

"You wrecked my family," Meacham said. "I could sue the balls off you, but I'm gonna get them another way."

His pace quickened. Chris had no idea how far they'd walked.

"How many have you killed?" Chris said.

Meacham glanced at Chris. He started chuckling; he couldn't believe Chris's questions. "That's none of your business," he said.

"They found the boy," Chris said.

Meacham grinned. "They found the *what*?" he said.

"Randy Loudis," Chris said. "Six years old. Todd left a note."

"Oh, sure he did," Meacham said. "And you probably believed it, too."

Chris again tried looking at Meacham, and this time he managed it. He was trying to make sense of Meacham's remark, and after a moment, Chris realizing something. Meacham didn't believe him. And that was interesting, because the only reason he wouldn't is if Meacham didn't know about Randy Loudis.

Chris considered this little observation.

William Meacham didn't know. He really didn't.

And now Chris wanted to laugh, because as things were turning out, he had been right the first time. Todd Meacham *was* a killer. Chris had just blamed him for the wrong murder.

Todd and William, both killers.

Like father, like son.

"Make a left," Meacham said.

They were in another alleyway. It was the darkest alley they had entered. Meacham walked him straight back, as familiar with the street as his own driveway.

"A friend showed me this," Meacham said. "I've got a bunch of friends in this city. One of them said all his friends like to come down here for fun. He said I could do the same. I've been here three times already."

Meacham led Chris between the garbage cans and opened a steel door. "Upstairs," Meacham said.

Chris obeyed. He knew where they were going. Before Meacham said a word, Chris made a left and stood in front of the door.

Meacham glared at him.

"I've been here, too," Chris said.

Meacham shoved him aside, then pushed the door.

The cutting room.

They stood at the doorway. Chris noticed the change in wallpaper while Meacham noticed the crowd on the bed. Two men and a woman were wrestling on it. At first Chris thought it was a rape, but the woman stretched back and flipped the finger at Meacham.

Meacham answered by tilting the bed.

There could have been a fight. One of the men looked angry enough to attack. Meacham, though, simply lifted the hunting knife and in minutes the trio gathered their clothes and left.

As for Meacham, he left Chris on the trunk, then locked the door.

"Someone told me there are cameras in here," Meacham said. "They thought it was police, but I don't think so. There's lots of reasons to film people. Isn't that right?"

Meacham grabbed Chris by the hair and dropped him to his knees.

"I liked those movies you took," Meacham said. "They're the only home movies I ever had." Meacham began walking the length of the room. He was searching the walls, looking behind the furniture . . . he was looking for the cameras.

Chris, meanwhile, stared at the trunk.

"Of course, this is Hollywood. What else do you expect except a roomful of—" He stopped and looked behind one of the cabinets. "Found one," he said.

Chris reached out and opened the top of the trunk. Inside was a whip, handcuffs, a few yards of rope . . .

"Where there's one, there's two," Meacham said. "That's something I learned from you. Look through all the windows. Isn't that right?"

When Chris didn't answer. Meacham turned. Chris was backing toward the door. One hand reached for the lock, the other dangled a chain.

Meacham took in the scene, then he walked around Chris and blocked his way. Chris stood there, waving the chain like he really would attack.

Meacham encouraged him. "Go on," he said. "Give your best shot."

Chris almost didn't have the nerve. He made one weak swing of the chain and barely brushed Meacham. Meacham could have knocked aside the weapon; instead, he stood there.

"I said do it," he said.

He again nodded his okay, and Chris struck harder, striking Meacham's chest, then coming around again. Chris found a rhythm. It was easy with Meacham asking for the pain. Chris brought it around once, twice... A burn ran across Meacham's cheek, and then a gash opened across the side of his head. The blood poured over his ear, and when Chris struck again, he heard a bone crack. He'd broken Meacham's nose. The blood leaked onto Meacham's lip, and Chris reared back for another full swing, bringing the chain across Meacham's chest...

After less than a minute, Chris was exhausted. He never had much strength in the first place; now he slid to his knees and dropped the chain. He also began crying.

Meacham looked disgusted. "My boy could do better than you," he said. "In a few years, he could've done better than me."

He lifted Chris and dropped him to the bed, then he reached in a pocket and pulled out a spool of wire. He raised Chris's head and began wrapping the wire about his neck.

"I'm gonna kill you now," Meacham said. His voice was calm and patient, as if he were talking to Todd. As if, despite everything, Chris was still a member of the fraternity.

Meacham knotted the wire to the bedpost, then held the knife beside Chris's face.

"I'd tie up your arms, but I'm gonna be rolling you around some," Meacham said. "See, first I'm gonna cut off your balls. Then I'm gonna make you swallow your balls. Then I'm gonna cut them out of your stomach and make you swallow them again."

Chris stared at Meacham. He thought of all the hate mail that had been sent to R.I.P. Productions. Meacham was waiting for a reaction, so Chris gave it to him.

"I've heard worse," he said.

Or so he imagined saying. Nothing came from his mouth, no matter how he tried. Chris was delirious.

Meacham twisted the wire. "Of course, anytime you wanna choke to death, feel free," he said. "Don't stick around on my account."

Meacham straddled him, the blood dripping off his face

and onto Chris. Chris looked beyond Meacham and toward the overhead lights.

The camera was pointed dead at him.

Meacham leaned even closer to Chris. "I got a gun, too. Maybe if you beg, I'll do it quick. You want to beg?"

Chris kept staring at the camera. Meacham thought he was staring into space.

"All right, don't beg," Meacham said. He began unbuttoning Chris's pants. "Tell you what . . . Let's get started."

TWENTY-EIGHT

D ON Campo knew something was wrong. It was late morning and the sun was out, yet someone was in his cutting room. This was odd, because the people who used the room—his *clients*, Campo called them—knew better than to stay until daylight. Campo tried the knob, knocked on the door and shouted. Finally, he reached in his pocket for the passkey. He turned the lock, and a moment later he was inside the room, absolutely stunned. He'd never seen such a mess, not even in New York. The overhead lights had been smashed, the furniture broken . . . Someone had left the place a junkyard.

He almost couldn't believe it; then Campo looked toward the bed.

That "someone" was still in the room.

Campo played it careful. Normally, he could handle psychos. In fact, he found them friendly and appreciative. But in a case like this, gratitude was out the window. It meant goodbye to handshakes and hello to hair grabbing and arm swinging and whatever else was necessary to get the jerk out of the building.

Campo approached until he was close enough to see the stranger's face.

"Chris?" he said.

It was him. He was hard to recognize, but Campo

somehow managed it. Campo also thought of an image. He thought of an artist or painter at the end of a day, when he'd be damp from sweat and dripping with colors.

This was Chris. Behind him lay his "art"—a body, sprawled on the bed; a straight-edge razor still in its neck. As for Chris, he wasn't only soaked in the victim's blood; in his hands was a gun. A gun that was loaded and cocked . . .

A gun pressed very deliberately into the base of his chin.

Campo stepped back. He was concerned—not about being shot, but with interfering. After all, this was the cutting room.

"Chris," he said.

Chris wouldn't stop staring at the gun.

Campo tried again. "Chris," he said, "are you done here? Do you want me to leave?"

Chris still wouldn't answer.

Campo decided to leave the room. He walked outside and waited for him to make up his mind. One thing he wouldn't do is stop Chris. Campo was an observer and he'd let things take the natural course. He waited perhaps ten minutes before the door opened.

Chris came out, the gun no longer in his hand.

Campo relaxed. He smiled and patted Chris's shoulder. "Good for you," he said. "A guy like you has too much to live for."

He unlocked the storage room and led Chris to a sink. Chris stood still while Campo washed him.

"What the hell happened anyway?" Campo said. "I swear, I've never seen this kind of mess. You're not hurt, are you?"

He tilted Chris's head and looked for cuts. Chris still wouldn't talk, but Campo had seen this type of thing. Soon Chris would break, and then there'd be no stopping him. For now, Campo killed the quiet.

"Don't worry about Meacham," Campo said. "I'll drop him off in the hills and call the police. No one's going to care how he died. No one's—" He stopped. "That is Meacham, right?"

Chris nodded.

Campo looked relieved. "Then it's not even a problem," he said. Once the hands were scrubbed, he washed Chris's face, wiped him off with a towel and led him out of the room. With great care, he helped Chris down the stairs. "You had me going there a minute. I mean with the gun. I thought you were gonna do it."

Chris stumbled, and Campo caught him. Chris looked like he wanted to talk.

"Don't say a word," Campo said. "I got it all on tape, remember? I can watch it later."

They reached the lower landing. Campo kept making conversation.

"I really thought you were gonna kill yourself," he said. "You had that look in your eyes. That death look."

Campo opened the door. He squinted against the sunlight, but not Chris. Campo stared at him. He still had it . . . the death look. One of Dorsey's Moments.

"You oughta see yourself in a mirror," Campo said.

They walked into the alley and toward the street.

"Am I going slow enough?" Campo said. "Do you need a doctor?"

Chris shook his head.

"Let me know if you do," Campo said. "In my opinion, what you really need is fresh air. We'll get you living again, and then maybe you can tell me what's it like. Killing someone, I mean. I've only seen it on film."

Chris slowed to a stop. Campo stared at him.

"What?" Campo said. "What's the matter?"

Chris returned the stare and Campo didn't move. For some reason, at this particular moment, moving seemed like a dangerous thing to do.

And then Chris walked away. He went to the nearest doorway and stepped inside—out of the sun, back and deep in the shadows. He stood there and waited to see if Campo would follow him, but Campo only watched. Campo seemed to know better.

Finally, Chris went inside. It was a dangerous, deserted building, but he didn't hesitate; after all, he was now a man without boundaries. He had held a blade and been under one; he had killed and almost been killed . . . He had proven, beyond any doubt, that he was Death's favorite son, able to pick and choose his worlds. And at the moment, he wanted to be alone, so he went where no one else would follow; he sought refuge in the shadows.

As for Campo, he watched Chris escape the sunlight, then turned and headed back to his own building. He didn't worry about Chris; anyone who could survive Meacham had destiny on his side. Besides, Campo had a full day ahead. There was getting rid of the body, plus Dorsey's business, plus his own, plus the cleanup. It was an impossible load of work, but Campo knew he'd manage. Somehow, he had a good feeling about all this. What happened to Chris was a sign. Things would be getting busy soon and then his cutting room would need a sign-up sheet. The place would be jammed with business, and Campo would have to worry about crowds. Who knows? Maybe he'd even have to franchise.

Yes, word was definitely getting out. There was no telling what awful things people would soon be doing.

Campo only hoped he had enough film.